SARAH KAMINSKI

SIX SECRETS

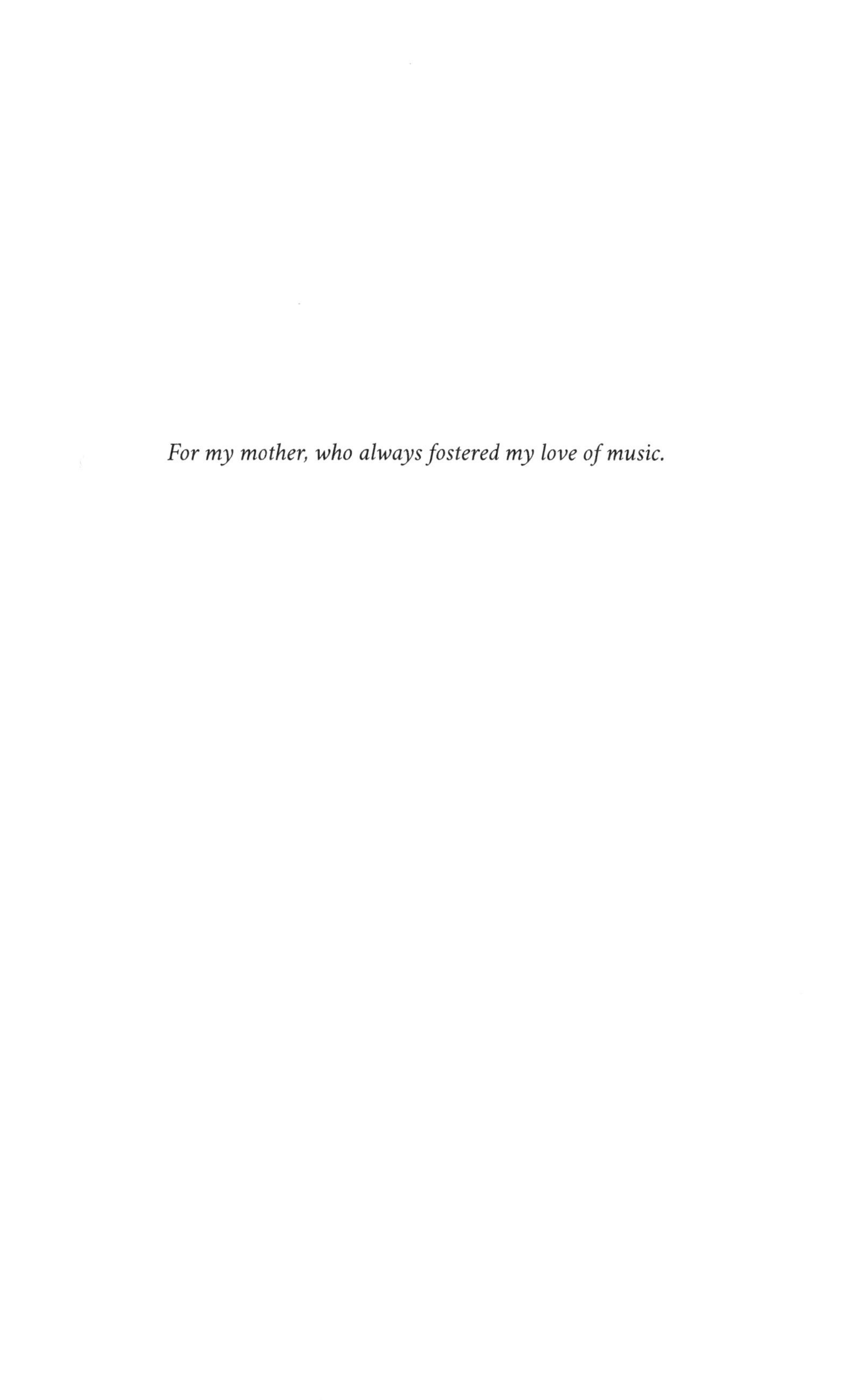

For my mother, who always fostered my love of music.

One

Brayden

When I run, the world disappears. I see the pavement in front of me and hear the even thud, thud, thud of my shoes pounding the road, and nothing else. My iPhone is strapped to my arm—its only purpose to alert me to the number of calories I'm shedding during my hours on the road.

Calories in. Calories out. The simple arithmetic makes sense to me, gives me purpose. Defines me.

Silence surrounds me. I need it. It takes away the pain. When I top that third hill from my house, the steepest one, I pause to check my pulse. My heart hammers in my chest. Now that I've stopped, the Brayden inside my head starts criticizing. It reminds me that I used to be different, ugly, unlovable. That I used to have no friends, no hope of a girlfriend. That everything I have now, beautiful Angie, my place on the basketball team, the school's adoration could all disappear. It tells me to keep running. To never stop. It conjures up visions of potato chips, brownies, ice cream, everything I used to love, and it labels them as trash and filth. Something I'll never let myself touch again.

My girlfriend, Angela, says I'm a deep thinker because I'm so quiet. Really, I just don't know what to say. I can't tell her about the never-ending criticism that runs through my mind and keeps me awake at night doing hundreds of sit-ups when I should be sleeping. I can't explain it, so I let her think I'm just a strong, silent type. I worry if she knew what really went on in my head, she'd break up with me.

Originally, I asked her out because I needed a girlfriend who was popular. I got moved up to varsity on the football team, and Coach said he'd name me captain of the basketball team this year, if I kept pulling my weight. Everything started falling into place. Image matters, and the right girlfriend completes that image.

Angela's great. She's quiet and sweet. It took me a long time to get up the nerve to ask her out, but I guess she was expecting it, because she didn't even hesitate. Three years ago, a girl that pretty would have laughed in my face, but I'm a changed man. She's real peaceful too. Sometimes it seems like we're hanging out in silence for hours, but I don't really notice it. Which I guess is kind of nice.

#

Three miles later, I am dripping sweat and panting as I open my front door. My dad glances up from his permanent seat on the sofa. "Good run, Bray?"

I grunt. "It's Brayden." Which he knows. Or he should. I haven't gone by Bray since middle school. Three years I want to erase from history, nicknames and all. He never listens.

"Uh huh." He turns back to the TV, cycling between procedural cop shows on three different channels. Dad's upper management at some boring company in St. Paul, but he acts like he was made for detective work, blurting out random legal terms in the middle of all his shows. Like anyone even cares.

I kick my shoes off and pull my phone out of its armband, but what I see makes me frown. My pace is slower. Slower pace means fewer calories burned – 367. I was aiming for 400. I sigh and climb the stairs, pulling my sweat soaked shirt over my head, my mind already racing with calculations.

I have to fit in more exercise, because it's Labor Day weekend and that only means one thing for my family—a huge end of the summer barbecue with burgers and homemade potato salad and my mom's famous brownies. If I don't eat at least one, she's going to think something's wrong. She perfected her recipe on me. I was her go-to taste-tester, but now that I've dropped all those extra pounds, I have to work even harder to keep them off.

She doesn't understand. She doesn't get what it's like to have to look through old yearbooks and see what I used to look like. Primo loser. Two hundred pounds of ugly.

Not anymore though. I flip the shower on and glance in the mirror while the water heats up. Does my jaw look rounder? No, I'm imagining it. A quick scan up and down reveals what I already know, toned muscle, sculpted abs, broad shoulders. Every pound of fat that haunted me for years has been carefully burned away. I'm on top now.

Still. Family barbecue.

One turkey burger, no cheese, no bun. I can fill up on raw veggies, then for dessert, half a brownie.

I'll run an extra mile tomorrow.

Two

Charlotte

My stomach churns every time I see the fryer. The smell alone will get me, but the way the chicken wings bubble and pop in the oil? It's half the reason I became a vegetarian.

I bobby-pin my paper hat to my short springy curls and scoot past the current fry-guy, another pimply-faced boy from my school whose name I should know. Not that it matters. People come and go at the Chicken-porium faster than you can say "would you like slaw with that?" Harvey and I are the only two who've lasted more than a month. We both need the money.

Harvey's already set up on the drive-thru which means I'm up front today. I hate being up front.

He nods at me as I sign into the register. "Running late, Charlotte."

I shrug. "Sorry." I'm not really sorry. I have more important things to do, and our manager is completely clueless. Harvey and I run this place. The entire fried chicken fast-food franchise will fall to pieces if we quit, so they let us get away with a lot. Like showing up ten minutes late.

"No biggie. I covered for you." He reaches across me to grab a handful of ketchup packets and tosses them into the paper bag he's holding. "You meeting up with the mystery boyfriend again?"

I bite back a smile.

"Cool."

Harvey slides his hand into the pocket of his apron and I avert my eyes, because what he's about to do next is illegal. I figure if I look away I can reasonably tell our manager I had no idea because I never saw him do it. It's a technicality, but one that could save my job if push comes to shove. Every man for himself in the fried chicken world.

I hear the window slide open and Harvey leans out, ushering another faithful chicken-eater through the line.

When he slams the window shut, I look back at him, frowning.

"You worry too much," he says.

"Aren't you afraid of getting caught?"

He shakes his head, shoulder-length brown hair flying up as he does. He's supposed to keep in in a ponytail. "I will eventually, but until then…" He shrugs.

I don't say anything. I'm a master of keeping quiet. Ever since my dad died, I just found it easier to keep opinions to myself. Opinions about my mom's sudden decision to pack up everything in our apartment in Oakland and move us to a no-name suburb outside of St. Paul, Minnesota. Because being the girl with a dead dad isn't bad enough, I also get to be the girl from out of the state.

Just one more year. I can keep my mouth shut and then go to college anywhere but here. Hence the job at the magical kingdom of grease and salt.

I lean my elbows on the counter and stare at the empty dining area. "Slow day."

"It's only four." Harvey stands next to me. "Haven't even got the dinner rush yet."

It's fine with me. I get paid the same either way, and it's easier when no one comes in for their daily dose of fried food. The only people here are Cynthia Marlow and that group of losers she calls a band.

They're sitting in the largest booth in the room, and from the looks of it, things aren't going well for her. The three boys are all crammed together on one side, leaving her all on her own. It looks like they're reading her the Riot Act or something. She slumps in the booth with her arms crossed and glares out from behind her choppy bangs.

Harvey leans close to whisper. "Looks like Steve-O's on one of his power trips."

"Which one's Steve-O?"

"Guy in the middle, bleach blond hair. He's the lead singer and he's had it in for Cyn for over a year now."

About once a week, the band comes in, orders a bucket of chicken, then argues for an hour about the stupidest stuff. No need to wonder what they're arguing about this time. Everyone in school knows about Cynthia and Jimmy and their epic breakup.

Jimmy's the bass player of the group. His hair is dyed bright red, not natural like mine, and he's got huge gauges in his ears which make me queasy when I look at them. Apparently, he had been cheating on Cynthia all summer. No one knows who with, but they do know she found out last week and nailed him for it.

Literally. Knee right to the junk.

I'm not a gossipy sort of person by nature, but even I paid attention to that story. He's been slinking around school looking permanently offended for days.

Harvey lays a five-dollar bill on the counter. "Bet she storms out."

"No bet. Too easy."

"Bet she throws her drink."

I nod at the new stakes and place my own five on top. "You're on, but you have to clean it if she does."

"Deal."

We shake on it under the counter then lean closer to watch. Good thing no one's at the drive-thru because Harvey'd probably just ignore them at this point. Sure enough, ten minutes later, Cynthia's on her feet, large soda in hand.

Harvey and I suck in simultaneous breaths, waiting, and for a second, it looks like I might win the bet, but then she hurls the Styrofoam cup at her band mates with a loud, "fuck you," snatches her bag off the seat and makes a beeline for the door.

I sigh. "Dammit." I should know better. Harvey's lived here his whole life. He knows everyone in town.

Harvey takes the cash with a grin and stuffs it in his pocket, then grabs the mop, while I watch the three boys clamber out of the booth. Steve-O flicks his hand, sending droplets of dark syrup flying, then looks at me.

Our eyes meet, and I wish desperately I were invisible. In Oakland, I could disappear in a crowd, but this town is so small, and I stick out.

He saunters over, his eyes dropping from my face to the name tag pinned on my polo, perched just above my left breast.

"Hey, Charlotte." He's still talking to my boobs. "Can I get some napkins?"

I point to the drink station where dispensers overflow with napkins.

His eyes linger longer than necessary, then he licks his lips and looks back at me. "Thanks."

I wrinkle my nose and look away.

Three

Cynthia

Punk rock is loud. Punk rock is ugly. Punk rock is in your face and it's not gonna back down.

And punk rock might be dead. At least to me.

I can barely lift a drumstick these days. I just sit on my stool and mope while *Black Parade* blares in the background and Jason watches me from across my basement.

"Cyn, c'mon. Bang your drums. You'll feel better," he says in a cajoling voice.

I slump even farther in my seat. My life is over. No more band. No more boyfriend, not since I found out he's been screwing someone else. I gave him a well-deserved knee to the groin and became single. Less than twenty-four hours later, Steve-O boots me out of the Stinks. Apparently nailing the bass player in the balls is grounds for being ousted. As if they'll find another drummer as good as me. I've been playing forever. I'm a beast with the sticks. I'm like Keith Fucking Moon. You don't kick Keith Fucking Moon out of the band.

But, as Steve-O liked to remind me, no one comes to shows to see the drummer. Especially a girl drummer. They come to see him, the front man. He's sexy as hell and doesn't wear a shirt while we play. I used to sit behind him, obviously, so I can verify for a fact that he has a nice ass.

Jason crosses the room to stand behind me, then leans over to grab my hands and to force me to play, tapping out stupid rhythms a half a beat behind the stereo.

"Am I doing this right?" he asks.

"No."

He hits one of the toms at a bad angle, so it doesn't resonate.

I roll my eyes. "You suck."

One more pretend run which mostly just consists of banging the sticks against the rims while missing the beat entirely. He drops my hands. "Show me how it's done, then." He puts his hands on his hips and raises an eyebrow sardonically.

I can't resist the urge now. It's a good album, and I already know most of it by heart. The rest I can pick up by listening. "Turn up the volume," I say.

When the music is so loud I can feel it in my teeth, I start banging. You gotta play punk loud. Anything less is a travesty. It doesn't take long to get into the swing of it, the rhythm. I know it when I feel it, that moment when drumming stops being about playing and is more like a dance, my whole body moves in time with the music and the rolls just flow out of me. I can let go.

And I do.

For the first time since Jimmy and I broke up, I actually start to feel kind of good about drumming again. Screw them. I'm going to be famous someday, then they'll be sorry.

Jason smirks from across the room and flops onto the couch, listening as I pound my way through the first half of the album, but then *CANCER* comes on. It's kind of slow, so I leave the sticks on the stool and collapse on the couch next to him, leaning my head against his shoulder.

"Thanks," I whisper into his black T-shirt.

"Jimmy's a douchebag, by the way."

I snicker. "Wish you'd said something a year ago."

"Pretty sure I did."

I nod. I should listen to Jason more. He's pretty much my only friend these days. We've been best friends since middle school, basically from the moment I kissed him outside the gymnasium and he pulled away in disgust and told me he was gay.

At first, I guess I was kind of hurt. I mean, who wouldn't be? But it's not like being gay is a choice, and it doesn't change the fact that he's got excellent taste in music, a killer sense of humor, and actually helps me in math so I don't flunk out.

I'm the only person who knows he's gay though, because Jason's dad is one of those freaky, super strict, evangelical pastors. I'm pretty sure his parents would try to Bible thump the gay right out of him if he ever came out. It's gotta suck. I mean, he's never even had a boyfriend, which means no making out. Poor guy.

Not that I'm making out with anyone these days either.

Just like that, I'm back to pouting.

The song ends, and in the little moment of quiet before the next one begins, we hear it.

PING!

PING!

Our phones light up with identical new alerts. His first, because his plan is better, then mine a half-second behind. He flips his floppy brown hair out of his eyes, then swipes the screen.

"JJ posted a new video."

We both groan. Everyone at our school knows about Julie Jenkins's YouTube channel. It's a pretty big deal. JJ is a huge gossip and every once in a while, she makes a video about the latest buzz around school. Some stupid tidbit she picked up by listening around corners or interviewing girls in the locker room. You gotta be careful when you talk to JJ, because anything you say can and will be used against you. The worst part is, even though I know it's stupid and I hate her, I can't help but watch her channel.

"You think she'll call out Jimmy for being a gigantic douche?" I ask as I dig around in the couch cushions for the remote to mute the stereo. I don't like turning the music off. It feels wrong to cut out in the middle of an album like this.

Mostly though, I don't like turning the music off because when things get too quiet, it sets me on edge. I get jumpy, like something might go wrong. I'm the kid in class who's always drumming on the desks with my pencil. Teachers hate me.

Jason shrugs and scoots closer to me so we can watch together. The video loads with her irritating pop/hip hop theme music that she had to have sampled off some real artist's hard work. Then, the picture centers on her face, perfectly made up with a high brown ponytail. She gives an exaggerated wave.

"Hello, Foxboro High!" Her voice grates. "Have I got a treat for you today!" Every single sentence she says ends with a squealing uplift in her voice. Kind of like how Steven Tyler punches the end of every Aerosmith song he's ever sung, but he can get away with it. He's Steven Tyler.

"I've spent the past few weeks investigating some truly interesting stories, and it turns out," she pauses for effect, "some of our classmates are not who they say they are. Some of them are pretending. They're liars. They're fake."

Jason rolls his eyes. "What sort of God complex do you have to have to think that delivering gossip is a noble calling?"

On screen, JJ straightens her shoulders, throws a stupid grin at the web camera, and says, "Today, I'm going to reveal six secrets of the senior class." She draws a breath, as if steeling herself for an unpleasant task. As if she doesn't love every second of this. She looks deep into the camera lens. "Secrets can be so harmful. Secrets tear friendships apart. They are walls between us. I do this for the good of our school. Because we deserve the truth."

There's a long pause, and the uncomfortable feeling of silence crawls up my back. Then the picture pixelates and refocuses on the yearbook picture of last year's varsity basketball team. It zooms in until only one player is on screen.

"Brayden Matthews," JJ's voice dubs over. "Captain of the basketball team. Mr. Popular himself. How many girls have tried and failed to catch his eye, until he finally settled on beautiful, popular Angela White?Wilkinson It seems like a match made in heaven, right? The two stars of our school united in love? Yet, sources close to Brayden have revealed that while the two seem devoted to each other at school, he remains…"

The screen cuts back to JJ's face. "…a virgin."

Jason rolls his eyes. "Big deal. Lots of people are."

"Maybe he's gay?" I suggest.

Jason gives me a look, like 'girl, you are so dumb.' "He's not."

JJ's voice interrupts our back and forth. "I know what you're thinking. Not possible, JJ! Remember how he told everyone about the cheerleader from South Mission Hills last year? Not to mention, he and Angela have been together for how long again? Surely, by now they've done the deed?" She gives a dramatic sigh. "Alas, no. Brayden is indeed, a virgin."

Up next is a face everyone in our school recognizes, Lindsey Banford, Student Body President and all-around queen bee, smiling serenely behind her dad who is mid-interview with a reporter. She has the locker next to mine which means I have to suffer through her prattling on about cost-effective solutions to who-even-cares every time I need to grab something. She is the worst.

JJ's voice dubs over. "Lindsey Banford. She's perfect, right? Untouchable. Her father, a representative in the House? Her mother, an attorney at one of the biggest law firms in the city? She makes straight As, goes to church, follows every rule. No one would ever suspect her of petty theft. Right?"

The picture flicks to a shot of Lindsey at a department store, clearly pocketing a tube of lipstick, dubbed over with JJ's voice. "Wrong. Lindsey likes to steal things. Trinkets. Those big soiree fundraisers her parents put on every few months? Somehow the caterers are always a little short on silverware at the end of the night or the hosts are missing some small family heirloom. And let's not talk about the stash of lipsticks and mascaras she's lifted from shops at the mall. Look hard enough, and you'll see Lindsey isn't as perfect as she pretends to be."

I'm having a hard time hiding my glee at this. Not that I have anything against Lindsey, but some people are too perfect. It's nice to find out she has faults like the rest of us.

Jason's body shifts next to me and he groans. They go to the same church.

I don't think they're friends, really, but maybe I'm a little jealous that he cares.

Another fade, and the next student's picture shows up. Or rather no picture at all. One of those blank gray faces they put in the yearbook with the words "not pictured." The camera pans across to the names, and JJ's voice cuts in.

"Harvey Plessinger. He's practically invisible. No pictures in the yearbook, slinks through the school hallways unnoticed by teachers and students alike. But is it possible his complete lack of notoriety serves a greater purpose? Helps him in his business schemes."

At this, Jason and I both groan. We know about Harvey's business, and now so does the entire school. It's only a matter of time before he's expelled.

JJ's voice sobers slightly. "I'm speaking, of course, of the business of selling drugs. It turns out Harvey Plessinger is the perfect drug dealer. Money exchanges hands at school, and product gets delivered through the drive-thru window at the Chicken-porium where he works." Sure enough, a picture of Harvey leaning out of a drive-thru window with a paper bag of fried chicken in his hand pops up.

I reach across Jason to press pause on the video. "This is stupid."

"You think the principal watches YouTube? If so, Harvey's screwed."

I hadn't thought about that. They'll search his locker, flush his stash. Maybe even press charges. I don't know if he's eighteen yet, not that it matters. If they want to bring you down, they'll find a way.

Jason nods, reading my expression perfectly. "My guess is your supply just got cut off, cupcake."

"Whatever," I say. "Press play. Let's get this stupid thing over with."

He does, but our resolution lasts about five seconds because after JJ delivers the last of her Harvey-speech the picture fades and it's replaced with…

"ME?!" I screech, snatching at the phone in Jason's hand.

It can't be me. Except it is. The picture is taken from one of the band's summer gigs. Not professional, it's clearly a cell phone photo, and as if zooming in on me drumming wildly in the background isn't enough, she's fucking edited the photo to draw a bright red circle around my drums and me.

Then her irritating voice pipes up. "Cynthia Marlow."

Four

Jason

"Turn it off!" Cynthia screams, scrambling over me to get to the phone which threatens to fly out of my hands. "Turn it off, turn it off!"

"Jesus, Cyn, I'm trying!" I manage to extricate myself from her clawing hands and press the pause symbol. We collapse back into the couch cushions next to each other, panting, and I open my mouth to say something, but before I can get a word out, the basement door opens and Cynthia's mom pokes her head through.

"You guys okay down here? I thought I heard a scuffle."

Cynthia looks like she's about to explode. Like how toddlers hold their breath sometimes during a tantrum, she's red in the face and won't even look at her mom.

"Yeah, Mrs. Marlow. We're all good," I say.

She glances around the room. "No music today, sweet pea?"

Cynthia groans and peels away from me, grabbing her discarded drumsticks and starts banging on her drums. It's not music. Not by any definition of the word. It's anger. Her mom takes the hint because she nods grimly and smiles at me. "Well, come upstairs if you get hungry, okay?"

The second the door closes behind her, Cynthia rounds on me. "What the hell?" she hisses, waving a drumstick wildly. I'm glad I'm across the room. I don't feel like getting jabbed with one of those.

Again.

Long story.

When Cynthia gets like this, there's really only one thing to do, let her cuss her heart out until she can be rational again. Her record is fifteen F-bombs after she found out Jimmy was cheating on her.

Sure enough, she starts pacing the room like a madwoman, kicking things out of her way and letting expletives fly. Better words than objects. A few minutes later, she's finally able to sit, but she's still upset. Not that I blame her. I wouldn't want to be in JJ's stupid video either.

I take a deep breath. "We have to watch it, Cyn."

"No," she snaps. "No way. I don't want to hear whatever that bitch has to say about me."

"Wouldn't it be better to hear it now, when it's just the two of us? Instead of at school on Monday?" I catch her eye and offer what I hope is an empathetic smile.

She considers it. She really does. When Cynthia thinks hard about something, she runs her tongue over the inside of her lower lip so her lip ring dances back and forth. I watch it flick left and right while she mulls it over. Then she shakes her head, and I know there's no use trying to get her to see reason.

The entire day's been ruined by JJ's stupid video. Cyn's not in the mood to drum or listen to music or anything. She's just curled up on the couch looking murderous. No sense in sticking around.

The alarm on my phone beeps, signaling the end to my brief freedom. I stand up and grab my bag off the floor next to the couch. "You cool if I head home?"

Cynthia looks up at me with those icy blue eyes of hers. Normally they're cold and hard, but right now they're swimming in tears.

Jesus Christ. She really doesn't need any more added to her plate right now. I'm actually pissed at JJ for including her. It's just evil to kick a dog while they're down.

Not that Cyn's a dog.

I reach over and ruffle her jet-black hair which is kind of awkward, but once I start I have to commit to it. "Don't worry about what she says. She's just an attention whore. She'll get what's coming to her one of these days."

Cyn scowls harder, which I guess is my cue to get the hell out of her basement before she really loses it.

Probably for the best, because I have about a billion chores to do when I get home. I sneak out of the house most Saturday mornings to hang with Cyn. I kind of have to. Dad's the associate pastor at the biggest church in town, and Cyn looks like a walking billboard for the Satanist revival. All black clothes, a ton of piercings in each ear and hair dyed black except for a chunk of blue that almost matches her eyes in the front.

Saturday afternoons, I do chores, because on Sunday we have church, then Bible study and as it's "God's chosen day of rest" we can't do chores on Sunday. We have to keep the day holy. I'm not even allowed to do homework on Sundays which means double the work on Saturdays.

Mom and I run around the house all day scrubbing and mowing and making sure everything is perfect. Dad doesn't help because "his work is God's work" which means he gets to hole up in his office all day writing his sermon for Sunday while we do all the heavy lifting.

"God's work" apparently doesn't stop him from being able to step out of his office at nine o'clock on the dot to inspect our work. And woe be to the son who fails to meet his standards, lest he be grounded until eternity. I hate being grounded. Grounding for normal teens means they lose their phones or their cars or whatever. For me, it means weeks upon weeks of copying Bible verses then sitting in Dad's study with him and going over every inch of those Bible verses to discuss the lessons I should have gleaned from them. The lessons are almost entirely that I'm a bad son and I should do better to make him happy.

I'm kind of an undercover atheist these days, so anything I can do to get out of Bible verses, I'll do it. Even if it means scrubbing the shower until the skin on my knuckles cracks open.

Before I go home, I have to watch the rest of JJ's video. At the very least, I have to be prepared to help Cyn deal with whatever JJ said.

I climb into my car and pull out my phone, glancing around before I remember there's no way my Dad is on Cynthia's street watching me. If he found out I was watching this type of stuff… well… Bible verses.

This is stupid. I press play and slouch into my seat to watch.

"Cynthia Marlow," JJ says. "Rocker chick extraordinaire. She'd have you believe she gets by on talent alone. That her status in the local punk rock scene is due to her prowess on the drums and nothing else. She struts around school like she owns the place, all because she can bang her sticks on her little drum set."

"Of course, she'd be nowhere without Steve-O and the Stinks. And what did she have to do to earn their loyalty? It's simple really. Have sex with Steve-O's drug dealer to score free pills. Enough energy to keep on rocking another day. Sad really, when my sources tell me she wouldn't even put out for her own boyfriend."

I grit my teeth. That's pretty bad. I know everything about Cynthia, so I know exactly what JJ's talking about. That wasn't sex for drugs. That was… something else. Cyn was really messed up for weeks afterward. I had to drive her to the Planned Parenthood in the city for the morning after pill, but no amount of begging on my part convinced her to quit the band.

Honestly, I'm glad Cyn didn't have to hear that.

Cynthia's picture disappears and is replaced with a shy looking girl with a bob of black curls and medium brown skin shrinking into the corner of the bleachers at a pep rally.

"Charlotte Waters" JJ says softly into the microphone. "The new girl from the coast. And that's about all anyone knows about her. But why should she get to know her new classmates? Why should she make friends? When she's too busy fooling around with her English teacher, Mr. DuPont."

This video is starting to make me feel sick. JJ's spilling secrets that could ruin lives. At first it was kind of funny, laughing at Brayden for not getting laid, but this is serious.

My head swims and I completely miss what else she has to say about Charlotte. The picture switches and I glance at my phone again to see my own face staring back at me.

I'm not like Cynthia. I'm not going to rant and rave. I'm not going to cuss out every person I know.

I can't. I'm too paralyzed with fear. There's only one secret JJ could possibly have dug up on me. The big one. The one I've been hiding from everyone.

Sweat breaks out on my skin, making me feel cold, even in the summer heat. I can't hear JJ's voice anymore, but I don't need to. I already know what she's telling the whole school

Jason Sanders is gay.

Five

Lindsey

From my bedroom window, I have the perfect view of the sunset. Every evening, I sit at my desk and watch as yellow turns to gold, then to brilliant orange. Reds and pinks transition smoothly, almost imperceptibly to purples, then a deep dark blue that tells me night has fallen.

"Lindsey Marie!"

Mom's voice pulls me out of my reverie. It's not a voice I can ignore. I've never heard her shout, yet her voice still manages to travel from our front sitting room through entrance hall, up two flights of wide, winding stairs, down the hallway of empty bedrooms that once belonged to my older siblings, to resonate in mine at the very end. I have precisely twenty-two seconds to walk downstairs. She knows exactly how long it takes. If I hurry, I can make it in fifteen, which gives me seven seconds to check myself in the mirror, to make sure every strand of blonde hair is smoothed neatly into a low bun at the base of my neck, my dress is wrinkle free, and my makeup perfect.

I can't be caught hurrying. Banfords do not hurry. The world waits for the Banfords. When there are two Banfords involved, like my mother and me, the younger Banford must bend to the elder's will. As the youngest Banford of seven, not including my parents, I've had some practice bending.

I am like clay. I can be molded in my father's image, I can be sculpted into perfection.

And I can still be found wanting.

I pause at the entrance of the sitting room, cross one ankle over the other, rest my arms straight by my side, and smile. Years spent in the cotillion circuit have taught me how to stand in the most becoming way.

"Yes, Mom?"

She turns in her seat, her eyes traveling up and down. "Don't slouch, Lindsey."

I'm already standing as straight as I an, but that doesn't stop me from aiming higher. My back lengthens so far an ache builds between my shoulder blades.

"Come. Sit next to me." She pats the vacant seat. This should feel welcoming, but it doesn't. My mother's never been known for being warm. Not even to her children.

I sit, ankles crossed, hands in lap, back straight, head cocked slightly to the side, and a demure smile on my lips. The checklist runs through my mind, how to appear pleasant at all times.

She nods approval than hands me a paper. "The itinerary for the next two weeks. I will be flying out on Monday morning, before you wake, and I won't return until next Thursday. Your father is still in Washington for the next three weeks. You'll have the house to yourself. Loretta will still be here to cook meals and clean, of course. I've included phone numbers for the hotel where I'll be staying, and of course you know your father's line at the Capitol, but that's only to be used for emergencies."

I nod. "Of course."

"When he returns, his campaign for reelection begins. It's all hands on deck, Lindsey. He's had a good run, but poll numbers have him down. People want change, someone more in touch with the everyday man." She purses her lips. "We'll have to work even harder this election cycle. Which unfortunately means less time together as a family."

I should have known. My face is blank, but still, she reaches over and grips my hand. "It's only for a few months, Lindsey."

Only a few months out of my senior year in high school. The last year I'll be home.

"Yes, of course. It's not a problem." I square my shoulders, and force my lips not to twitch and break the smile still plastered on my face. "I'm awfully busy these days, too. I've got Student Council, college applications, three AP classes. I'll make do."

"Excellent." Mom stands. "Don't forget, while your father and I are gone, you are the face of this family."

"Of course, Mom."

"Church every Sunday, a calm and welcoming demeanor, but not too welcoming. Remember, friends are just enemies who want something from you."

My phone dings, a text message coming through. There's a small pause, then another two dings. I feel so foolish. I should have left it upstairs.

Mom frowns. "Do you need to get that?"

"It's nothing."

Two more dings.

"Lindsey, I insist. It could be Student Council business."

"It's not."

"Well then, what is it?"

I run a finger through my hair, pushing a loose strand behind my ear. "It's silly really. There's a girl at school, she makes these videos."

"What sort of videos?"

"Idle gossip mostly. It's all so petty. I don't know why she does it."

My phone pings again, and Mom's lips tighten, a thin pale line of judgment. "I don't understand the connection between her gossip and your phone going off like firecrackers on the fourth of July."

Words fail me, but not her. Mom holds out her hand. "Give me your phone."

"Mom, it's nothing. It'll all blow over."

"I won't ask twice, Lindsey."

I pull my phone out of the pocket in my skirt and hand it to her, along with all semblance of freedom. She unlocks it with my password, and begins reading texts.

"Thief," she reads aloud. "Liar. Thief." She frowns. "This one calls you a bitch."

I wince.

"Well," her prim voice cuts through the haze I am in. "I suppose I'll need to watch the video."

Mom stops the video after JJ finishes my secret and sets the phone on the end table beside her. "Well then."

I know better than to speak before she's decided what to do. Interrupting will only make things worse.

"Is this true?"

Emotions are a weakness, so I force myself not to have them. I try to think about nothing and I pray to God to keep my face void of any hint of the shame that is bubbling up inside my throat. Staring at my lap, I offer a simple nod.

I don't need to look at her to know her lips are pursed, her neck stiff. And I certainly don't need the speech that follows. Not that anything I say could matter. There's a reason she has such a great track record for litigation at her firm.

"I'm shocked. Your father and I did not raise you to be some common thief. You have everything you could possibly ask for, and so many opportunities. Why would you stoop so low? No, don't answer that. I don't want to know." She stands up, hands on her hips, and stares into the fireplace. "This isn't good. Not for you. Not for your father. It's an election year! Do you realize what will happen to his poll numbers when the news gets hold of this?" This is a rhetorical question. If I answer, I'll be in worse trouble. "Your brothers and sister never gave us this sort of trouble. And you're a fool if you think Princeton will admit you when they find out about this."

I look up, worried, and she fixes me with a stern look. "Every Banford for six generations has gone to Princeton, and you'd throw that legacy away for what? A few silly trinkets? No, there's nothing else to do about it, except to head this off as much as possible. Formal apologies. We'll have to return anything we can, pay for what we can't. You'll need to be seen doing something charitable. Giving back to the community. Show proper remorse."

Her disappointment cuts through me, a knife to the heart. Her shameful youngest daughter. None of her other children put her through such torment.

"Okay," I say.

Her eyes flash angrily.

"Yes, ma'am."

Six

Brayden

As a general rule, I don't watch JJ's videos. I don't even follow her channel. I'm not a fan. As soon as I walk into school Monday morning, I can tell a new video dropped because everyone's looking at me like I'm Godzilla or something.

It takes some searching, but I find my best friend Mark in the library. I'm surprised, because it's pretty much the last place he would ever be—until I realize he's there bullying an underclassman into doing his math homework.

"C'mon man," he says, shoving the back of the geek's shoulder. "I need that before class starts."

The kid is kind of scrawny, all wiry with hunched shoulders and a nervous look in his eye. When Mark nudges him again, he scribbles even faster on the paper, copying equation after equation out of the book and solving them nearly as fast. I don't really approve of Mark cheating on his homework, but he's a starting player on the basketball team and if he doesn't make at least a C, they'll kick him off. Mark's not exactly Einstein or anything.

I thump Mark on the back to let him know I'm there and he turns around and grins. "Dude…" He has a look in his eyes that makes my stomach feel like it's filled with lead.

"What's up?"

He starts to laugh. "Didn't you see JJ's new video?"

"No."

"Oh, man." Mark pulls out his phone. "You're going to be so pissed."

First the lead stomach, now my heart is doing back flips. "Is it about me?"

"Not just you."

The sophomore with the Algebra book snickers, and I scowl. Cred is everything. And if some geek who can't even drive is laughing at me, then I'm losing it fast. Mark gives him a look, and he goes back to the math.

"I don't get it," I say, pulling my phone out of my pocket. "I haven't even done anything."

"That's the point, man."

I find the video and press PLAY, turning the volume up so I can hear it, which I immediately regret because the second JJ's voice blares out of my phone's speakers, everyone in the vicinity looks over, sees me, and bursts into laughter. My picture pops up on the screen, JJ declares me a virgin, and I groan.

"So what're you gonna do?" Mark asks.

I close the app. "Nothing."

"Seriously man, you gotta get laid."

"Shut up!"

Mark puts his hands up all innocent like. "Don't snap at me, dude. I'm not the one who doesn't know where to stick it when he gets the chance."

The math geek has abandoned Mark's work and is full on watching us. I could just kill Mark for pulling this with an audience. What I really want to do is skip school and hide at home, but then I'll get suspended, which means kicked off the basketball team. No can do. As captain, I really have to look like I have my act together. Which in this case, means I gotta go about my day like normal. Starting with getting out of this library and to first hour as fast as possible.

Mark snatches his homework and catches up with me, throwing an arm over my shoulders. "Dude, it's just a dumb video. It'll blow over."

Everyone is staring at me and not in a good way. They're not even bothering to hide their smirks behind their hands.

I try to ignore Mark and shoulder my way through the crowd to my first hour, but he grabs me by the arm. "Brayden!"

"What?"

He looks serious now, like he's finally realized I'm not amused. "You're not the worst one on there, okay? There's six of you, and trust me, you're like the least interesting one. No one's gonna care. And if anyone tries to give you shit, you send them to me. I got your back."

I roll my eyes. "Whatever man."

He leans in. "So your girlfriend's a prude, so what? Here's what you do. Next party, we get Angela a little drunk. A little liquor will loosen her up, then you take her upstairs. You can make it real romantic you know? Flowers or whatever. Bam. Problem solved."

I shake my head. I can't do that. If I could do something like that, I wouldn't be in this situation in the first place. I'm pretty popular. Girls want to get with me, it's just when I get into a situation like that, like what Mark's talking about, I start thinking what if my mom could see me? Which is about the last thing you want to be thinking about when you're about to hit a metaphorical home run in the sack. Then I chicken out.

I thought getting a girlfriend would help, but if anything, it made it worse. Now, instead of thinking about my mom, I'm thinking about Angela's feelings. The last thing I want to do is mess up what we have.

So yeah. I'm a virgin, and now the whole school knows.

#

Angela waits for me in our first hour class, and the second I sit next to her, she pulls her braids over her shoulder and leans across the gap between our desks.

"Brayden, I'm so sorry."

"Why?" I ask. I'm attempting to act nonchalant about this whole situation, but my voice cracks slightly. "It's not your fault."

Her big brown eyes fall to the floor. If her skin weren't so dark, she'd be blushing a bright pink. "I feel like it is."

I reach out and grab her hand, leaning close so our conversation stays private. Not that anything is private in this school. "It's not a big deal. I swear. I don't care what anyone's saying, as long as you're happy. That's all that matters, right?"

Her lips curl up in the corners, and I guess in that moment, it really doesn't matter to me. Like Mark said, it'll blow over. If the worst thing people can say about me is that I'm a virgin, oh well.

Seven

Cynthia

All day, in every single hour, I get stares. It's bad enough that most of my classes are sophomore or junior classes, thanks to the semester I flunked a couple years ago, putting me behind with the other school idiots. I'll have enough credits to graduate, but I'm not exactly surrounded by fellow seniors. As Jason says, "get the C, get the credit, get the hell out of here." Jason gets it. I don't need Algebra to drum, I just need a new band. Maybe all girls so there won't be any of that screwing around with the bass player drama that got me kicked out of the old one. Once we've signed a label, all these dumbass high school classes and even worse people will mean nothing.

Which doesn't exactly help right now, because today still sucks.

Pretty much everyone around me is either dying of laughter when they see me, or looking at me like they've never seen anyone so trashy. I've been cultivating this vibe with the underclassmen, like I'm too tough to touch, but now I've been knocked down a peg. I can see it in their eyes.

It'd be okay if Jason were here, but he's not. Which has me worried. I assume it's related to the video, but I don't find out for sure until lunch. Cat calls sound from every corner of the cafeteria while I make my way to my usual table and sit. It's all guys, and the second I put my tray down, the one next to me slides across the bench and drops his hand to the inside of my thigh.

"Hey Cyn."

I elbow him hard in the ribs. "Back off."

The whole table starts hooting with laughter and I feel heat rising to my ears which can only mean one thing. I'm about to lose my temper. Ask Jimmy how that goes. Luckily, one of the teachers with lunch duty strolls by and tells the boys to knock it off and get to eating. Thanks, Ms. Whatsername. I really appreciate it.

Usually Harvey sits with us, but today he's halfway across the cafeteria staring at his phone screen so he doesn't have to meet anyone's eyes. Smart. I should have done that.

Once everyone's calmed down, I venture my question. "So, where's Jason?" I try to sound like I don't care, which is a total joke. Everyone knows Jason's the only reason I even bother coming to school. He said he will personally kill me if I don't get my diploma, and since it's important to him, I guess it's important to me.

More snickers.

"You didn't watch the video?"

"I watched half of it."

"Jason was the last one."

I shrug. "So? Jason doesn't care what other people think."

Cory, who is sitting across from me and is a slightly decent person from time to time, leans forward. "JJ said he's gay."

Speechless. My mouth just hangs open. How the hell did she know? I'm the only one who's supposed to know!

Even Cory looks confused. "So it's true?"

"Fuck off," I mutter, which is as much of an admission as anything else, I guess.

"She said he's been fooling around with some guy at the park near his house. Sneaking out and stuff."

Now I don't even know who to be pissed at because even worse than JJ outing Jason, which is pretty fucking bad, is the fact that Jason was seeing someone and he hadn't told me. We tell each other everything.

"Is it true?" I ask. Stupid question. How would they know if I didn't?

"Is it true what she said about you?"

Hell if I know. I didn't watch.

They all start laughing again at my obviously confused face.

"She said you sometimes have sex to score drugs for the band."

Did the temperature in the room just drop a thousand degrees or did I just get doused with ice water? I'm dying. There's only one thing this could refer to, but I don't even understand. Where did drugs come into any of this?

I never even told anyone, except Jason. Because I was hurt bad. I was bleeding and everything and Jason was pissed. Said that it was rape and I should quit the band. Said that Steve-O was bad and I needed to stay away from him and his band and everything.

So we got into one of our rare screaming matches, because he didn't understand what it's like to be a member of the best band in town, to play, to have the audience scream at you. To want you. And it wasn't like I was permanently scarred or anything. But he was still pissed, and he never really liked Steve-O all that much.

My lip starts trembling, like it always does when I get really upset. If JJ knows this about me, she probably knows everything about everyone. I clamp my teeth down over my lip ring, sucking on the cool metal and taking deep breaths to calm down.

When I trust myself, I speak. "So what? Jason's gay. It's not that big of a deal."

"Apparently, someone told his dad yesterday."

Every noise in the cafeteria stops.

Not really, but it feels like it does. I can still see all the other students talking and laughing, but it's like slow motion. Like I'm outside of it all. For me, it is deathly silent. All I can hear is ringing in my ears. All I can feel is my own rage.

I stand up slowly and walk to the trash can, dumping my uneaten food before making my way to the back corner where we're supposed to drop off our trays. Before I get there though, I pass JJ.

I don't think. I just swing that plastic tray as hard as I can, crashing it onto the back of Julie Jenkins's stupid fucking head.

Eight

Lindsey

The deafening CRACK resonates through the lunch room, and the entire senior class turns in their seats in time to see JJ slump forward and Officer Hawkins, our school resource officer, pull Cynthia out of the cafeteria.

The people closest to JJ jump out of their seats. Well, most everyone does. Not me. I just watch as teachers pull students away and fight their way to her. Within moments they've ordered everyone out of the cafeteria, into the courtyard. We watch through a wall of windows as paramedics rush her out of the building.

While everyone around me mutters about how awful JJ looked, the blood, or wonders whether she'll be okay, I stand in silence. I don't feel a thing.

You can't blame Cynthia. You don't blame a rabid dog for biting and spreading the disease. It can't help itself. It's simply too brain damaged to know better. You blame the human who poked the rabid dog with a stick.

And while my name was on JJ's list of nefarious doings, you would never find me losing control like that. It would never be allowed.

Once the paramedics are out of the building, the teachers tell us all to get back to class and quick. The halls are filled with gossiping voices, everyone filling in their friends about what happened. It is utter chaos. Teachers keep telling us all to get to our classes, to clear the halls, to stop talking about it.

Through it all, I walk calmly down the hall, my hands neatly folded behind my back, and try not to smile.

Because, I have a plan.

Mom thinks contrition is the only way to move past this. It may work on Sephora, enough contrition and a hefty sum of money to smooth it over, but my schoolmates will be harder to impress.

For them, there's only one option. It's all about power. Mine may have taken a hit, but all I have to do is prove I'm still in charge. I rule this school. Not JJ.

The thing is, JJ thinks she's an investigative journalist, but she's not. She's a gossip monger, nothing else. No one takes the gossip column seriously. No one stands in line at the store reading headlines in tabloids and thinks "gee, what excellent journalism!"

JJ spreads rumors, then watches as the people around her crack, and I'm going to use that against her. That and every litigation trick I've picked up from my mother over the years. Deny, then offer a counter fact. Deny, then ask a loaded question for which there is only one answer. Deny, then suggest that JJ's credibility is lacking. Whereas I, Lindsey Banford, have a pristine reputation, thank you very much.

I don't intend to lose that reputation over something as silly as a YouTube video.

Nine

Cynthia

This isn't the first time I've been trapped in the principal's office waiting for my parents to show up, but this is by far the worst. Dr. Pritchard keeps mentioning that JJ has to go the hospital and she might need stitches and don't I feel terrible?

I definitely don't feel bad. JJ got what she deserved. The bitch.

I do feel kind of bad when my parents walk in twenty minutes later with that look on their faces. *What did she do this time? Our messed-up daughter.*

Then Dr. Pritchard explains to them what happened in the cafeteria, and even though he's trying to be unbiased and all, I guess it's pretty tricky to tell someone that their kid sent another kid to the hospital without sounding a little pissed.

Dad pinches the bridge of his nose and Mom sighs, "Oh Cynthia." Then they both look at me like I'm a monster, and that makes me feel pretty shitty.

"Why'd you do it?" Dr. Pritchard asks.

At first, I'm not sure if he means attacking JJ or having sex for drugs, then I realize he hasn't seen the video yet, so I explain to him all about JJ and her stupid YouTube channel. Normally, I'm no snitch, but since it's JJ, I don't care. Let her deal with the fallout for once.

"So there was a video over the weekend?"

"Yeah," I say, scowling. "I was pissed about what she said in it."

Dr. Pritchard unlocks his computer and starts typing into YouTube. It takes him about three minutes of searching to find the offending video, because adults really don't know their way around the internet. It's kind of hilarious. Except, then I realize he's going to watch the video, right here, right now.

With my parents in the room.

All my insides start squirming around. I don't even know what the video says about me. Not exactly. But I'm pretty damn sure it's about the last thing I want my mom hearing.

I guess Dr. Pritchard thought it'd be dumb stuff, like the first secret, all about virgins and stupid things that adults think don't matter. But when JJ gets to Harvey and his drug business, he goes a little pink in the ears and pulls out his walkie talkie.

"I need Officer Hawkins to my office, ASAP."

But he doesn't stop the video, which means I'm forced to listen to everything JJ has to say about me. It's bad. Way worse than I imagined. She makes it sound like I fucking volunteered for the job. Behind me, Mom says "Oh Cynthia, oh Cynthia" again and again. I could just kill Dr. Pritchard for making her listen to that.

I know Jason's coming up, and I really want to know exactly what JJ said, but before him is Charlotte. Even I wasn't prepared for her secret affair with Mr. DuPont. Dr. Pritchard about falls out of his chair scrambling for something to write with and the closest piece of paper, which happens to be an old McDonald's receipt. Egg McMuffin and a large coffee.

He gets on his walkie again, tells the front office to phone the local police department, and asks that Charlotte get pulled out of class. Then, after a pause, he suggests the school counselor come as well. He's not looking red anymore. He's looking green.

We don't even listen to Jason's story. I don't think Dr. Pritchard can stomach it, but I fill him in.

"JJ told everyone Jason's gay." I glance back at my parents, but neither of them looks surprised. "His dad didn't even know, and he's like the biggest gay-bashing evangelical asshole there is."

"Watch your language please, Ms. Marlow."

I slump in my chair and fold my arms. "I don't even care what she said about me, but she had no right to do that to Jason. He's like the only decent person in this whole fucking school."

Dad clears his throat next to me, and Mom mumbles, "Oh Cynthia," again.

Dr. Pritchard sighs, and I know he wants to tell me off again, but he's restraining himself. He looks up at my parents. "She'll have five days out of school suspension. Normally, I'd have our SRO escort her around school to get missing work, but we have other matters to attend to, so if you could just take her home. She can return next Monday." He looks at me like he wants to offer some stupid platitude about not letting gossip get me down and remember that life goes on after high school. The total bullshit that adults always try to shove down our throats. But I give him a death glare and instead he just grits his teeth, nods, and tells me I can go.

Mom drives me home in my own damn car, which I paid for by the way. She tries asking about the video, but I can't talk to her right now. The ride takes damn near forever, and when we get home, she pockets the keys. Then she and Dad spend the rest of the afternoon tearing through my room searching for anything and everything to prove I'm a massive disappointment.

Pot stash, gone. That sucks. I thought I'd hidden it pretty well, but they found it. Mom starts asking about my drug usage like I'm some hardened criminal instead of a normal kid who likes to get high on the weekends. Like I'm doing the hard stuff like Steve-O. She's about to start crying. She just keeps saying "Oh Cynthia" over and over again in this pitiful voice that makes me feel like total shit.

They take all my drumsticks too. Every last pair. Even the ones I broke on my first ever gig because I was so excited. I kept them as a memento, but now they're gone. They say I can't play for a few weeks, that I need a break from drumming. When they lock my drum set in the basement I feel like I'm dying. This is what death feels like. Not being able to drum. I don't even know what to do.

Mom can tell I'm about to lose it, because she rubs my back and tells me that we'll "discuss our options" in a few weeks once this all blows over, but without drums I have no options. Without music, I am nothing. They know that.

My room is completely gutted. No cell phone, no laptop, everything is gone except my textbooks and a biography about Amy Winehouse I bought a few weeks ago because she's a fucking goddess. I guess I should be happy they let me keep that, but it feels like a pretty small consolation prize.

That's not the worst part about this day. Not by a long shot.

The worst part is after my parents go to bed, I sneak downstairs to use my dad's cell to call Jason. He answers on the first ring, so I guess he must have known I'd try to call.

He tells me all about his day, which apparently was spent watching his dad contact all his pastor friends to find the best "specialist" for young Christians who are confused about their sexuality.

"That's code for gay conversion therapy, Jason!" I hiss into the phone.

"I know."

He sounds so damn scared and sad and lonely that I really do start crying. I'm not normally a crying sort of a person, but it's been a really stressful day.

"Please don't let them change you," I say. "Please, Jason, please, please don't let them change you. Say whatever they want to hear, do whatever they want you to do, but don't let them fucking change you. Because you're perfect Jason, exactly the way you are. You're perfect."

I'm getting all emotional right now, but Jason is completely silent. I start to wonder if he hung up on me or if he hates me because I'm being so pathetic right now. I start to ask if he's still there, but he interrupts me.

"Thanks, Cyn." His voice cracks, and he gulps a few times then says, "I should go. I'm not supposed to be on my phone, ya know?"

I nod, which is stupid because you can't see a nod over the phone. Then I say the only thing I can think to say, which probably sounds kind of idiotic, considering, but I tell him that I love him.

He sniffs loudly, and I think he may have started crying too, because his voice sounds really funny when he responds. "I love you, too."

Then there's a beep and he's gone.

39

Ten

Charlotte

About thirty minutes after the spectacle in the lunchroom, I get called into the counselor's office. It was only a matter of time, I guess. I go in prepared to lie. I have to lie. I can't let Mr. DuPont get in trouble for this. For what I made him do.

Our principal is already there, standing with his arms folded and a grim look on his face behind the counselor's desk.

I knock on the door frame as I enter. "Am I in trouble?"

Mrs. Cooper hops up to guide me into the chair, then instead of sitting in her own behind her desk, sits in the blue plastic chair right next to mine. "No, not at all! We just have a few concerns."

Concerns. Could she just say what she means, like a normal person? Concerns makes it sound like she actually cares about me, which quite frankly, isn't true. I've been at this school for a semester now, and she doesn't even know my name. None of them do.

Dr. Pritchard clears his throat. "Um… Miss Waters…" He looks nervous. "As you may know, there was a video released by one of your classmates over the weekend."

"Yeah, I saw."

He glances at Mrs. Cooper who jumps in, turning in her seat to face me and placing her hand on mine. I pull my hand away.

"Charlotte," she begins. I guess she does know my name. "There are some things that were said about you that we are very concerned about."

"Lies." I force myself to maintain eye contact.

Mrs. Cooper cocks her head. "We need to verify. These are troubling accusations." She's really dancing around what she wants to say. "The video suggests that perhaps you were sexually involved with a teacher."

I look at Dr. Pritchard, but he's staring intently at the ceiling.

"I told you, it's not true."

But Mrs. Cooper isn't backing down. "Can you think of why this other student would say something like that about you if it wasn't true?"

"I don't know," I shrug. "I don't really talk to her. Maybe she's mad at Mr. DuPont for giving her a bad grade or something. Why is it my problem if she's lying?" I'm talking too much. I feel it, the way the blood rushes to my head. I get a little light-headed when I'm lying.

She closes her eyes and takes a long breath, then leans in closer. "Are you absolutely sure nothing happened between you and Mr. DuPont? He never propositioned you in any way? Never touched you? Made you feel uncomfortable?"

My lip twitches. "No," I repeat, but I guess my eyes tell the truth for me, because Mrs. Cooper looks like she's going to throw up and Dr. Pritchard starts twisting a chunk of his hair maniacally, so I start to understand why he's got such terrible male pattern baldness around his temples.

"Charlotte—"

My heart is beating about a thousand times per second at this point, and my face feels burning hot, so I'm guessing it's red enough to match my hair. I open my mouth to speak. "I... uh, I..." I swallow, but my mouth is so dry, it just sticks in my throat. "I... he never forced me to do anything, okay? I... I wanted—"

Mrs. Cooper reaches out for my hand, and this time, I don't pull away. "Can you tell us what happened?"

Tears slide down my cheeks. This isn't fair. Mr. DuPont is an amazing teacher, the head of the English department. In the six months I've known him, he's inspired me more than any other teacher I've had. And now his name is getting dragged through the mud over what? We have a real connection. It's not his fault no one else can understand us.

But my mouth has a mind of its own. It opens and truths come tumbling out. The way I used to stay in his classroom after school every day last semester to chat. The first time we kissed—in the storage closet while he was searching for some printer paper. I followed him in. It was my fault. I made the first move. This isn't fair. The way we used to meet up after I got off work, or how during the summer, when my mom was working, I drove into St. Paul to meet him at his apartment. And how, for a couple of glorious months, we had a real relationship, an hour away from everyone else in this town. We could explore museums, hold hands, eat lunches at outdoor diners, then return to his apartment for the afternoon. With the right clothes and makeup, I look twenty-something. And with him, I felt it.

By the end of it, I'm sobbing. I can't help myself. I manage to choke out the stupidest excuse ever. "We waited until I turned seventeen to actually do anything."

"That doesn't matter."

I stare at the fake wood pattern on Mrs. Cooper's desk while they decide what to do with me. The decision is made for them when there's a knock at the door. The school secretary opens it to reveal two uniformed police officers and behind them, my mom.

Not sure which of them makes me more sick to my stomach.

Dr. Pritchard excuses himself to "discuss next steps" with the officers, and Mom and Mrs. Cooper trap me in her office where I have to explain the entire situation all over again to Mom.

"What's going to happen?" I ask.

"I don't know."

"Is Mr. DuPont going to lose his job?"

Mom snorts, like she can't believe I'm concerned about Mr. DuPont.

Mrs. Cooper gets a pained look on her face and doesn't answer for a while. Then she sighs. "Yes."

My lip starts shaking. "That's not fair. I'm just as much to blame. Maybe more!"

"No," she says sadly. "No, Charlotte. You're not."

We sit in Mrs. Cooper's office for most of the afternoon. I don't say anything. Mom wants to hash this all out with me, but every time she starts to question me, Mrs. Cooper reminds her that I'm still processing things and that she should be patient. She says it half to her and half to me, reminding me I can talk in my own time.

I don't want to talk. I just want to sit here and stew in my own anger. I make a list of everyone I'm angry with. First, JJ for posting that video. Next, Mrs. Cooper and Dr. Pritchard for making me say all those things about Mr. DuPont, for not just accepting my initial lie and moving on. And, Mom, of course, for moving me all the way here in the first place. I was happy in California!

Really, everyone at this school makes me so angry because not one of them ever really bothered to get to know me last year. I was brand new, halfway through my junior year of high school, literally the worst time ever to move across country. No Dad, my mom worked all the time. I was alone.

Mr. DuPont was the only person in the entire building who actually spent time getting to know me.

We sit there until Dr. Pritchard comes back to tell us the officers have left, which of course means Mr. DuPont has as well. They must have dragged him away in handcuffs. Mr. DuPont. Literally took him out of his own classroom, hands behind his back. Like he was some criminal and not a highly educated man of thought and reason. I wasn't even there for him.

Mom wants to take me home, but I refuse to go with her, and we have one of our patented silent mother-daughter fights, which normally she wins. But this time she just grimaces, then leaves.

I start gathering my things. "Can I go back to class?"

Mrs. Cooper nods. "If you ever need to talk, you know where to find me."

Never going to happen.

I spend the last hour of the day sitting in the back of the classroom listening to my classmates gossip about Mr. DuPont. Of course they've all seen the video as well, but to them it's just a joke. A man's life has been ruined and they're just excited to get to watch a movie in class for the next few days.

I sink lower in my seat as a dozen athletes, in their letter jackets and matching haircuts all turn to look at me. Looks like I'm finally getting noticed.

Eleven

Jason

I've missed three days of school, and I'm knee-deep in intensive at-home Bible study. Every morning, I wake up, eat breakfast, get dressed, and meet my dad in his office for my daily "assignment." I'm dying to ask to go back to school. It's crazy to miss this much time, but I know if I ask, he'll just keep me home longer. Dad's standing in the doorway to his office when I get there Thursday morning, arms crossed over a barrel chest that can only come from years in military service "fighting for our freedoms." Insert mandatory southern accent, even though he's Minnesotan born and raised.

He watches me slink down the hallway until I'm standing right in front of him, then says, "you're late."

Gulp.

"My alarm didn't go off?"

I made that sound like a question. Big mistake.

His eyes narrow. "Don't lie."

I force myself to face him. "Okay."

"Okay?"

"Yes, sir."

His eyes bore holes into my head. I'm ninety-five percent sure my dad can read minds, or would be if reading minds were condoned by the Bible, which I'm pretty sure it isn't.

He gives a curt nod. "Get in here."

Nothing good has ever happened in his office, at least not for me. I've been forced to copy passages of the Bible in that office, been smacked in that office, been expected to recite from any number of verses directly correlated to my many transgressions. The office is where my dad feels most powerful, where he "receives our Father's message," and that message is usually that I'm a failure in every sense of the word.

But I can't exactly refuse.

I follow him in.

For as much as Dad talks about God's light, his office is dark and intimidating. A large oak desk faces the doorway, and bookshelves of dark wood flank either side. A large cross hangs to the left of the door, a painting of the crucifixion to the right. Real uplifting stuff. The only non-religious decor in this room is the pair of dog tags hanging from his desk lamp, a reminder that he serves his country as well as his god.

For me, it's a reminder that if he hadn't met my mom while stationed in Guam, I might never have existed. And maybe that wouldn't be so bad.

He paces the hard wood floor in front of his desk. "Shut the door."

Obedience is my life-preserver. I have no choice but to do what he says and pray. Scratch that, prayers are for the religious, which I am not. Hope. Hope for the best.

Hope is universal.

I know better than to sit without being told to. Instead, I stand in the exact center of the room, with my shoulders squared and my chin parallel with the floor. My hands clutch each other behind my back. I funnel my fear to them, hidden out of his sight, because my face can betray nothing. It must be a blank slate. Emotionless.

Dad settles into his office chair and works, or pretends to work. He makes me wait. This is one of his tricks. I must stand perfectly still, at the ready, like a soldier awaiting his orders. Any hint that my legs are tired or my shoulders sore, or my mind wandering, and he's on me. I've had seventeen years, ten months, and eleven days of practice. I know what's expected of me.

He types at his computer for several silent minutes, then out of the blue says. "Recite Leviticus."

He doesn't need to say the chapter or verses. I know what he wants. The homophobe's favorite verses. Man lying down with another man. Big sin and all. I rattle them off no problem. Not like I haven't had the practice.

"Look at me when you're speaking."

I meet his eyes and say them again, slower this time.

"Do you understand what that passage is saying?" he asks.

"Yes." He frowns, so I add on a "sir."

He eyes me for a long time, trying to detect a lie, but there's no lie to be found here. I know exactly what the passage is saying. I just think it's crap.

"I spoke to Mr. Murphy from the Youth Salvation Center in St Paul. He believes your case to be particularly urgent." His eyes fix on mine. "And I agree. So, starting Monday, you will be meeting with him two evenings a week for spiritual guidance."

I force a nod. The muscles in my jaw ache from the way I'm clenching my teeth to keep from talking back.

Dad pulls a stack of books from beneath his desk and sets them in front of me. "On top of your work with him, I will expect you to study these during your spare time."

I tear my eyes away from him to glance at the titles.

"You're a smart boy." The closest my dad has ever come to complimenting me. "It should take you no more than a few weeks to finish a book. I expect a full report on the first one by the end of the month, and an additional report every three weeks following. We will meet to discuss your reports on the Saturday following."

"You want me to write you a book report every three weeks?" I regret the words a second after I blurt them out. Rule number one of dealing with my dad: never question his orders.

His jaw clenches, and he stretches the muscles in his neck, suppressing the anger that's building up behind those dead eyes of his. "What did you just say to me?"

I steel myself, gathering up whatever little grains of courage still exist somewhere in me, way down deep. The ones that haven't yet been beaten out.

"I'm taking two AP courses this year, and I have to apply to colleges, and—"

"And," he interrupts, "all of this is more important than the fate of your eternal soul?"

I have to swallow back all the bile in my voice before I can speak. "No, sir."

He stands up and walks around the desk until he's standing next to me, like a drill sergeant, his mouth inches from my ear. I expect him to bark orders. Drop and give me fifty, you best not be talking back to me, private! But he doesn't.

"It seems to me," he says in a voice barely above a whisper, "that if you have time to sneak out of this house and pervert yourself with another boy, then you have time to read a book or two." He snatches the top book and slams it against my chest. "Start with that one."

I steal a glance at the title as he returns to his desk. *The Lord's Plan: Defeating the Inner Demon.* That's what my sexuality is to him. An evil that must be vanquished. My stoic resolve weakens, the muscle below my right eye twitches, betraying my own anger as I raise my eyes again to meet his gaze.

"Yes, sir."

A part of me wants him to see the hatred inside me. To recognize this for what it is. We are nothing, him and me. Not father and son. There is no love here, not even respect. Just determination on both sides to despise. But Cynthia's words ring in my ears. Do whatever I need to do, then get the hell out. I'll meet his damn counselor and read his damn books, then I'll get the hell out of here. I'll apply to every college in the country, just so I can get away from him.

California might be nice, or New York.

Several seconds of tense silence pass, neither of us wanting to lose the staring contest between us. Then in his gruff, loveless voice, he tells me I'm dismissed, and I can breathe again.

Twelve

Cynthia

JJ's words whirl in my head nonstop. Mom and Dad are both at work, and I'm home by myself with nothing but a pile of chores and JJ's words. *Have sex to score the band free drugs.*

It sounds disgusting and wrong. It *is* wrong. I didn't do that. Not even close. Every time the words run through my head, I scrub the mixing bowl in my hands a little harder. Like I'm trying to scrub it out of existence. I tell myself that if I keep busy, I won't have time to think about what JJ said, but it's not working. I want to talk to Jason. I *need* to talk to Jason. But I can't, because his parents suck.

The doorbell rings and the bowl slips from my hands, landing with a loud clatter on our linoleum floor. I start to head toward the front door, then pause. My phone's been lighting up nonstop the past few days. Pretty much everyone at school has something shitty to say to me. What if one of them is there? Technically, they should be at school, but it's not that hard to skip. I do it all the time. I don't want to see anyone from school right now. Especially some asshole trying to corner me in my own home.

I've just about decided not to answer the door when a knock comes from the door off our kitchen, and Harvey's face appears in the window.

"Cyn, let me in," he hollers.

I breathe a sigh of relief. Harvey's harmless. A bit of an idiot, but a harmless one. I yank open the door and he hurries inside, glancing over his shoulder as he does.

"What's wrong with you?" I ask.

He throws himself into one of the chairs at the kitchen table and lays his head down. "I owe money."

I sit across from him.

"The school flushed my stash. Right down the drain. Now I got people breathing down my neck because it hadn't exactly paid for itself, ya know?"

I sigh. "Yeah, I know."

He lifts his head a fraction of an inch to look at me. "You couldn't have waited until after school to bash JJ's head in, could ya?"

I shrug sheepishly. "My mom says I'm too impulsive."

"No shit."

Now I feel kind of bad. I guess I probably should have waited until after school. Dealt with JJ outside of school. Would have saved me the suspension too. I don't get how she's allowed to say shit like that about me and Jason and all of us, and gets away scot-free. Maybe because she lives on the good side of town, and Harvey and me are over here in Crummyville, MN.

"I got like fifty bucks upstairs," I offer. "I know it's not a lot. My parents confiscated my stash." I didn't have much anyway. Not like that's going to pay for what Harvey lost.

I start thinking about Steve-O and his pills, and how much money those would go for. As soon as I start though, I can't stop. I think about his apartment and his dealer, and it feels like I can't escape or breathe. I feel cold and sweaty at the same time, like I'm going to throw up.

"Cyn?" Harvey interrupts my panic, and I jerk out of it.

"Yeah, what?"

"You okay?"

"Yeah," I shake myself a little, try to throw off the chill. "Yeah, I'm fine. I'll go grab that cash, okay?"

#

Sometimes I feel bad that my parents got stuck with such a shitty kid like me. I'm not exactly the dream daughter. Lindsey Banford. Now she's a dream. Straight A's, Student Council president, off to some big shot college on the east coast. So I figured during my week off, I'd try to at least pretend to be a good daughter. You know, doing all the housework and stuff. I even made dinner on Tuesday night, just to prove I'm not a complete waste of space. My parents are good people. It's not their fault I'm a screw up. They don't deserve my gigantic ball of shit.

Harvey beats it as soon as he has cash in hand. Good.

I still can't get JJ's video out of my head, and seeing Harvey just brought it all back full force. I need answers, and there's only one person who can give them.

Steve-O.

Mom took my keys when she grounded me, but I made a copy months ago, and because I knew my room could be stripped at any time, I hid it somewhere they'd never think to look - the junk drawer in our kitchen.

My hands shake the entire time I drive over there. I gotta get that under control, play this cool. What I really need is a smoke. I'm not like a real smoker or anything, but when I'm really freaking out, like right now, it helps. I dunno, maybe I'm going through withdrawals. I'm not even sure you can get withdrawals from weed. I sure as hell never did anything harder. That shit will mess you up. I got my career to think about. I can get wasted when I'm famous.

There's barely any parking around Steve-O's apartment building. It's one of those really dumpy places that would make my mom flip if she ever found out I was at. I end up parking on the street a few blocks over and carrying my keys between my fingers in case someone tries to grab me. You can't be too careful in this part of town. Seriously.

Outside his door, I take about a billion deep breaths before knocking.

There's music playing inside—The Clash—and at first I think maybe he didn't hear me knocking, so I lift my fist to bang again, but the door swings open right as I'm about to hit.

"Whoa," he says, dodging out of the way.

I drop my hand. "Sorry."

"Well, don't you look like shit."

I probably do. Still, kind of a dick thing to say.

He leans in the doorway, clearly not letting me in. "What's up?"

I shrug. "I just needed a break from suburbia is all. That a problem?"

"Heard you got yourself kicked out of school."

"Yup."

Steve-O stares at me for a few seconds, then shifts out of the way to let me through. "I have to work in an hour. You can hang until then."

"Cool, thanks."

As soon as I'm inside, I make a beeline for the spare drumsticks I'd left over there. I'm always leaving them all over the place after shows, and sure enough, there's a set poking out of the corner of his couch, just waiting for me to hold them.

It just feels right, having sticks back in my hand. I twirl the left one. Good, I haven't lost it. People like to say petting a dog or cat can lower your blood pressure? Well that's me with drumsticks. Already, I feel calmer. Safer. The weight, the balance, it's comforting.

I sink into the couch and close my eyes, listening to the music in the background. It doesn't take me long to pick up the beat, then I start tapping on Steve-O's coffee table. Lightly, because I don't want to break the damn thing. If I had my set, I'd let loose. But this is almost as good.

Steve-O sits next to me and laughs. "Feel better?"

"Yes."

I sigh and sink back into the couch. It's stupid, but I do feel better.

"It's bullshit, them taking your drums from you."

"You heard about that?"

He shrugs. "Ray mentioned it."

"You know," I say, sneaking a glance out of the corner of my eye. "It was kind of bullshit taking my band away from me."

"It was never your band." He says it so fast, I'm sure he must have had it prepared.

"Whatever." I tap a few more beats on the coffee table, just to vent my frustration. Plus, I gotta work up some nerve. "So," I say, trying to sound casual. "You heard why I got suspended?"

"Fighting."

He's playing it cool. I know he knows. Well, I'll just have to play it cool too.

"Yeah, you ever met JJ?"

He shrugs.

"She posts videos about kids at school. Shit like that?"

"Yeah, so?"

"So she posted one about me."

"You and a few others," he says. Then, he realizes his mistake. "Or so I heard."

I stand up and walk across the room. "C'mon Steve-O. You watched it. I know you did."

"Fine, I did."

My drumsticks thump against the sides of my legs, sending little shots of pain through my body, enough to relax me, enough to keep my voice from shaking. "So you know what she said about me?"

"Yeah."

"Say it."

He glares at me, like he's going to refuse, then he scowls and looks away. "You used to bang Grayson to score free drugs. Big deal. Lots of chicks do it. I don't know why you're so bent out of shape."

"That's not what happened."

Steve-O raises an eyebrow, daring me to go on.

"JJ's video mentioned pills. I never did pills. I didn't even drink back then." And I really hadn't. I was still so innocent. Until that night. Steve-O was the one who as into all that shit, pills and all. He was the one who would want the drugs. He was the one...

I look up slowly. "You knew," I whisper.

He doesn't say anything, but the corner of his mouth twitches. Enough to let me know I'm onto something.

"You knew," I repeat a little louder. "You were the one into pills. You were the one who—" I can't finish the sentence. I can't be near him anymore. I cross the room, stopping to catch my breath next to his bookshelf.

"You're probably remembering it wrong," he says.

But I'm not. Not at all. I remember everything. I just didn't have all the pieces. Not until today.

He keeps going, digging his own hole a little deeper. "You got wasted, made some stupid decisions, whatever. Get over it."

My temper flares and I snatch a book off the shelf next to me and hurl it at his head. "Tell the truth!"

"What the hell, Cyn?" He leaps off the couch and scurries as far from me as he can get. Good.

"Tell me the truth!" I chuck another book. "You set me up." The book hits his shoulder.

He grabs his arm. "Fuck, man. Stop it!"

When I grab a third book, he throws his hands up defensively. "Fine. Shit. You want the truth. Here it is. I owed Grayson money, and he said he'd forget it if he got some time with you. I figure what the hell. What you and him do, that's your business."

"You didn't think, I dunno, maybe you needed my permission?" I snap.

"You were being a bitch. He offered to put you in your place, I took him up on it. And hell, you must have been good, because—"

I throw the final book, smacking him square on the nose.

"What d'ya want me to do, Cyn?" he cries, "I can't take it back okay? I felt like shit afterward. I really did."

"That doesn't change anything!" I scream. We stand across the room from each other, both of us in fighting stance. My breath comes quick and heavy, and my entire body shakes.

Steve-O relaxes slightly, rubbing the back of his neck and looking down. "God, you don't know what he's like."

"YES I DO!"

I can't breathe. I'm hyperventilating. I gotta get out of here before I explode. I fumble for the door handle, but my hands are shaking bad, and I can't see straight. I struggle long enough for Steve-O to cross to the door and grab my wrist.

"Don't touch me," I snarl, yanking myself free and bringing a drumstick down hard on his hand. Hard enough to leave a red welt.

"Look," he says, "I'm sorry. I am. Honest. What do you want from me?"

"I want you to suffer," I spit out.

I throw the door open and make a run for it. Not like he's going to chase me down the street or anything, but I can't be near him. My skin crawls, my sweat feels freezing on my skin. I make it to my car, then double over sick to my stomach, dry heaving as I wrench the door open and crumple inside.

Oh god, it's true. It's fucking true. JJ's video was true.

Thirteen

Charlotte

Chicken-porium is deserted. Harvey was good for business. It's Saturday night, and usually the drive thru is packed full of teenagers looking to party. Not anymore. He is closed for business. I lean over the counter and scroll through pictures on Instagram and try not to feel sorry for myself when I see everyone from back home having fun. I tell myself I don't care. But I do.

The bell over the door jangles, and Harvey walks in.

I'm not going to lie, I'm surprised to see him.

He clues me in pretty quickly. "Gotta pick up my last paycheck."

"Oh." I stare down at my apron. "I'm sorry you got fired."

He shrugs.

There's really not much to say after that. The dining area is dead. I feel like I should say something else, but I don't know what to say. His situation sucks, but I guess I think he kind of had it coming. I mean, he knew what he was doing.

He checks the time on his phone. "Hey, do you mind letting Mr. Lempke know I'm here?"

"Oh, yeah."

Mr. Lempke is our manager. Well, not Harvey's manager anymore. I find him in the back going over some paperwork with a calculator in hand. I know he saw the video, because he fired Harvey in record time, so he has to know what it said about me. Lucky me, he doesn't seem to think my secret is a fireable offense. He has been really weird with me ever since it came out. Like, way too nice but also really distant. Like he thinks I'm a victim or something.

I let him know Harvey's waiting then beat it, because I can't stand his sad looks. He reminds me of a basset hound, big ears and drooping eyes.

"He said he'll be out in a few minutes," I tell Harvey when I get back to the front counter.

He nods and leans against the counter opposite me.

"You hungry?" I ask.

"No." His stomach lets out a loud grumble.

"I'll get you a chicken sandwich."

He shakes his head. "I can't afford it, Charlotte."

It takes a while for me to process that, not even being able to afford a two-dollar sandwich. I mean, I guess I never thought about Harvey's situation all that much.

"On me," I say. I grab one of the paper-wrapped sandwiches from the heater and shove it into his hand before he has a chance to argue.

He tears into it immediately, muttering "thanks" around a mouthful of food. The whole sandwich is gone in about thirty seconds, then he wipes his mouth with the back of his hand. "You're pretty cool, you know that?"

"Uh, thanks, I guess."

"I'm really sorry about, um, well you know... Mr. DuPont and... everything," he says.

I don't want to talk about it. Not with Harvey. Not with anyone. Everything is ruined, and I'm more alone than ever before.

Harvey, however, doesn't pick up on the hint. He just keeps going. "I mean, damn, Charlotte... if I had know your secret boyfriend was our teacher. Shit. I don't even get it. He's like twice your age."

"He is not!" I snap.

"It's kind of gross, that's all I'm saying."

My face burns. "You don't know anything about it, Harvey. He's a good person. He was nice to me, he treated me like… like I actually mattered."

I didn't mean to say all of that. As soon as it's out, I wish I could take it back.

Harvey stares at me with his eyes all wide. "Wow," he says, "wow…"

I'm saved from responding by our manager who shows up with Harvey's check, which he basically shoves into his hands before retreating back to his office. I'm so mad at Harvey for calling Mr. DuPont gross, I can't even look at him.

I fold my arms and stare at the counter. "You don't know anything about me and him, okay? You don't get it. He was all I had. My mom's always working. My dad is dead! I don't have any friends—"

"I thought I was your friend," he says. I look up in time to see him shove his check into his hoodie pocket and head for the door. He gives me a half-hearted wave over his shoulder. "See ya, Charlotte."

#

Mom's asleep on the couch when I get home. She clearly tried to wait up for me, but didn't make it. I know I should wake her up, let her know I'm home and safe. That's what she'd want me to do, but I don't. I can't stand the way she looks at me now, like I'm damaged, about to break.

The television is still on, local news, and that's something. Ever since Mr. DuPont's arrest, Mom's been guarding the TV remote with her life, quickly changing the channel away from the news when I walk into the room. Keeping everything lighthearted. It's better to avoid the problem, I suppose, than to actually talk about it.

Not that Mr. DuPont is a problem.

The real problem is that I haven't seen him in weeks.

As if the news channel has read my mind, Mr. DuPont's school picture pops onto the screen, followed by the footage I've seen a thousand times on my laptop screen—him in handcuffs walking out of the school's front doors, head ducked, but still so unmistakably him. His jaw, his lips, his…my breath catches and I pinch my eyes shut so I don't have to see it.

"Local teacher who was arrested earlier this month has taken a plea deal," a brusque female news anchor says. "The prosecutor's office released a statement earlier today."

The video feed that follows was clearly shot in the afternoon, probably while I was at work far from any screen. It shows a middle-aged man with bored eyes reading dryly from a paper. I catch a few phrases like "reduced prison sentence" and "registered as a sex offender," and I know I'm going to cry or throw up if I listen any longer.

I grab the remote off the arm of the couch and turn the TV off.

Somehow the sudden silence wakes Mom.

"Charli, baby?" she groans, lifting herself up and yawning widely. "When did you get home?"

"Just now."

"Are you okay?" She catches sight of the remote in my hand and her eyes widen with worry. "Was there something on the news? Was it...?"

I toss the remote onto the cushion next to her. "It was just one of those annoying car ads. You know, lots of screaming about credit approved and all." I force a shrug. "My head kind of hurts."

I turn toward my bedroom, and she rushes to her feet intent on following.

"Do you need anything, honey?"

"No," I say, "I just want to go to bed."

As soon as I say it, I feel so dead tired it becomes true. I just want to go to bed. I'm not sure I want to ever leave it.

Fourteen

Lindsey

It's been three weeks since the video, and in those weeks, so much has changed. I no longer command the respect around school that I've grown accustomed to over the years. Underclassmen now talk back during Student Council meetings, suggesting I might not be fit to run the school because of my "moral failings." Dad came back to town and brought with him a whole army of public relations experts to handle my situation.

Then we spent an entire weekend being seen around town doing the right thing: serving food at a homeless shelter, reading books to children at the library. For a few short hours, I became a puppet to my parents' needs, smiling and waving when necessary, standing quietly in the background, propping up my father's campaign for reelection.

At home, Mom reminds me that everything is hanging by a thread. She doesn't elaborate on what "everything" is, because I already know. Dad's election, my chances at Princeton, even her potential partnership at the law firm. Anything that goes wrong can and will be pinned on me.

In many ways, the only times I can breathe freely are at school, though of course, my perfect image must be maintained. The mere glimmer of possible failure on the horizon would send my mother into a conniption. She combs through my online grade book every Friday, looking for any hint that my shortcomings extend past shoplifting and into school.

I am not permitted to leave the house unattended.

I discovered this the first Saturday after the video. Mom was still out of town, leaving just me and Loretta, our cook, who must have been told to keep an extra eye on me, because the second my hand descended on our doorknob, she came bustling out of the kitchen, insisting that I help prepare vegetables for dinner. And when I insisted I just wanted to go shopping?

"Oh, your mother wouldn't like that." She couldn't outright tell me no. Not when my family employs her. But the threat was there. If I leave, she would tell Mom, and I would hear about it.

Three weeks of house arrest. I can leave for school, church, and election business. Nothing else.

"I don't understand why they keep punishing me," I complain to my older sister on the phone. "Why can't they get over this?"

I can hear Beth bustling around her own kitchen, telling my niece to move so she can put dinner on the table.

"Are you still there?" I ask.

"Huh?" More sounds of casserole dishes landing on bamboo trivets. "Yeah, sorry. It's a little hectic here. What's up?"

"I'm tired of Mom and Dad treating me like a convict. How do I get them to stop?"

"Oh, Lindsey…"

Beth is my oldest sister, already twenty-six. She went to Princeton, just like every other Banford, where she met the perfect husband—a med student with dreams of private practice. She got her MD a year after him, and now they work at the same hospital in downtown Des Moines. She is, without doubt, my parents' favorite daughter, the one against whom I am constantly compared.

She's also the only sibling willing to talk to me.

"Please, help me," I say desperately. "I can't spend my entire senior year trapped at home with Loretta."

"You're being hyperbolic."

"Am I?" I say. "I just want to go to the mall."

She snorts into the phone. "So you can steal something?"

"Of course not!" It's preposterous that everyone thinks I go to the mall for the sole purpose of stealing things. Ninety percent of the things I own, I purchased with my own money, or rather, my parents' money. But with their money, comes their scrutiny. They go through receipts and shopping bags, to approve every purchase.

Sometimes, I want something different. Lipstick that is a little too red, earrings that are a little too garish. Things I know they would never approve of. I know it's wrong, but when every second of your life is dictated, you have to take back something.

All I wanted was a little independence from the Banford name.

"Lindsey?"

I sigh. "Maybe they'll let me drive out to see you some weekend?"

"Things are really busy here. It's not a good time."

She doesn't want me around. Maybe she's afraid I'll take something of hers, but I never would, not from her.

I sit on my bed and curl my feet beneath me. "But you're still coming for Thanksgiving, right?"

"David's requested off, but you know how it is. Senior doctors get the best vacations."

My silence speaks for itself. It is uncomfortable and long, and it forces her to speak.

"We'll drive up sometime soon, Lindsey. I promise."

I hear my mother's voice in my head. *A smile can be heard through the phone.* Her advice is for speaking to campaign donors, but it's just as true here. I force a smile. "Of course, Beth. Sounds wonderful."

Then I hang up.

#

At least at school, I have a little freedom. My grades are perfect, naturally, and my behavior nearly so. Good enough that no teacher would ever dream of calling my parents to complain. Which means I can easily sneak into an empty classroom and swipe one of Mrs. Stenson's puppy figurines off her desk. I know it's wrong, but she's terrible, and I just need to feel in control of something. With Mom and Dad breathing down my neck every second of every day, I just need to know I still have it in me.

I tuck the figurine into the pocket of my dress, trusting the folds of fabric to hide the shape as I move through the hallways. No one even glances my way.

Why would they? When the train wreck called Cynthia Marlow walks the halls.

Her locker is next to mine, so I've enjoyed a front row seat to her complete self-destruction. Her normally spiked and styled short black hair hangs limp these days. She's traded in the ripped up black leggings and tank tops for an oversized hoodie that falls well below her bottom and plain blue jeans. She's given up on real jewelry and has instead replaced the earrings that used to travel up the sides of her ears with a row of safety pins that look like an infection waiting to happen.

She looks like a mouse that got stepped on and is now limping its way back to its hole to die. I kind of feel sorry for her.

I might be the only one. The boys at our school have been pigs.

For example, once I stow my latest acquisition in my locker, I turn around to find that complete boor, Carlos, staring at Cynthia's bottom. For thirty-six seconds, he stares. I watch him watch her, and every time she bends over to rifle through the stack of books on the floor of her locker, he nudges his group of friends and they all guffaw like idiots.

I smell trouble.

Sure enough, when she straightens, he saunters across the hall until he's standing directly behind her and slaps his palm on the locker frame next to her face. A folded twenty-dollar bill pokes between his fingers.

Cynthia's entire body tenses. "Get lost," she growls.

Carlos doesn't even bother to keep his voice down. The whole hallway can hear him. "You're up for anything, right? For the right price." Then his free hand drops to her side, tracing the outline of her hips.

She looks like she might explode. Her hand flies to her backpack and digs in the front pocket. I have to intervene.

I grip his wrist and gently pull it away from her. "Leave her alone," I whisper, "or I'll make sure every girl in this school knows you picked up chlamydia last summer when you were staying with your cousins."

He scowls. "Back off, Banford. This doesn't concern you."

"Sadly, your uncontrollable sleaziness is a concern for us all."

Cynthia snorts, which makes him angry. He backs away, stuffing his twenty in his back pocket, but not before declaring Cynthia "too skinny anyway."

She glares at the inside of her locker until he's long gone, then slams the door shut and turns to leave.

I catch up with her. "I'm sorry about that. Carlos is a jerk, but he's harmless."

"Sure."

"By the way," I drop my voice to a whisper and pull her close so no one can hear. "If you pull a knife at school, you'll be expelled. Zero tolerance policy."

She yanks her arm out of my grasp. "Don't pretend like you care, Blondie."

"I just thought, we're kind of in the same boat."

She scoffs. "We're not in the same boat. Not by a long shot. You're in some fancy yacht your daddy bought you, and I'm clinging to a life preserver, trying to keep my head above water while my asshole ex-boyfriend drags me down by the ankles."

"Cynthia…" I begin.

"We have nothing in common. Just leave me alone."

#

She's not the only one who feels this way. In seventh period, our overly eager new English teacher has decided to assign research projects, to be completed in teams of two and turned in at the end of the semester, along with a twenty-minute presentation.

My partner?

None other than Charlotte Waters. Cynthia may be in self-destructive mode, but Charlotte is completely flattened. I sit at the desk next to her, back straight, shoulders back, ready to brainstorm ideas for our project, but all she can say is "I don't care, you decide" in a monotone voice.

I suppose I'll be doing this project on my own.

Just what I need. More weight on my shoulders.

Fifteen

Brayden

About two weeks into October, some poor freshman on the football team gets forced to throw a party for the upperclassmen, and because it's tradition, almost everyone from school shows up, whether or not they're on the football team.

I show up about an hour after the party starts. Only the losers show up right on time. Things are already well underway, which is good, because I can just blend in. I'm not a huge drinker. For one, beer has a ton of calories, and the more you drink, the more you have to run to burn it off. Mom says I'm obsessed with calories and that I take my physical fitness too far. But she's crazy. Boys can't be anorexic, that's a girl problem. I eat plenty. I just like to make sure I don't get too chubby. I like feeling good about myself. Big deal.

Rock music blares from the living room. It's the kind of thing where the lead singer feels the need to scream every word. Pretty angsty stuff. It'll give you a horrible headache if you listen too long. I'm more into the classics. The Beatles, the Rolling Stones, that kind of stuff. My parents got me into it pretty young, and I guess it stuck.

I skirt the edges toward the kitchen where Mark and the gang are already filling red plastic cups from the keg and passing them around.

"Thanks," I say when someone hands me one. "Anyone seen Angie?"

"Dude, she's *your* girlfriend."

"Yeah…" I shrug. Parties aren't really her thing. I was hoping she'd still come, since I'm the captain of the basketball team and all. Guess she decided not to.

Mark swallows a large gulp of beer. "Look on the bright side."

"What's the bright side?"

"Without that prude weighing you down, maybe you can finally get laid."

I narrow my eyes. "Show some respect. That's my girlfriend you're talking about."

But he's clearly not sorry, so I head into the living room. Sometimes Mark is too much. He's not great at reading the mood of the room. Sometimes he just says stuff like that without thinking. He'll figure it out eventually and apologize, or forget about it. Either way, we'll be cool by the end of the night. But I'm not going to let someone talk like that about my girl.

The lead singer of the band takes a swig of his drink and turns around to nod at his drummer, who counts off a few beats, then they launch into a new number.

Mark sidles up next to me. "Hey, sorry about that."

"It's cool."

Mark's alright.

He nods toward the stage. "Looks like they got a new drummer."

"Huh?"

"That's the Stinks. Remember Cynthia Marlow, from the video?"

Oh yeah, sex for drugs. This must be her old band. I scan the crowd. Sure enough, she's there, arms folded and looking murderous. It can't feel good, seeing yourself replaced like that. The song moves into the chorus, and I catch the words for the first time:

> *Sick as sin, sick as sin, Cynthia*
> *Sick as sin, sick as sin, Cynthia*
> *You're a liar, you're a tease, you're a whore.*
> *Cynthia*

"Wow," Mark says. "That's cold."

"Yeah."

We watch Cynthia's reaction. Her eyes grow wide and she looks around. Everyone in the vicinity is staring at her. So are we, I guess, but at least we're far enough away we can get away with it. Boy, if I were that band, there's no way in hell I'd mess with her. She'd probably kill anyone who got in her way. I was there when she smashed the lunch tray over JJ's head. Scary crazy.

Mark starts laughing, and he's not the only one. But I'm not laughing. I just watch her. I half expect her to climb up on stage and start pummeling the lead singer, but she doesn't. She just chews her lower lip and her whole body starts shaking. Really shaking. She's that angry. Then, after the second verse starts, she raises both hands and gives a double middle finger salute to the band, then turns and walks away.

Maybe she's learning self-control.

Everyone near her scurries to give her space. Smart.

Mark nudges my shoulder. "C'mon man, let's go shoot some hoops."

"Yeah," I agree. "Let's go."

* * *

Most of us basketball guys hang outside for the majority of the night. We play three-on-three for a while, Mark and Darrell and me against a few of the JV kids. It isn't exactly fair, and eventually we get kind of bored. Plus their cups are empty—I haven't really touched mine—so we head back to the kitchen for a refill.

Cynthia is already there. Sick as sin, Cynthia. It'll be hard not to think of her that way from now on. She looks pretty wasted, leaning over the counter, nursing her half-empty cup of punch and tottering dangerously. I'm guessing she spent the last half hour drinking cups non-stop. Sure enough, she gulps down what's left in her cup and goes to pour another, tipping so far to the left as she does, I think she might fall.

The door slams when we enter, and it takes her a couple seconds to register the noise. She blinks wearily at us, like she's not a hundred percent sure we're even real. Her eye makeup has run, sending solid streaks of black down her cheeks, so we all know she's been crying.

Mark smirks. "Sick as sin," he croons with a mocking tone. "How's it going?"

"Back off," she mutters.

He makes his way across the room to her, blocking her into the corner where the counter top turns to make a little island-like thing in the middle. It's a nice kitchen. My mom would kill for a kitchen this nice. I'm weird. I notice these things.

"Now this," Mark says as he presses his body against hers, "is the answer to all your problems, Brayden."

Blood rushes to my face. The rest of the basketball team guffaws at his joke. Emboldened, he leans down and whispers something into her ear.

Her reaction is instantaneous. She yanks drumsticks out of her hoodie pocket and jams them hard into his stomach. "I said back off, asshole!"

Mark doubles over, groaning, and she slides away and out the back door. I catch her eye as she leaves. I don't know. Maybe I want to apologize or something. But she just glares.

Mark winces. "Ah, bitch."

He's getting no sympathy from me. He had it coming.

"I think I'm gonna head home." Suddenly this party feels like the last place on Earth I want to be. I guess I'm a little naïve. Realistically, I know that this kind of stuff happens, girls getting drunk and manhandled and what not, but I can usually turn a blind eye. Not have to actually see it. But Mark took this to a whole new level tonight, and I need some space.

No one seems to care that I'm leaving early. That's the nice thing about popularity. You can basically do whatever and people accept it. If I were still the shy, fat boy I was in middle school, I'd be hearing it for weeks. Brayden the loser. But now my friends just wave me off and let me go.

When I get to the front porch, Cynthia is there, doubled over, emptying her stomach into the bushes.

I reach out and touch her shoulder. "Hey, you okay?"

"Don't touch me!"

My hands fly up, because I don't want to share Mark's fate. "Sorry."

Something roots me to the spot. I know I should just leave her behind. I mean, if anyone doesn't want to be helped, it's her, but I feel kind of bad for her. So I just stand there and stare at the sky while she vomits over the railing.

When she's finished, she turns around and wipes her mouth with the back of her hand. "What do you want?"

"I dunno. Um… do you want a ride home or something? I haven't really been drinking, and I don't think you can drive."

She shrinks into herself. For the first time ever, I notice how small she really is. Barely over five feet and maybe a hundred pounds. I could lift her easy. Not that I'd try. I guess she's got enough personality to make up for her size.

Except now, she looks like a wounded animal. Not dangerous at all.

"I'm not having sex with you," she says, right out of the blue. "Don't think you can be nice to me and I'll fuck you or something, because I won't."

I shake my head nervously. "I didn't think that."

"Okay."

"Okay, what?"

"I need a ride home. Just don't talk to me or whatever." Like I'm the embarrassing one to be around, not one of the best-looking guys in school. Angela's words, not mine.

I sort of expect her to say thanks when we reach her house, but she doesn't. In fact, she doesn't say a word to me the entire way, except to grunt and point as we navigate the roads. She lives across the train tracks, not the greatest of neighborhoods over there, but not too far across. Her house is still decent looking, at least on the outside. Two stories, paint job looks nice, what you can see of it through the trees in her front yard. Makes me think her parents might be relatively normal, even though she's kind of a mess.

Anyway, I pull into her driveway and she practically leaps for the door handle to get away from me.

"You want me to walk you to the door?"

"No," she snaps.

Still, I wait until she stumbles her way through the front door before I back out of the driveway. I don't want to find out on Monday she never made it and wandered into the street and got hit by a car or something. That would suck.

#

Mom's waiting for me when I get home. Looks like she's been up this entire time, making sure I make it home alive. Kind of sweet, but mostly annoying. I'm almost eighteen, after all.

She jumps off the couch. "It's past midnight, you know."

"I know."

"How was the party?"

I shrug. "Normal, I guess."

She follows me into the kitchen and watches as I fill up a glass of water and chug it down.

"Did you drink?"

"One beer. What's with the third degree?"

Her eyes dart around the room, like she doesn't want to admit she's questioning me.

I sigh. "The answer is no."

"What?"

"No, I didn't have sex with some poor drunk girl and do something I'll regret for the rest of my life. That's what you're wondering, right?"

She breathes a long sigh of relief. "I can understand the pressure, Bray—"

"Yeah, I'm sure you can," I say sarcastically. "For what it's worth, I had the chance." Then I explain all about Cynthia and what a drunken mess she was, and how Mark was pestering her and all. How I drove her home to make sure she didn't die or whatever. "I'm sure I'll be catching shit for it for the rest of the school year."

Mom smiles. "Better to be a shit catcher than a shit thrower." I guess she kind of gets it.

Sixteen

Cynthia

J ason's been back at school for a couple weeks now, but I'm still practically glued to his side. For one, we never see each other outside school anymore. His parents have him on extreme lockdown. Mine do too. School isn't exactly a picnic. I'm used to being called all sorts of crummy names. Punks don't need to fit in. We do our own thing. But Jason? He's been flying under the radar for so long, all this attention is really getting to him.

He leans against the locker next to me while I fish around in my backpack for a pencil. If I show up to Algebra 2 one more time without a pencil, I'm pretty sure Mr. Hartsell will flip his shit. I slam the locker door and turn to find Jason staring at a group of jocks who are goofing around across the hall. I watch Jason watching them for a few seconds. His mouth quirks up into the first smile I've seen on his face in weeks.

I snap my fingers in front of his face. "Who're you checking out?" I tease.

His eyes go wide and he turns away quickly. "No one, geez."

"It's okay. I mean, they're kind of hot, I guess. If you're into sporty guys."

"Shut up, Cyn."

He starts walking off and I skip a few steps to catch up. "You know Brayden drove me home from that party the other night?"

"So?"

"He didn't even try anything. I was pretty drunk too. Like, completely out of it. He could have gotten away with it."

Jason shoots me a disgusted look as we walk.

"He seems nice," I say. Not that nice will get anyone anywhere in this world. Still, if you're gonna be drunk in a car with some strange guy, it helps if he's nice enough to leave you alone.

"Why were you even at that party?" Jason asks.

I loop an arm into his as we walk, leaning against him a little as we navigate the crowded halls. "I heard the Stinks were playing, and I, uh, I guess..."

I can't really explain it. I wanted to see what it was like, them without me. I didn't expect it to hurt as much as it did. Even now, it still hurts.

Jason starts to say something back, but words fail him, because when we turn the corner, we see the word "GAY" in huge letters on his locker. When we walk closer, I realize that it's written in chewed up wads of gum. Some asshole sat there and chewed a dozen packs of gum so they could spell out the word "GAY" on Jason's locker.

The worst part? They left a huge wad of slimy, slobbery gunk on the locker dial, so if he wants to get anything out, he has to touch it.

He stands there staring speechlessly at the mess, and I slide my hand in his. "Want me to go get a teacher?"

"No."

The bell rings, and we're still staring at his disgusting locker. I wanna hit someone. I wanna know who did this, so I can punch them in the throat, but Jason's calm. Or maybe he's just so stunned he can't move. I'm kind of afraid he'll start crying or something, but he doesn't.

"Jesus," he says, "I hope their jaw hurts."

In the end, I go get paper towels from the girl's bathroom, and we spend about ten minutes cleaning the worst of it off. Even so, there's enough residue left that anyone who walks by can still see the word "GAY." Rubbing alcohol, that's what we need, or nail polish remover.

"You wanna use my locker for a while?" I offer while he pulls a heavy textbook out and stacks a spiral notebook on top.

He shakes his head and stands up.

"Darrell," he says. "I was checking out Darrell. He's who I was meeting all summer."

I should feel relieved he finally told me, but mostly I feel sad. He sounds like he's given up.

#

When I finally stroll into class, Mr. Hartsell gives me a look like he can't decide whether it's worth breaking his teaching stride to lay into me for being so late. In the end, he decides it's not worth the fight, and I slink to the back of the room where I sit alone. The only senior in a room full of eager sophomores and resigned juniors.

On the first day of school, Mr. Hartsell tried to use me as an example. A real "look at what happens if you don't apply yourself" teaching moment. But that backfired, because I made it pretty clear that math is pointless and I didn't really need his stupid class to get by. To graduate, sure. To drum? Never.

Now we exist in a state of mutual hatred. He doesn't call on me, or expect anything of me, and I keep my mouth shut and let him teach his pointless subject.

It works.

I prop my feet up on the desk in front of mine and pull my phone out. One new message. Interesting. I thought everyone had given up trying to fuck with me. I click it open.

Jimmy: Meet me fifth hour. Our spot.

My thumb flies to the delete button before I even have a chance to process the request. Once I do, I can't get it out of my head. Jimmy wants to meet with me? What the fuck? I've got two hours to figure out what I'm going to do.

We haven't spoken since the band booted me. Maybe he wants to say sorry. He should. He really screwed me over. It's his fault I can't drum. It's his fault I don't have a band. It's his fault…

It's his fault.

Fuck.

What are the odds that video came out less than a week after the we broke up and the band booted me? Seriously. How have I been so blind? He's the reason JJ put me in that video. Revenge. He wanted revenge on me for what? For nailing him in the gonads? Which can only really mean one thing. I know who Jimmy was cheating on me with, and it's so much worse than I figured.

Not some floozy from a show, but the gossip queen herself. Julie Jenkins.

Oh, I'm meeting him. When I do, he's going to wish he'd never met me.

#

Our spot. That can only mean one place in the entire school.

This school has too many cameras. Way too many. It's like they don't trust us or something. So, if you're like me, and you're looking to break rules, you gotta figure out where those cameras are and how to hide from them.

The classrooms are safe, no cameras in there, but the teachers keep them locked up. They think people like me will steal stuff, but really, they should worry about Lindsey Banford. Harvey sneaks out back twice a day to smoke, but that's risky. If you let the door close all the way, you get locked out and you're really screwed.

But Jimmy and me? We found out that the little hallway between the gym and the boy's locker room is completely hidden from sight. A trick with the camera angles. We figured it out when we were both sitting in the principal's office watching the video feed of us making out, and bam, we had a spot. So much PDA happened in that hallway last year, and we never got caught.

We're not kissing this time. We're fighting.

He launches into it as soon as I round the corner, doesn't even give me a chance to breathe. The asshole.

"Look, Cyn, we need to talk."

"I don't give a shit about anything you have to say."

I pretend like I'm walking away, but he grabs my wrist, yanking me back. "I know you think I told, but I didn't. How could I? I didn't even know you were cheating on me."

"I wasn't cheating on you," I hiss. He's got a decent grip on me, but I could get loose if I tried hard enough. Not without a bruise though, then I'd have to explain it to Jason, and he'd find out I met with Jimmy.

He scowls and drops my wrist, folding his arms and pacing away. "You were fucking some other guy. That's cheating."

"Like you and JJ?"

The way his jaw drops in shock is priceless. "Who told you?"

"I figured it out." I close the distance between us, aiming to land a hit but he pushes me away. "You're a real piece of shit, you know that?" I spit out.

"Shut up." He's so witty.

"Personally, I can't figure out which of you to feel sorry for. You or JJ. You're both disgusting."

"I said shut up!"

Before I know it, his hands are on my shoulders and my back slams into the concrete wall behind me. We're back to grappling with each other, like we did for months. Hands tearing at each other, both of us trying to get a fistful of something, shirt or hair or flesh. Even when we were together, love felt more like hate.

He shoves me into the wall again, harder. It knocks the wind out of me, but we're interrupted before it can go further.

"What's going on?"

It's Mr. Nice Guy himself. Brayden Matthews.

Jimmy scowls at him. "Get lost."

Brayden's eyes skim over the scene, and it ain't pretty. Jimmy's hands are clenched around my upper arms. So much for avoiding bruises. I can give as much as I take, so I don't care.

I just need to get rid of Brayden so I can finish the job. He's the sort of guy who will run to get a teacher over every little thing. I don't need that in my life.

He turns to look at me. "Are you okay?"

My eyes narrow. "Look, I don't know if all those steroids are making you stupid or what, but we told you to get lost. So get lost."

Brayden opens his mouth, then closes it again without saying anything. Then he nods and makes his way across the hall to the locker room.

Jimmy keeps me pinned against the wall the whole time. His hands are familiar in all the wrong ways. He thinks I'll take off if I have the chance, but I'm not going anywhere. I want to have this out as much as he does.

We watch Brayden in silence until the locker room door closes behind him, then I yank my arms out of Jimmy's grasp and give him a solid shove back.

I may be tiny, but I'm not weak.

Seventeen

Brayden

Maybe I'm a bad person for eavesdropping. I just figure I should stick around in case things get out of hand. I close the door then lean against it to listen in time to hear Jimmy confess it all.

"It's not like you think. Yeah, okay I started hooking up with her, but I only did it because you were holding out on me."

I roll my eyes. What a loser.

He keeps going. "You changed, Cyn. You know that, right? You used to hang out with us after the shows, partying and all. It was good. Then out of the blue, you stop coming over to Steve-O's place, you stopped being one of us. Like we were just a band, not your friends.

"So yeah, we were all at Steve-O's place and he had some girls over and JJ was there and that one guy, Grayson or whatever his name was. I guess I got a little drunk because I started bitching about how you don't put out and for fuck's sake how long was I supposed to go without getting laid, Cyn?"

There's a loud smacking sound, and I sincerely hope Cynthia just let him have it because c'mon, what a jerk. Except, then I feel kind of guilty because violence is violence, even if it's from a girl.

"Anyway," Jimmy says, "Steve-O started messing with me, him and

Grayson. All laughing and saying I needed to get control of my girl because you might not be giving it up for me but you were doing it with Grayson. Then when I got all pissed, they said to chill because it didn't matter, because you were just doing it for the drugs."

At first, I think that's the end of it, then I hear Cynthia's response. Her voice is so soft I have to press my ear to the crack in the door jamb to hear her.

"Good story. Wanna hear mine?" Her voice shakes, and I think she might be crying. I shouldn't listen to this, but I can't help it. I'm engrossed.

"You remember the first time we played Battle of the Bands?"

"Yeah, Steve-O lost his voice, so you sang."

"He was all pissed at me for stealing his spotlight, so he sent me back to his apartment to order pizza. He failed to mention Grayson was waiting for me there."

The phrase "awkward silence" comes to mind. Because this is awkward.

Cynthia sniffs loudly. "At first, I thought whatever, you know. We'll just sit around listen to music. Then we started to make out, but whatever. It's nothing. Just kissing. No big deal. And I was single. Then..." she draws a breath, and I imagine her standing there looking weak and helpless.

"It happened so fast. I didn't even know what was going on until it was happening. And I..." Her breath comes faster and frantic. "Sometimes, I can still feel him on me, and... God, I didn't even know about the drugs until that stupid video came out. It was like... every time he was around, he found some way to get at me. I couldn't get away." Her breathing is loud and fast. I can hear it through the door. "I had to get away."

"Jesus." Now Jimmy's the one sounding weak. "Why didn't you tell me?"

"Why didn't you care enough to ask?" she says. "Why did you believe them?"

I hear a soft thud, like maybe Jimmy has slumped to the floor or something.

"I was the only girl in the band," Cynthia says. Her voice ice-cold. "I was sixteen. I guess I thought that it was just a part of the deal. Like if I really wanted to make it, I'd have to put up with some shit."

"Cyn... c'mon..." I can feel Jimmy's discomfort through the door. Heck.

I'm uncomfortable, and I barely know this girl.

"Yeah, I stopped hanging out after the shows. I stopped partying. So fucking sue me." She sounds so dangerous. I don't envy Jimmy one bit. I'll take my safe virginity, thank you very much.

There's a sound of scurrying feet down the hall, and Jimmy calls out, "Cyn, wait!" A second passes, then the locker room door slams open, nailing me in the jaw.

"Aw, man!" I clutch my face, peering through my fingers to see Jimmy's angry red hair and even angrier face.

"Were you listening to us?"

"No!" I am an awful liar.

He pushes past me. "If you tell anyone, I'll kill you."

#

I can't stop thinking about Cynthia. It's making me feel gross all over, what she said. How she said it. I keep hearing the shaking in her voice, the way it rose to near hysterics with the words, "sometimes I can still feel him on me." When I hear it, I get a sick feeling in the pit of my stomach like I'm going to throw up.

Something Mom notices as soon as I walk in the door after school.

"What's up with you?"

"Nothing." I dart up the stairs, but she's hot on my heels.

"Where are you going?"

"Uh…" My mind scrambles for an idea. "Over to Angela's."

If she can sense a lie, she doesn't say anything. But even she can't keep her mouth shut when I peel off my T-shirt and turn to rummage around in my closet for something clean to wear.

"You've lost weight."

"So? That's a good thing. Remember how heavy I used to be?"

"What did you have for lunch today?"

"I don't remember." I do, but if I tell her the truth, I'm going to get a lecture, and I'm not in the mood. "Mom, stop worrying, okay? I'll eat dinner at Angie's. Double helpings. I swear."

I'm not sure she believes me, but I'm not sticking around to find out.

82

Eighteen

Jason

Darrell and I haven't spoken since JJ's video came out. I guess I should be grateful, but mostly I'm just confused. I know I should avoid him. I know I should forget all about him and focus on getting through my dad's stupid books and even stupider "counseling sessions."

Except, it's kind of hard when he catches my eye across the hall from Cynthia's locker. He wouldn't smile at me if there weren't something there, right?

Was there ever something there? During the summer, I took emotion out of it. We were hooking up for fun, that was it. He didn't even exist outside of that park. Out of sight, out of mind.

Now, he's constantly in my line of sight, and constantly on my mind. It's like he's doing it on purpose. He knows I can't act on anything, not now, not with my dad breathing down my neck. Talk about cruel and unusual punishment.

It's totally unfair.

A smarter person would have avoided him like the plague, because that's what he is. A plague sent to destroy any semblance of normalcy I've got left.

A smarter person would have done everything in their power to forget about being gay until they had graduated or moved away, preferably both. Except, you can't forget about being gay. It's like forgetting your eyes are brown, or your height, or something mundane like that. Someone will casually ask you, "how tall are you?" and you'll answer without even thinking, "six foot even." Then you're trapped, because now, forever, they'll know. You're six feet tall.

Except no one cares about height. Apparently, everyone cares if you're gay. You try to suppress it, you try to forget. You try so freaking hard to push that part of you away, because you know, you know without a shadow of a doubt, that if your dad catches you in even the tiniest, most minuscule lie, you're done for.

I keep thinking if I can just get alone with Darrell, just once, I'd know for sure if this is just a game for him, or if it's something more.

Until then, I'll resign myself to raised eyebrows and knowing smiles. I'm thinking about that smile as I walk around the track after PE class on Friday to help our teacher gather cones. It's supposed to be a rotation, but I've noticed I get held back more often than anyone else. Maybe he's protecting his basketball team from my predatory gayness. Because you know, we homos just can't help ourselves.

Maybe he thinks he's protecting me.

Either way, when I get back to the locker room, I find a whole crowd of dudes laughing their asses off next to my locker. It takes a second to realize what's happening. They're all standing there watching Mark piss on a pile of clothes.

My clothes.

One of Mark's cronies has Jimmy pinned against a locker, so I guess I should be grateful he was trying to help, but he's not putting up much of a fight. My locker is hanging open. The lock looks like it's been pried open.

"What the hell?" I yell.

Mark stuffs himself back in his basketball shorts, and keeps laughing as he and his friends saunter out of the room. One of them gives me a hard shove into a nearby locker on his way out. The smell of urine mingles with the Axe body spray and sweat that we've all grown accustomed to over the weeks.

I sink onto the bench just in time to hear the dismissal bell ring. My mind races with options. Wear my gym clothes for the rest of the day and let everyone know something happened in gym. Try to desperately scrub my clothes clean in a sink and dry them under an air dryer? That'll take forever. No way I'll get to class on time. Plus, I'll spend the last two hours of school thinking about how I'm wearing piss-clothes.

Jimmy sidesteps the pile to stand in front of me. "Want me to get Mr. Maddock?" His kindness makes me hate him more. I hate that the friendliest face in PE is Cynthia's ex-boyfriend.

"No," I say. I'm practically an adult. If I go running to a teacher for help because of a bunch of idiots, I'm never going to hear the end of it. I still have six months of this place to survive.

"I have an old Nirvana t-shirt in my locker, if you want it."

I look up at him, and he is all sincerity. But we're not friends, and it feels disloyal to Cynthia to accept his help.

"No. I'll just wear my gym clothes for the rest of the day. Three more hours. Big deal."

"What are you going to do with that?" He points to the soggy pile on the floor.

I know I should take them home and wash them, but the idea of putting those clothes on again, after what I've just seen makes me sick to my stomach. I shake my head. "I don't want them anymore."

Then Jimmy does something I never would have expected. He reaches down and picks up the dripping clothes and shoves them in the big trashcan by the door. Doesn't even seem fazed by the pee. He shuffles over to the sinks on the other side of the locker room and washes his hand, then returns a few seconds later.

I stare at him in shock, and he shrugs. "You see it all backstage. Kind of stops bothering you after a while."

"Right. Well, thanks." I offer the tiniest smile possible.

"No problem."

For a second, I guess I kind of almost see what Cynthia liked about him.

Even if he is an idiot, at least he's a nice idiot.

#

I show up late to my sixth hour, and everyone turns to look at me as I walk in. Brayden's eyebrows knit together when he notices what I'm wearing. Of course, he's in the same gym class, but he's also Mark's best friend, so I don't know why he'd be shocked. Surely, he knew what Mark was up to.

Even Mrs. Salisbury looks confused. I'm not a jock. I don't wear shorts to school. It's jeans and a hoodie every day. She looks like she wants to say something, but thinks better of it. All the better. Maybe she'll forget to mark me tardy, and I won't have to explain it to my dad. Something tells me "sorry Dad, the guys in gym peed on my clothes because I'm gay" won't cut it with him.

I can't pay attention at all. Here's hoping that whatever Mrs. Salisbury is talking about up there doesn't end up on our final, because all I can think about is Mark's stupid laughing face and the way my clothes smelled when Jimmy picked them up. I lay my head on my arms and stare out the window.

"Jason Sanders!" Mrs. Salisbury's voice cuts through me, jolting me awake.

"Huh?"

"Are you ill?" There is absolutely no concern in her voice. Just accusation. How dare I put my head down in class!

"No." My voice is this weird mixture of pitiful and surly that catches even me off guard.

Her face softens. "Maybe you should go to the bathroom. Splash some cold water on your face, so you can pay attention."

"Yeah," I say, nodding. "Whatever."

Only the second I get to the bathroom, I start crying. I try not to, but I'm just so stressed these days. It kind of bursts out of me at random. Luckily, I'm alone, because if anyone saw me crying over Mark and his idiots, I'd never be able to show my face around here again. I shut myself into one of the stalls and try to be as quiet as possible so even if someone comes in, hopefully they'll think I'm just taking a crap.

I don't know how long I'm in there, but apparently long enough because the next thing I know, the bathroom door is opening and I hear my name.

"Jason?"

I can tell from the voice it's Harvey, and I kind of hope he'll just ignore me and go away. But he doesn't. He nudges on my stall door, and it swings open. I forgot to lock it. Our eyes meet, and I can't even help it. I start crying harder.

Say what you will about Harvey. He may not have much between his ears, but he takes one look at me and says, "I'll go get Cyn."

All I can think is, *thank God.*

Nineteen

Cynthia

When you've flunked as many classes as I have, they start putting you in the waste of space classes. They call it remedial, but we all know what it means: waste of space. The nice thing is, they put the waste of space teachers in charge of those classes.

For example, sixth period, I have American History, supposedly taught by Mrs. Hoeckeroff. What it actually looks like is Mondays through Thursdays, she runs through some barely accurate PowerPoint slides she made a thousand years ago, then on Friday, we take a quiz and watch a movie while she falls asleep behind her desk.

Every week is exactly the same, and they wonder why kids like me fail.

It's nice though, because we can basically go in and out of her room as much as we want and she never notices. It takes a while to get the underclassmen on board. They're still eager to please or whatever, but by mid-November, they get into the system as much as the rest of us. Only one or two of us can leave at any given time, because if Dr. Pritchard passes the room, we have to look like Mrs. Hoeckeroff has some semblance of order or else he'll fire her and put some do-good, first year in charge of our class and we'll actually have to work.

Anyway, as soon as Ol' Hoeckeroff zones out, Harvey sneaks out for his daily smoke break. She's still sleeping when he creeps back in a mere two minutes later and comes straight to my desk.

"Done already?" I say, keeping my voice low.

"No," he whispers, kneeling beside me so we don't attract attention. "I saw Jason in the bathroom. He's real upset."

"What happened?"

"I don't know."

I look around. Most of the class is asleep. Good enough for me. I slide out of my desk and grab my bag. "Which bathroom?"

"Just down the hall." He points to the left of the classroom door, and I nod, darting out of the room. I hurry to the bathroom as fast as I can without running, because I swear Dr. Pritchard can detect running from a mile away.

Then, I stop in front of the entrance and holler in, "cover your dicks, boys. I'm coming in!"

The sigh from within barely contains its annoyance. "It's just me, Cyn."

He's curled up on the toilet in the closest stall, and he looks like shit. Face all puffy and red from crying. He looks… defeated.

I drop my bag on the floor and squeeze into the stall with him. "Hey."

Then, I kiss his forehead, which makes me feel stupid and affectionate, but it's just Jason. He won't make me feel bad about it.

He forces a smile. "I'm having kind of a bad day."

"No kidding?" I grin. If he can joke, he'll be okay. I back out of the stall and start yanking paper towels out of the dispenser, wetting them in the sink. Then, I squat next to him and begin wiping snot and tears off his face.

"What happened?"

"Some of the guys from the basketball team happened." Then, his voice shaking, he tells me all about it. Them breaking into his locker and peeing all over his clothes. I hate them. All of them.

"Who?" I ask, "I'll kick their asses for you."

"No offense, but that's kind of emasculating," he says.

Eventually he calms down, but it's pretty obvious he's been crying. As soon as that bell rings, the halls will be filled with snooping kids, and it'll be obvious what happened. Just more ammunition for those assholes, or for JJ's videos.

"I think you should go tell the principal," I say.

Jason shakes his head. "No."

"Fine, I will."

"No, please. God. They'll call my parents." He suppresses a shudder. "My dad… I don't want to make it a big deal, okay?"

It is a big deal. It's a huge deal. He looks so pitiful with his arms clutched around his body.

"Fine," I whisper. "You gonna go back to class?"

He shakes his head.

"Hide in here the rest of the day?"

"Maybe," he mumbles. "Who cares?"

I sigh and lean against the stall door behind me. "You're eighteen, Jason. Just sign yourself out and go back to my place for the rest of the day." I pull my keys out of my bag and unhook the house key and hand it over.

He stares blankly at the key in his hand for a bit, then closes his fingers around it with a forced laugh. "Thanks."

I walk with him to the back door that leads to the student parking lot. As soon as he's gone, all the anger that's been building up since I first saw him starts pouring out. I'm pissed. I can't remember a time I've ever been this pissed. Jason may not want to get back at those assholes, but I do. And I know exactly who to start with.

Twenty

Brayden

I barely make it back to my locker after class when a hundred pounds of angry drummer chick barrel into me out of nowhere. Don't get me wrong. It's not like she can hurt me. Cynthia's tiny, and I'm pretty solid, but it still takes me by surprise.

"What the hell?" I cry out, spinning around to face her. Her ice blue eyes blaze dangerously like the hottest part of a flame, and her whole body actually shakes with anger.

She shoves me again. "Have you seen Jason? Do you know what your precious team did to him? Do you know what they did?"

She somehow manages to cram all these words into a screaming fit of rage that probably only lasts a second or two, but feels like forever. Each question is punctuated with a push or a hysterical punch to my chest. Everyone in the hallway turns to stare. I try to grab her arms to stop her hitting me, but she's fast and surprisingly strong. She pulls away and stumbles a bit. Newton's Second Law at work.

"Look, Cynthia," I say, hands held up in front of me, defensively. "I wasn't involved, okay?"

She aims a punch at my face, but I dodge.

"You knew!" she shrieks. "You knew what they were doing. How could you let them do that to him?"

"I didn't know." I grab her arms and swivel her around, pinning her to my chest so she can't move. "Mark said he had a bone to pick with the…" I break off. Cynthia will positively kill me if I call Jason that word, even if I am just repeating what Mark said. "It's not like I agree with him, but I can't control him either, alright?"

She keeps flailing like a wild animal, screaming curse words as she struggles to break free. Saying I'm supposed to be a nice person, and how I obviously don't care about anyone but myself. Which is pretty rich, all things considered. We definitely have an audience now.

"Let go of me!" she cries. Then, she lands a pretty solid kick to my groin, and I go down, with her beneath me.

This literally could not look worse.

"Ah, god dammit, ah shit," I groan. I normally don't cuss, but I'm pretty sure a kick to the balls is a cuss-worthy moment. The girl has a pattern, that's for sure.

I feel Cynthia's body scramble away from me, and when I finally open my eyes, she's curled up in a ball, leaning against the lockers and sobbing into her arms.

"Cynthia," I say, but I don't have a chance to get anything else out because a strong hand closes on my upper arm and hauls me to my feet, and I know our security officer has arrived.

Across the hall, the school counselor lifts Cynthia off the floor and wraps her arms around her, which is annoying because she attacked me. Everyone's acting like she's the victim here.

"Get to class," the security officer barks, and just like that, the hallway starts moving again. Kids scurry out of the way, and teachers rush to pretend like they weren't watching as well.

A minute later, and we've been successfully deposited into the empty chairs in Dr. Pritchard's office. Cynthia curls her legs into her chair and folds her arms around them and chews her lip ring so hard, I'm pretty sure it's going to start bleeding. Dr. Pritchard has a framed photo on his desk of himself shaking hands with Lindsey's dad and another of a woman with two preteen kids. Above his desk, he has two diplomas framed, one from his Master's degree in education, another for his Doctorate. His laptop is open, but the screen is blank. Altogether, his office looks boring. No personality whatsoever.

They've left us in here alone, which is probably a stupid idea on their part, but they still have eyes on us. Through the window, I can see Dr. Pritchard and the counselor arguing about something.

I sigh. "I'm going to get kicked off the basketball team."

"Just shut up," Cynthia snarls. "Just shut the fuck up."

Dr. Pritchard coughs from the doorway. "Language, Ms. Marlow."

She chews her lip some more and stares at the wall.

He walks inside and slides into his rolling leather chair. "Perhaps one of you could explain what happened in my hallway today?"

I glance at Cynthia, but she doesn't move a muscle. Just clamps her mouth shut and refuses to speak. I take my cue from her and keep quiet. She's the expert after all.

Dr. Pritchard nods. "Alright, Cynthia. We'll start with you."

"Why?"

"I watched the tapes. You hit first." He folds his hands on his desk. "Please explain."

She casts a furious glare my way. "I'm mad at him."

"Why?"

Then she snaps, spilling it all. "Because his idiot friends from the basketball team broke into Jason's locker and peed all over his clothes, just because he's gay. In the boy's locker room after class, because everyone knows they can't put cameras in the locker room and you can get away with anything." She rounds on me, jabbing her finger at my chest. "And you let it happen. You knew they what they were going to do, and you let it happen!"

"Okay," Dr. Pritchard cuts in. Cynthia sinks back into her chair. He turns to me. "Is this true?"

"I wasn't there."

He gives me a look that plainly says that plausible deniability isn't going to work here and pulls out a piece of paper and a pen. "I need names."

"I don't know," Cynthia says. "Jason wouldn't say."

I take a deep breath. "I'm not rolling on my teammates." Cynthia lets out a loud "hmph", but she doesn't get it. Fact is, some of those guys are our best starting players. If they get suspended, the whole team suffers. I need us to make it to regionals if I want a chance at a scholarship. If we get to state, I might even be able to pull a full ride. I know it makes me look selfish, but that's life, right?

Cynthia won't look at me. I know I shouldn't care. I mean, I hardly know her, but it kind of hurts. I'm not used to being hated. Especially when I didn't do anything wrong.

Dr. Pritchard waits in silence for a full minute, then gives up and pulls the paper back toward him. He turns to Cynthia. "I'll watch the tapes and see if I can figure out who did it, but it's like you said. No cameras, no evidence. Without names, my hands are tied."

She sniffs loudly.

"Okay," he says, "Cynthia, please step outside. I need to speak to Brayden alone."

As soon as Cynthia's gone, he picks up his phone and dials my mom's phone number. They talk for several minutes, I can hear my mom's voice saying, "I'm so sorry" through the receiver, then he says "goodbye" and drops the phone.

"So," he says, "I'm not going to suspend you, and I'm leaving it to Coach Maddock to decide whether you ought to be suspended from the team. Personally, I think you just got caught up in her drama." He waves to the window in his office, where we can see Cynthia sitting on a bench chewing her lip ring. "So here's the deal. Saturday detention tomorrow. It'll be community service. The bathrooms need repainting. You get here by eight, and not a minute late. You stay and work until five, or until you're finished. You get thirty minutes for lunch. If you don't show up, you're getting three days OSS, and you get kicked from the basketball team. Capiche?"

I nod.

"Good." He writes something down in a folder and slides it into the filing cabinet. "You may go back to class. Send Ms. Marlow in on your way out."

Twenty-One

Cynthia

Brayden's only in Dr. Pritchard's office for a few minutes, then it's my turn. He barely looks at me as he leaves. Just mumbles, "he wants to see you," and walks out of the office. I know I should be brave, but honestly, I'm sweating bullets. Mostly, because I know he has to call my parents, and once he does, I can kiss my drums goodbye forever. I have basically no chance of getting them back before Christmas.

The worst part is, I really have been trying to stay out of trouble. I haven't snuck out of school once this semester, and I'm obviously not making out with my boyfriend between classes anymore.

I'm still really pissed at Brayden. Neither of us would even be here if he hadn't let his friends gang up on Jason in the first place. I really thought he was a decent guy, maybe a little vanilla, but that's not his fault. I thought he was the sort of guy who cared about other people, even if they're a little different. And Jason? Jason's harmless. He's not like me. He doesn't get mad, and he doesn't explode. He doesn't defend himself, so it really pisses me off that Brayden knew Mark was planning something and didn't at least give Jason a heads up about it. I mean, ideally, he could have stopped his teammates, but short of that, he should have warned him.

Brayden's just another asshole guy. Just like the rest of them. Only looking out for himself.

I sink into the seat opposite of Dr. Pritchard, but before my ass has even touched plastic, he's got the phone up to his ear and is dialing my mom's phone number which, apparently, he has memorized.

They talk for a while, then he hands the receiver to me so I can tell Mom what happened. I really want to explain about Jason and how scared he was, but she's not in the mood to listen. She'll see him when she gets home from work. Then she'll understand. I hope.

When he hangs up, Dr. Pritchard gives me a real pitying look and opens up my grade book to show me my grades. As if I don't already know.

"You need to pass every course if you want to graduate this spring, Cynthia."

"What about summer school?"

"That's an option, but," he pauses, shaking his head, "if you don't earn the credits during the school year, you can't walk at graduation."

Like I care. Except Mom and Dad would be so disappointed. I start racking my brain trying to think of what to do. I could try cheating, but I'd have to get ahold of the tests somehow, and make it look convincing. That's a lot of work. Jason's too busy to tutor me, what with his dad being a gigantic dickweed these days. I'm itching to pull my drumsticks out of my boots, because sometimes it's easier to figure things out when I'm drumming on something.

I'm pretty sure if I start banging on Dr. Pritchard's desk, I'm out for good, so I suppress the urge.

Then the door opens and Mrs. Cooper walks in. She and Dr. Pritchard exchange a look as she sits in the chair next to me.

Dr. Pritchard nods back, then says, "I'm not going to suspend you, Cynthia."

I breathe a sigh of relief.

"Mrs. Cooper believes," he continues, "and I admit, I agree with her, that a suspension would only set you further back in your academics. Believe it or not," he fixes me with a stern look, "I care about you graduating. I want to see you succeed. So, in lieu of suspension, you will be serving Saturday detention tomorrow. Eight to five. Bring a sack lunch, because we won't be feeding you, and wear clothes you don't care about. You'll be painting."

I bite down hard on my lip ring, but not because I'm upset. I'm trying to hide my smile. This is just about the best punishment I could hope for. Schools are weird. Most of the time, punishments are about wasting your time or getting rid of you. But every once in a while, they give you something fun to do. My dad's a painter. He does this all day. I like painting walls. I change the color of my bedroom all the time, just for the hell of it, and I'm pretty damn good at it. I can knock this chore out in record time and do it better than the custodians who clearly don't give a shit.

And hell, I may even put my own mark on things for once.

Dr. Pritchard types something into his computer then gestures for me to leave. When I get to the hallway, I practically run headlong into Jimmy who is clearly waiting for me. Great.

"Cyn, hey, can we talk?"

"Leave me alone."

"I will, I just heard what happened." He tries to block my path toward the stairs. "I wanted to make sure you're okay."

"I'm fine."

"Did you get suspended?"

"No," I say, "Saturday detention."

"Oh, cool." He glances around the empty hallway. "Um, is Jason okay?"

I shrug. Not like he actually cares.

Jimmy scratches the back of his neck, the way he used to do between songs. Back when we were part of the same band. I used to think it was kind of cute.

"Look," he says, "I tried to stop them. They cornered me. Held me back, ya know?"

I look up. "Do you know who did it?"

He nods his head

I sigh. I gotta be all sorts of desperate to be asking Jimmy for a favor, but, "could you tell Dr. Pritchard for me?"

I lean on a set of lockers, and Jimmy joins me, an inch away. I can feel the warmth radiating off his skin, and for a second, I almost miss it. Then, I remember he cheated on me, and was sometimes kind of a dick. Like whenever we had an argument during band practice, he told the guys I was on my period. And one time, he kicked over my drum set in the middle of a gig and called me a fucking show off. So I mean, it wasn't all great. I guess I kind of miss the good parts. Like when I was cold and he could just hug me and I'd feel fine again.

He takes a deep breath. "I broke it off with JJ, just so you know."

"Great, whatever. I don't care." It's like he read my fucking mind. That's what I get for reminiscing about him.

"I miss you," he says.

I shove off the lockers and start heading back to class. "God, Jimmy, just stop. I can't be around you, okay? I just can't."

For once, he does the decent thing and doesn't follow me.

#

I make it home in record time. I want to check on Jason, but Mom's waiting for me on the front step when I pull into the driveway, and Jason's car is nowhere to be found.

Gulp.

"Where's Jason?" I ask.

"I sent him home." She purses her lips. "We need to talk." She steps aside and points down the hallway toward the kitchen. "I'll make you some hot cocoa."

Serious conversation ahead.

"Fine," I mumble as I make my way to the kitchen. She follows a step behind. She can talk all she wants, but she can't force me to talk.

I sink onto a chair and fold my arms. "What?"

"A respectful tone of voice would go a long way, first of all," she says as she busies herself with the cocoa mix. "I'd like to talk about how school is going."

I shrug.

She sighs. "I checked your online gradebook. You're still failing Algebra."

"Math is for bitches. No one actually uses it in the real world."

"Well, you can't graduate if you don't pass."

"So?"

I may have a killer death glare, but Mom's the real artist in the family. She holds my gaze without blinking, so I have to turn away.

"Fine, I'll work harder."

That's not enough for her, she wants some sort of blood oath, I guess.

"Is it because of the video?" she asks softly. She's dropped the death glare and switched to overly concerned. Which is way worse.

"No, Jesus, Mom! I don't care about the video!" I leap up and start pacing the floor. "Just once, I don't want to have to think about that stupid video!"

"We haven't really talked ab—"

"I don't want to talk about it!" I shriek. "I want to forget everything it said." I can feel myself getting hysterical, that fuzzy feeling in my head when I just hear ringing, and my heart is racing, and I'm about to lose it.

Mom tries to hug me but I pull away. "Okay, it's okay. Cynthia. Calm down."

Then I sink into the kitchen chair and start crying. It's so embarrassing.

"I just want to drum again." I sob. "Please just let me play again and I promise I'll do anything you want. I'll take drug tests and I'll pass Algebra, and I'll graduate. Whatever, I don't care. I just want my drums."

This is pathetic. A part of me is watching myself cry like a baby over a set of drums, and that part of me is shaking her head, thinking that the girl at the table is a loser and she's ashamed that we even share the same name. I'm not sure which of us is the real Cynthia Marlow. The girl in the chair crying her eyes out, or the one at the counter wishing she'd shut up.

I guess I kind of hate both of them.

Twenty-Two

Charlotte

Everyone's talking about Cynthia attacking Brayden in the hallway. Everyone except Lindsey. The only thing she wants to talk about is our semester project. She makes me meet her in the library after school to discuss a thousand and one things we need to do over the weekend.

"You're making this way harder than it needs to be," I say.

She frowns. "I know what Mrs. Cameron wants to see in this project."

"Yeah," I say, as I open my laptop and start typing. "But you can do the research so much easier. Look." I type in some quick code and pull up information from the Smithsonian's website.

Lindsey leans over my shoulder. "Wait, you can hack?"

I roll my eyes. "No. That's not hacking. That's just knowing that most websites build in shortcuts for people who know their way around computers." She gives me a dubious look. "It's not hacking, I swear. I don't do anything illegal."

That was the wrong thing to say. All her manufactured confidence falters and she ducks her head.

"No, I didn't mean it like that! I'm not judging you, I swear." I chew on my thumbnail. No one at this school likes me, but if I can get any sort of sway with Lindsey. Well, I need what I can get. "Let's just get some research done, okay?"

She nods, flipping open her notebook and immediately taking charge. I click through the site while she takes notes, and in practically no time, we've gotten enough information to call it a day.

I shut my laptop and slide it into my bag, hopping up as fast.

Lindsey smirks. "You got somewhere to be?"

"No," I shrug, "just… it's the weekend, right?"

She doesn't look excited. If anything, she looks worried. Interesting. The family man act her dad puts on for his campaign aside, looks like there's trouble in paradise.

"No plans for you then?" I ask.

She shakes her head. "Just family obli—, I mean stuff."

"Yeah, me too. Not like I have any friends, right? Just me and my mom."

She opens her mouth for a second, like she wants to say something then thinks better of it and just nods grimly.

#

Thank God I got home when I did, because there's a letter from Mr. DuPont waiting for me. If I hadn't beaten Mom home, then she would have burned it before I ever had a chance to read it. She's really overreacting about this whole thing. She hardly speaks to me, and when she does, it's with this weird concern, like she still can't believe that some vicious predator attacked her precious daughter.

Sometimes, I guess I have a hard time pinpointing how it all began as well. When we first moved here last February, I didn't know anyone. I started eating lunch in Mr. DuPont's room because he seemed nice. It was less awkward than trying to find a place to sit in a room full of strangers. He was always easy to talk to. I told him all about how Dad died and how Mom barely waited a week after he was buried to ship us across the country. Then things just kind of grew from there.

I lock myself in my room with the letter, just in case Mom gets home earlier than usual. It's not very long. Just says that he moved a couple towns over and that he doesn't like to leave his apartment much because people recognize his face. That he wants to talk about everything that happened.

At the bottom, he left his phone number and said to call when I get this.

My heart starts beating violently. He's never given me his phone number before. Said he didn't want there to be a record of our conversations, just in case. Could this be real?

I guess I could probably get a cheap phone from Walmart or something, but even that can be traced.

I pick up my phone and call Lindsey instead.

"Hello?"

"Hey, Lindsey. It's Charlotte."

"I know," she says, all prim and proper. "Is this about the project?"

I jump right in. "No, actually, I got a letter today. From Mr. DuPont."

She sighs. I can almost imagine those pursed lips of hers. "Throw it away and pretend he never contacted you."

I sigh. "Look, if you add to him to a conference call, then drop out, it won't look like it's coming from my number. It's been months since I saw him. I just want to know how he's doing. Nothing bad."

There's a long pause on the other end of the line, then she speaks. "No."

"Seriously?" I snap. "I thought you'd understand."

Her voice is positively venomous when she responds. "No, Charlotte, I don't understand. What he did was wrong. It's gross. You shouldn't be around that." There's a pause, then her voice softens. "Can't you see he was manipulating you because you were lonely?"

"It wasn't like that."

It wasn't, I know it wasn't. Mr. DuPont and I had a real connection.

"Charlotte, listen to me. I'm really trying to be your friend here. Please don't contact Mr. DuPont. Just forget about him. He didn't care about you."

"He did," I whisper.

Before Lindsey can respond, I hear the front door open and Mom's footsteps coming down the hallway.

I cringe. "I gotta go. My mom's home."

"Okay." Then, she hangs up. No goodbye or anything.

Mom opens my bedroom door without knocking and looks around the room. "I thought I heard your voice."

"I was on the phone."

"Oh," her eyes narrow, "with who?"

"Lindsey Banford."

Her eyes narrow. "Why does that name sound familiar?"

I sigh. "She was in the video." I don't need to elaborate. She knows what video I'm talking about.

"Oh yeah, poor thing," she says. "How's she doing?"

I shrug. "Okay, I guess."

"Well," she says with a smile, "I'm glad you're making some new friends at school." She walks away before I have a chance to tell her that Lindsey is not my friend, but at least she doesn't notice the opened letter on the bed beside me.

Twenty-Three

Cynthia

My alarm goes off way too early for a Saturday morning, and I scramble out of bed to throw on some old jeans and my painting hoodie. It's actually Jimmy's. A trashy old sweatshirt he loaned me a year ago and I never gave back. At this point, it's mine.

There are tons of old cans of partially used paints in the garage, and I figure if I play my cards right, not only can I paint the bathrooms at our school, I can style them too.

They really need it, because, quite frankly, our bathrooms look like shit. The walls are bright pink. Like, Pepto Bismol pink. Clearly, some asshole thought, "girls like pink" and decided that every bathroom in the building needed to be Burn-Your-Retinas pink.

I end up pulling up late, because I'm always late, but Dr. Pritchard doesn't seem to care. He just nods his head at me and writes something on his clipboard before walking me inside. Brayden's already there dressed in joggers and an old basketball t-shirt, pouring light blue paint into a tray. How original.

Dr. Pritchard points along the hall. "There are three pairs of bathrooms in the building. Two on the lower level. One upstairs. The faster you get it done, the faster we all leave. I'll be in my office if you need me." He looks at us both sternly. "I don't want any drama."

I hate that word. Drama. Like it's a fucking play and not our real lives that we have to live every day. If life was a play, I'd drop out and hide in the basement playing my drums all day.

I glance at Brayden, but he just shakes his head and looks away. Fine, asshole. Be that way. I have my cell phone, I have my earbuds. I find the loudest, angriest music I own, so I can get into the zone and ignore everything else around me.

We end up working separately. Brayden takes the boys' rooms, and I take the girls'. Works for me. I don't give a shit about the boys' rooms. They don't have to look nice, but I'm going to make sure by the end of the day that every girl in this school has a happy place to pee.

With music, I feel like I can do anything. I can power through room after room of painting. I can make masterpieces. If they let me listen to music while I took tests, I bet a million bucks I'd ace every one of them. It just makes things easier. Everything makes more sense.

It takes an hour and a half to get the first bathroom painted. Brayden walks in right as I'm putting the finishing touches in the far-left corner above the mirror. I'm perched on a ladder, obviously, and I don't even hear him come in because I have my earbuds in. But I see him when I turn around and I just about fall off the ladder. Fucking boys, always sneaking up on you.

He's gaping like an idiot, and when I pull my earbuds out, he says, "whoa."

"What?"

"Dr. Pritchard is going to kill you."

"Why?"

He gestures at the walls. "You weren't supposed to paint a freaking sunset mural!"

I guess it is pretty extravagant.

"It looks nice!" I say, climbing off the ladder.

"Why didn't you just paint it pink like it was before?"

I glare at him. "Do you want to take a shit in a hot pink mess?"

"Who cares? It's just a stupid high school bathroom. It's not like we're going to be here next year or anything."

"I might be," I say without thinking.

Ugh, I wish I hadn't said that. Of course, he can't let it go.

"Really?"

I busy myself with cleaning out my paintbrushes in the sink. "Yeah, I'm flunking like half my classes, and there's no way my parents will let me drop out and get my GED. It's so stupid."

He doesn't respond, which I guess means he doesn't care. Whatever. I don't care either. People like that think they're so superior to everyone else. Like grades and college and stuff matter. I hate when people act like that. Like the future is so important, when I'm just trying to survive the right now.

Twenty-Four

Brayden

Cynthia drives me crazy sometimes. Take this whole Saturday detention thing. Really think about it. First, she gets into a fight with me. Then she acts like she's being rewarded by having to come to school and paint the bathrooms. Never mind that I had to skip my morning run because of her, so now I have to budget my calories even more than usual. Then, instead of just getting the work done and moving on with her life, what does she do?

She creates art. She can't do something normal for one second.

The girls' bathrooms look way better than the boys' bathrooms now. Embarrassingly better. Worse, after she finishes the first bathroom, she follows me back to the boys' room and points out all the spots I've missed because I was just slopping it on and not really taking my time.

The worst part is she listens to her music really loud, and she sings along even louder. I can hear her across the hallway the entire day, half screaming along with lyrics. She doesn't have bad taste in music or anything, but it's just so loud that I can't listen to my own stuff. I'm forced to listen to her belt out *Teenage Dirtbag*.

Girl needs to get her head fixed.

I'm about halfway through the second bathroom, and I'm actually trying a little harder on this one to make it look good, when she comes in to tell me she's hungry.

I drop my paintbrush in my tray. "We don't have to eat together, you know."

She narrows her eyes. "Nobody's around to see you. It's okay to eat lunch with a freak."

Truth is, I wasn't really planning on eating lunch. I brought something, in case Dr. Pritchard was going to make us sit in the cafeteria under his supervision, but after he disappeared into his office, I assumed I was home free.

She's not leaving though, so I go to the sink to wash my hands. "Just let me clean up a little, okay?"

"Fine, whatev—" Her voice stops.

I turn to check on her, and her eyes are trained on some graffiti above the second urinal. It's a crude picture of a girl on her knees doing well… stuff, and a long line of guys waiting in line to get serviced, with the caption: *Cynthia Marlow – Open for business*

Her mouth hangs open, and she can't seem to take her eyes off it. Not until I grab the paintbrush and swipe some blue paint over it. Then she shakes her head and glares at me like I'm the one who drew it.

"You don't have to pretend to be nice. I'm not going to sleep with you."

No good deed goes unpunished.

I return to the sink. "I don't want to sleep with you. It's your body. You have the right to make decisions about it." I take my time drying my hands, then turn to check her reaction.

Her eyes turn dark, angry, and she rolls her shoulders like she's gearing up for a fight. "Oh, do I? Do I really? Thank God, I have some big strong man around to tell me all about how rape is wrong because if you weren't here, I don't think I'd ever understand it!"

Then she turns on her heel and storms out of the room before I can defend myself.

#

By the time I get to the hallway, Cynthia's already slumped against the wall opposite me with earbuds in her ears and a bag of Takis open in her lap, her red powder-coated fingers sneaking in every few seconds to pull out a couple and stuff them in her mouth. She's on her phone, and doesn't look up as I sink to the floor across the hall from her, and I can't help but feel a little annoyed she made me come out here if she wasn't going to talk to me.

I clear my throat, and she looks up.

"What?"

Her dagger-like eyes are trained on me, and I gulp.

"Um, nothing."

She raises her eyebrows sarcastically and returns to her phone, occasionally shaking her head at what she sees.

"What're you looking at?" I ask in spite of myself.

"Band postings," she mumbles. "Trying to see if anyone's in the market for a new drummer. I figure I can Ringo Starr some unfortunate Pete Best out there or something."

I snort. "I'm pretty sure you're the one who got Ringo Starred."

Big mistake.

"What do you know?"

"Sorry," I mumble. "If it makes you feel better, their new drummer sucks."

"I know." There's a proud glint in her eye, so I know she's basking in the praise, even if she doesn't want to show it.

She shovels another handful of Takis in her mouth and cocks her head to the side. "What're you eating?"

I grimace and show her. "Can of tuna, apple, Greek yogurt."

She scoots across the hallway and picks up the yogurt. "This isn't even flavored. Are you crazy? It'll taste like shit."

"I don't care."

"Do you enjoy it? Eating like this?" She licks the Taki dust off her fingers.

"Food isn't supposed to be enjoyable. It's meant to fuel your body." I point to her chips. "Junk like that does nothing for your body."

"Everything is supposed to be enjoyable." She grins at me and waves the half-empty bag under my nose, so I get a whiff of chemical spice that can only be found in the cheapest of cheap foods. "Try one."

"No." My stomach flips. "I'm good."

"Right," she says with an exaggerated eyeroll. "You live on self-denial, huh?" she says. "Low-calorie, flavorless food. No sex." Her eyes catch mine, and I blush. "Have you ever been drunk?"

I shake my head. "Beer is full of empty calories."

"Never smoked pot."

"Of course not."

"Do you even cuss?"

I look away, refusing to answer. I try not to, but with her teasing me like this, it does feel kind of dumb.

It doesn't matter, she already knows. She laughs and sits up. "What's your favorite band?"

"I don't have one."

"I bet it's all Dad-rock with you."

"Dad-rock?"

"You know, that soft flavorless shit they play on Top 40 radio? You don't have any edges."

That does it. I snatch the bag of Takis out of her hand. "Fine, I'll eat your damn chips!"

I stuff a handful in my mouth, immediately regretting the decision. I haven't had Takis since, well, since I was a fat loser in middle school. My throat burns, and I race for the drinking fountain, Cynthia's derisive laughter ringing in my ears as I do.

Twenty-Five

Cynthia

The image of Brayden racing down the hallway for water keeps me pumped the entire rest of the day. I knock out the rest of the second bathroom—ocean scene, complete with a red octopus near the trash can—and the third bathroom with swirling music notes everywhere in record time. So fast that Brayden, who's just doing boring blue on all the walls, finishes at about the same time. We carry all the supplies back to the storage shed out back, and even though I have about three times as much stuff because of all the colors I used, Brayden helps me carry it all. It takes us a couple trips, then we're finally done.

He sinks onto the bench on the sidewalk next to the parking lot.

"Where's your truck?" I ask.

"My parents took the keys because of yesterday. My mom's picking me up at five." He shrugs. "It's not a big deal."

I'm not going to offer him a ride. Even though I guess I should, because he drove me home that one time. Still, I hesitate a little, I'm not sure why. I glance back, and his eyes are on me. He's not even trying to hide it. What a pig. I turn around to give him a piece of my mind, but he interrupts me before I can get a word out.

"I'm sorry about Jason."

I stop in my tracks.

"You were right," he continues. "I should have stopped the guys from messing with him. I was just… I don't know."

Scared. He was going to say scared. I guess I sort of know what he means. I bite my lip and stare at the ground.

He clears his throat. "You remember the talent show last year?"

"Yeah."

"You got up there and sang that one Rush song?"

I remember. How could I forget? I played guitar and everything. No one thinks I can play anything but drums, but I picked up the guitar pretty quickly.

"*Subdivisions*," I say.

"Yeah," he says with a grin. "Super appropriate for high school, by the way."

It totally is. It's all about cliques and acting fake just to fit in. It's a good song.

I smile.

"Well, you were really good. You're a thousand times more talented than the rest of the Stinks combined." He sounds so stupid, but I can't stop listening.

"I was thinking," he says, "I, uh… well, if you want, I can tutor you or something. I mean, I'm pretty good at math. I don't mind."

It's November in Minnesota, and I am dripping sweat.

"Jason says I'm impossible to teach."

He smirks. "I don't mind trying."

I nod. "Okay. Cool."

About halfway to my car, I decide to do something stupid and sentimental, because I am an idiot. I turn around and I walk back to him. He's so busy on his phone, he doesn't even notice me until I'm standing right in front of him.

When he does notice me, he looks up kind of surprised. Then, I kiss him. Full on the mouth. I kiss him.

I am so stupid. I should have just left him alone. I don't even know why I do it, except he's being nice to me, and I dunno. No one's been nice to me in a long time.

I pull back pretty quickly. I mean, I wasn't even thinking. It just happened. I figured I could just beat it and pretend it didn't happen, but he grabs my arm and holds me in place. Then he pulls me closer, so I'm kind of leaning against him and he kisses me back.

Hard.

I've made out with a lot of guys, but this is different. It's comfortable. Sexy, sure, and he's holding onto my elbow pretty tightly, but I can tell he doesn't want anything else from me. Just a kiss. One really long, really deep, really perfect kiss.

I run my fingers through his hair. It's so short on the sides, it just feels like fuzz. Not like most of the guys I hang out with, who keep it long. Brayden's a straight and narrow sort of a guy. He could join the army tomorrow and look like he'd been there for months.

How long I stand there, making out with him, I have no idea. I just know that Dr. Pritchard interrupts us with a loud cough and a real asshole remark.

"Please for the love of all that is good, do that off school property so I don't have to see."

I jump about a mile and then say something really dumb like "I'll see you later, I guess" and bolt to my car, slamming the door shut as fast as I can, so Brayden is stuck there on the sidewalk with Dr. Pritchard. Then, I blare the music and peel out of there, and I'm pretty sure Brayden's watching me the entire time.

Twenty-Six

Lindsey

For as long as I can remember, my family has gone to Jason's dad's church. It's the biggest church in town, and pretty much everyone there consistently vote Banford every election. From a purely numbers outlook, it's a smart move.

I'm just not a huge fan of the proselytizing.

According to Rev. Michael, pretty much anything can get you thrown into hell for eternity. It almost makes you want to give up trying to be a good person.

Jason and his mother sit in the first pew at church, the picture of obedient wife and son under the watchful eye of their patriarch.

My family sits in the second row – also for appearances – with straight backs and seemingly attentive ears. We used to take up the entire row. Father sat closest to the aisle, then each of us children in age order down to me, the youngest, with Mom on the end. She sat at the end so she could easily slip out of her seat to the piano and play accompaniment for the choir. Not just a church goer, but a vital member of the congregation.

Ever since the video, I've taken over the piano playing. Any chance to show the community how repentant I am.

I've taken to watching the backs of Jason's neck every service. The longer his dad goes on about sin and eternal damnation, the more the hairs on the back of his neck stand on end. Tiny droplets of sweat form between the strands of hair, and I time how long it'll take before Jason reaches back to wipe them off. The day after the video came out, he barely made it fifteen minutes.

Today, he's not doing much better.

Usually every Sunday, at least once, Jason glances over his shoulder at me, or we exchange pleasantries during the morning greeting. I suppose you could call us friendly, though not exactly friends. Because, of course, Banfords do not have friends.

When he turns around today, I mention that he wasn't in AP Chem on Friday.

"I went home early," he mumbles and rubs his neck. "I was sick." His mother shifts uncomfortably and turns away.

"Oh," I say. I can't think of anything to say. I know I should offer to share my notes or something like that, but the sad, empty look in his eyes has me flustered.

My mom grips my shoulder. "Lindsey, that piano isn't going to play itself."

"Oh," I smile weakly at Jason then scoot out of the pew. "Sorry."

I stumble over the steps on my way to the piano, and even from this distance, I can hear my mom's annoyed sigh. Rev. Michael gives me what should have been a comforting smile, but looks a bit more like a scowl.

"I'm sorry," I say as I sit at the instrument. "Sorry."

I try to focus on the sheet music in front of me, but all I can see is Jason, looking even more broken than he did two months ago.

After the service, I find him hiding in one of the unused Sunday School classrooms. I knock as I enter, but he still jumps.

"Hey."

"Hey," he says.

"Are you okay?" I ask.

He lets out a sad chuckle. "Not that anyone cares."

He's sitting on an old worn out couch, and I perch on the seat next to him.

"I care." At first it's just a thing to say. The way politicians listen to their constituents, say they care, then turn around and do the opposite. I've seen my father do it dozens of times. But once the words are out, I realize I do care. I really do.

"Friday," he mumbles. "Mark and his gang broke into my locker and pissed all over my clothes."

My jaw drops. "Whoa." Suddenly, the fight between Cynthia and Brayden makes a lot more sense.

"I'm sorry," I say.

"Don't be." He takes a long shaky breath. "As my dead dad would tell you, God has a plan for me, and apparently that plan includes locker room bullying. I still have the Devil inside me, you see? I need to work harder to be saved. Because God never puts something on you that you can't handle. Like Job, right?" He meets my eyes for the first time, like he actually cares about my opinion, but I don't know what to think. I believe in God and all, but I don't dwell on it. Not like this. For me, God simply exists within me without my even trying. Like blood. He keeps me alive, but I don't spend time thinking about how.

This God, the one Jason speaks of, doesn't sound like mine at all. At least I hope not.

"Do you actually believe all that?" I whisper. It feels blasphemous to ask in a normal speaking tone.

He hangs his head. "Honestly? I don't know what to believe anymore. I just want to stop feeling like this. I want to feel like I belong... somewhere."

I relax into the couch and sigh. "Yeah."

His head snaps toward me. "Don't tell me, Madam Stuco President herself doesn't feel like she fits in with the crowd?"

I sit back up and lift my chin. "Fitting in is so much work," I say, "I never get a break from it. Banfords don't do this. Banfords don't do that. Banfords definitely do not shoplift cheap little trinkets they don't even need." I fold my arms and gaze down my nose at him. "Banfords have a reputation to uphold." My resolve breaks and I slump back into the couch. "And I failed. I just needed to feel like I was in charge, just once. Then, once I felt it, I did it again. And again and again. Not anymore. I have zero room for error now."

When I finish talking, I look over to see Jason giving me a knowing smirk. "What?"

"Girl," he says, "you need to rebel a little."

I immediately straighten my back and cross my legs primly. "That has not worked out well for me in the past."

He rolls his eyes. "Forget shoplifting. Do something else."

"Like what?"

"I don't know. Pierce something, or dye your hair. Doesn't matter, but do something and quick before you go insane." He stands up gingerly and puts his hands on his hips. "Because there's only room for one teenage catastrophe in this church, and I call dibs."

Twenty-Seven

Brayden

Things I know to be true:

    Cynthia Marlow kissed me.

    I have a girlfriend.

It was sexy as hell.

I still have a girlfriend.

I shouldn't be thinking about her, but I can't stop. That kiss. It sidelined me. I completely missed my entire Sunday workout regime, and I can already tell. The mirror doesn't lie, and the mirror says I've got inches upon inches of fat around the middle. I wake up even earlier on Monday to get a run in before school.

At four in the morning, the streets are empty expanses of sleeping suburbia. It's just me, a smooth, even sidewalk, and a streetlight on every corner. Peaceful. Freezing, yes. But peaceful.

I'll take what I can get.

Peace doesn't exist at the school. All that bustling about, fighting with your classmates to get through hallways that are too crowded. There was talk of opening another high school, but the parents on the other side of the tracks got all up in arms because they were going to put it up north, further away, and they said they already had to bus their kids farther than everyone else anyway, and why can't they get a new school?

Because money talks. That's what my mom said. I think she kind of agreed with the parents on the south side. Personally, I think a second school would have been nice. I would never have met Cynthia Marlow then.

Anyway, the project got shot down before it was ever really underway, so I guess sometimes money isn't the only thing that talks.

Around five-thirty, I pant my way up my driveway and back inside, sweat dripping down my back in spite of the cold November air. Good. Every bead of sweat means weight lost. I need all the help I can get. Basketball season has started back up, classes are loading us down with homework, and I have to make time for Angela. But skipping my morning run? Not an option. All it takes is one off day, and everything I've worked for falls apart.

To top it all off, I agreed to start tutoring Cynthia. Why, why did I offer to tutor her?

#

I'm not the only one wondering. Angela's got steam coming out of her ears when I explain to her why I can't come over after school.

"Her?" she spits, eyes ablaze, "the freak?"

"Don't call her that. She needs help," I say, "I'm trying to be nice."

She narrows her eyes. "That girl is playing you, and you're too stupid to see it."

A lesser man than me would get angry. I've seen guys at school lose their cool over far less. Not me. Every time I start to get mad, I hear my mom's voice in the back of my head, and I can't stand disappointing her.

I just grit my teeth and tell Angela that I'm going to class and leave her standing there by my locker looking furious.

It's not like I'm blameless here. Cynthia kissed me, but I kissed her back. No way I'm telling Angela that. If she was breathing fire over me offering to tutor Cynthia, there's no telling what she'll do if she finds out we kissed. She just needs time to cool off, and I need to forget about that kiss.

In the meantime, I hunt Cynthia down, not that it takes much. She's leaning on her locker with her earbuds in, playing on her phone in spite of the fact that class is going to start in less than a minute. The hallway is emptying around her, but she doesn't care. I can hear her music blaring as I approach.

I stop in front of her, and she looks up, her angry eyes turning soft the second they see me.

She pulls her earbuds out and fiddles with her phone to stop the song. "Hey."

"Hey," I say. "You know listening to music that loud could result in permanent hearing loss."

She shrugs.

So much for getting a smile. I pull my phone out of my pocket. "Um, I was thinking maybe we should have each other's phone numbers. So we can decide when to meet and all that... for tutoring, obviously."

She raises an eyebrow sardonically.

"I'm free any time," she says. "I have literally nothing to do with my life right now."

"Except your homework," I joke.

She grunts, then hands me her phone. We spend a few seconds typing numbers into the other person's phone, then hand them back over. She shoves hers into her bra, and I catch a glimpse of creamy white skin as she pulls her shirt down, averting my eyes as fast as I can before she catches me.

"Cool," I say, "After school, I have basketball practice, then I'm free for the rest of the night. You want to come over around five?"

"Don't you have a girlfriend?"

"Yeah, but she understands. You know, helping a classmate out. It's practically community service. You can't really argue with that, right?" I'm rambling, because I know for a fact Angela does not understand, and she did argue with it.

Cynthia nods. "Fine. Text me your address."

"Great, see you then." I turn away, then pause. "First hour starts soon. You might want to go to class."

Oh man, the look she gives me. I should have kept my mouth shut.

Twenty-Eight

Jason

Cynthia grabs me as soon as I arrive at school Monday and drags me down the hall toward the girls' bathroom. "I have something to show you," she says as she stops breathless at the doorway.

"I can't go in there, Cyn," I say.

She rolls her eyes and pulls me in after her. The bathroom is an explosion of color. Reds and golds, pinks and purples. It's vibrant and beautiful.

Next to me Cynthia smiles broadly, ecstatically. "I painted it!"

I turn to her dumbfounded. "Really?"

She nods. "Saturday detention. We painted bathrooms."

"We?"

"Oh yeah," she says and launches into an explanation about fighting with Brayden and getting assigned detention. She sounds gleeful through the whole thing, talking so fast her words stumble over each other.

Her excitement is infectious, and I grin in spite of myself. "It's really cool, Cyn."

#

By lunchtime, Cynthia's bathrooms are the talk of the school. The girls are all in raptures, and the boys are grumbling that our bathrooms are still boring blue. It doesn't take long for everyone to figure out who was responsible for our sudden upgrade in decor, and it seems like everyone is coming up to Cyn with praise. Our lunch table has never been this busy.

She is basking in the attention. That's the Cynthia I know and love. The creative brilliant one. The one who lives for her audience.

When Lindsey stops by our table, Cynthia's smile fades.

"Is it okay if I sit with you?" she asks quietly. She directs the question to me. Big mistake. Cynthia's the natural leader here.

"Uh…" I glance in Cyn's direction. "Sure."

Harvey freezes in shock as Lindsey slides onto the bench next to him and starts to carefully unpack her lunch. The chicken nugget dripping in barbecue sauce hangs a couple inches in front of his gaping mouth, completely forgotten.

Cynthia snaps her fingers in front of his face. "You're dripping."

His ears turn bright red, and he hastily shoves the chicken into his mouth and starts wiping drops of barbecue sauce off the table with his sleeve.

It's hilarious. Prim and proper Princess Lindsey and her bento box of perfectly balanced cuisine sitting elbow to elbow with Harvey and his school issued slop.

An awkward silence falls over the lunch table. Cynthia seems determined not to speak to Lindsey. Harvey looks like a deer in headlights. He's clearly starving for the free lunch in front of him, but also not sure he wants to be caught eating garbage. And Lindsey just looks nervous.

"You know, Lindsey goes to my dad's church," I say, attempting a conversational tone. "She's actually pretty cool. Once you get to know her."

Cynthia snorts.

Lindsey clears her throat. "I really love what you did with the bathrooms." She sounds like a grown up trying to talk to a toddler, her voice sweet and calm and slow. "I went around to all of them this morning. My favorite is the sunset. I love sunsets." She catches my eye and blushes deeply. "It was exquisite."

Next to me, I feel Cynthia relax. "Thanks," she says.

Lindsey keeps going. "At first, Dr. Pritchard was angry about them, saying that he never said you could paint murals and that he was going to have the custodians paint over them, but I convinced him not to."

"Why?" Cynthia asks. "Who cares about some dumb bathrooms?"

"Obviously you care a little," Lindsey says, "or else you wouldn't have done it in the first place."

Then she gives me a quick smile and stands up. "I have to stop by the Stuco office before my next class. I'll see you later."

#

Once Lindsey leaves, my stomach starts churning. I've got gym next, which means facing Mark and his gang of Neanderthals.

Actually, that's kind of insulting to Neanderthals.

"What're you going to do?" Cyn asks.

I shrug. "I'm not afraid of them." It's total bullshit. I'm incredibly scared. But I'm not about to admit it.

She walks with me to the locker room. I tell her not to, but she says no one cares if she's late. She's got a point. And if I'm completely honest, having her there makes me feel a lot better. Even though I know she can't exactly join me in there. It's something just to have a friend by your side.

I wait until everyone else has filed into the locker room before I go in. Brayden hangs back for a second, looking like he wants to say something. Weird.

The bell rings and Cynthia gives me a hug. "If anyone tries anything, kick their asses."

I roll my eyes. I have no fighting skills at all, but I don't argue.

Here goes nothing.

Twenty-Nine

Brayden

The first thing I notice when I open the front door is that Cynthia has dyed her hair. Sometime between when we spoke this morning and when she rang my doorbell thirty seconds ago, her hair went from faded dye job to jet black with the ends mind-numbingly bright blue. She looks up, her lip ring hidden between her teeth in what I've come to realize is her nervous habit. The blue in her eyes almost matches the blue in her hair, and with the black eyeliner, the effect is intense to say the least.

This is one of those times when I know I'm supposed to say something so she knows I noticed, but I can never think of the right thing to say. If I tell her she looks nice, she'll think I'm hitting on her. I can't just say that she dyed her hair, because duh, she knows. She's the one who did it.

So I just stand there staring stupidly until her eyes narrow, and her hip juts out. "Are you going to let me in?"

"Yeah," I scurry out of the way. "Sorry."

"Why?"

"I don't know."

Yeah, this is going to be a piece of cake.

She pushes into the entryway, clutching the strap of her black backpack as her eyes roam around, looking at family photos on the walls, peering into the living room. When her gaze returns to me, I can tell that she's feeling what I'm seeing as well. She doesn't belong here. She's the exact opposite of every person who has ever set foot in this house.

But, that's kind of okay.

"My mom wants to meet you," I say.

Her eyes widen.

"It's not a big deal," I hurry to add. "She just likes to meet all my friends, not that we're friends, not that we're not either, just well, she does this with anyone I bring over. She just wants to make sure you're not like a murderer or something."

Her look of fear gives way to amusement as I stumble through this speech. "How do you know I'm not a murderer?"

"Um…"

Then she grins. Thank God. It was a joke.

I lead her to the kitchen where Mom sits at the table perusing a magazine and sipping a cup of hot tea. She looks up as soon as I walk in. I swear, she has some sixth sense only moms have, knowing when their kids are around.

"Hey, hon," she says with a smile, then peers around me. Cynthia is literally hiding behind me. "Who's your friend?"

It's weird. I'm used to Cynthia being loud and argumentative, but here she's acting shy and nervous.

"Uh, Cynthia, this is my mom. Mom, Cynthia." I suck at introductions.

Mom stares at Cynthia, clearly dumbfounded. I get it. I've never brought someone like Cynthia home before. She forces her voice to be cheery. "How did you meet?"

"Um, you know, we, um…"

"We were in the Senior Secrets video together," Cynthia finishes for me. "I'm the slutty one who had sex for drugs." She catches my eye. "What? She's seen the video, right?"

"Yeah."

"So, she already knows who I am." It's an accusation, not a question.

Mom doesn't help. Her lips tighten into a thin line, and her skin goes pale, and she says absolutely nothing.

"You shouldn't talk about yourself like that," I say, lamely.

Cynthia rolls her eyes. "Whatever." And with that, she walks right out of the kitchen.

"Um, well I'm tutoring her in math. She's failing."

"That's really sweet of you," Mom says, but I can tell she disapproves. "Leave the door open."

I feel my ears grow hot. "Nothing's going to happen, Mom."

She gives me a look. "That girl is damaged, Brayden. She's been through the ringer." She sips her tea. "Don't expect anything great from her, because she's got a lot of issues."

"Don't psychoanalyze my friends," I start to argue, but she cuts me off.

"I'm not. Just offering my motherly advice. Don't put a lot of effort into fixing her, because you might not get much back. I know you. You're kind, you care about people. People like you get hurt."

This is the second conversation about Cynthia I've had today, and I'm sick of it. I grab some snacks off the counter, for Cynthia obviously, and hightail it out of there, but not before offering my own bit of wisdom.

"You shouldn't judge people on how they look."

I'm still fuming when I get to the living room, where Cynthia stands clutching her backpack to her chest and staring at a huge family portrait above the fireplace. There's no way she didn't hear that entire conversation.

"You want a pop?" I ask.

"What kind?"

I glance down at the can in my hand. "Cherry cola."

She shrugs. "Sure."

I hand her the can.

"Thanks," she says, not moving. She's just staring at me with those cold blue eyes, and a shiver runs down my spine. "Jason said you moved your gym locker to be next to his."

I nod. "Yeah. And I talked to the guys. If they pull something like that again, I'll make sure they get kicked off the team."

Her mouth twitches, like she wants to smile, but she doesn't want to give me the satisfaction. "How come they didn't get suspended?"

Because sports rule the school, but she doesn't want to hear that. I sigh. "No cameras in the locker room. No witnesses."

"Besides Jimmy," she says.

"Besides Jimmy. Dr. Pritchard said it was up to Coach to discipline them, which basically means running laps."

Her mouth tightens, and she sucks the lip ring into her mouth, clamping hard before blurting out, "that's fucking bullshit."

"It's not my decision."

"It's still bullshit."

I don't want to argue with her, so I point to the stairs. "Maybe we should get to work. I'm the second door on the left."

She turns back to the family photo, like she's scrutinizing every inch of it. It's a few years old, so it still features chubby me.

She grins, pointing. "Is this you?"

"No," I say sarcastically, "it's some random kid my parents found on the sidewalk that day. Of course it's me."

"You look so—"

"Fat," I snap. "I know."

"No," she says. "I wasn't going to say that."

"Yeah, right." I throw my hands up in disgust. "That's my big secret, Cynthia. I used to be an overweight loser with no friends and no life. Are you happy?"

She can't stop staring at the picture, my rounded cheeks and awkward haircut. I'm about to die. I wish my parents would throw away every picture of me from middle school. The worst three years of my life, and I feel like I'm reliving every second with her. I shouldn't even care what she thinks.

She cocks her head to the side. "Brayden, you're not fat in this picture. You look healthy, and cute, and happy."

I shake my head. "There's nothing healthy about that kid. I'm so much better off now." Then, because I can't stand to have this conversation a second longer, I head upstairs to my bedroom and pray she'll follow.

Thirty

Cynthia

Brayden's an idiot. He's not fat. He's just insane. I don't get it. He acts like I insulted him when I told him he was cute.

The first thing he does when we get to his room is point at his desk and say, "you sit there" like I don't know what a desk is for. Then he sits on the complete other side of the room and launches into this big lecture about how he has a girlfriend and that this was schoolwork only, nothing else, and how he wasn't interested in me romantically or anything.

Romantically.

He actually says that. As if sex has anything to do with romance.

It's pretty insulting, the whole thing, and I want to fight with him, really I do, but I'm kind of scared he's going to kick me out and not help me and if I don't pass Algebra, I'll never my drums back.

So I just lean back in his chair and twirl my drumstick while he goes on and on, then as soon as he stops, I slam the feet back to the ground.

"Gonna be kind of hard to help me if you can't even see what I'm working on."

He looks so taken aback that I can't help but smirk, but it's a short-lived feeling because when he sits down on the bed next to me, he opens up his laptop in front of me and tells me to sign into the school website to look at my grades.

"Why?"

"To see what you're missing."

I guess that makes sense, and my hands are kind of tied. I have to do it. But shit, it's pretty embarrassing. First of all, I haven't taken a school picture in three years, so the picture that pops up is all sweet and innocent looking Cynthia Marlow with ugly brown hair and no makeup. Back before the Stinks and Jimmy and all that shit.

I click quickly to the gradebook so I don't have to look at that stupid little girl, then slouch in the chair with my arms folded. "There, are you happy?"

He peers at the screen, and starts scribbling down assignment names. "Click on Chemistry."

"Why? I'm passing."

"No," he says, "you're borderline. And," he reaches over to click for me, "you're missing ten assignments."

I scoot even further down in the chair.

"It's okay," he says, "we have a few weeks before Winter Break. We can still salvage this."

"If they even accept my late work."

"I'll talk to your teachers for you."

I stare at him. "Really?"

"Sure, why not?" He smiles sheepishly. "Most of the teachers like me."

He's being way nicer to me than I would have ever been to him. There's an awkward silence, then he points at my bag. "Did you bring your textbook?"

"Yeah." I dig it out and drop it onto the desk.

He picks it up. "Okay, let's start at the beginning and just work our way through." He flips open the book. "Okay, what do you know about the quadratic equation?"

I stare at him blankly. "The what?"

He smiles. "Look, there's a song and everything." Sure enough, he leans over my shoulder, so I catch a whiff of his cologne, and types quickly into the Internet bar and a YouTube video pops up. I've had about enough of YouTube for the rest of my life, but this one is a really dorky looking math teacher with a guitar, and when he clicks the link and he starts strumming and singing about x equaling some shit or another.

"This is awful."

"Then write something better," he shoots back. Screw that, maybe I will.

He makes me listen to it three more times so I can't get it out of my head, then writes the formula on the top of my paper and tells me to copy the first problem. Then, the real work begins.

#

Brayden's actually a really good teacher. He's patient and he doesn't care if I have my drumstick out, so I can sit there and write out equations with my left hand while I tap out rhythms on my leg with my right. He says if it helps me think, then why would it bother him? He won't let me listen to music though, because he thinks I'll stop working and just jam out.

He's probably right.

I spend basically every evening for a week at his house, then on Friday I turn in a huge pile of homework. Mr. Hartsell looks at the stack like he thinks I'm insane, but I figure if he even counts them for half credit, I have a decent chance of passing. Then, my parents will have to let me have my drums back. I'm dying to play them. I can practice all night long and try to find a new band. I swing by the guitar shop every once in a while, to check for fliers. No luck yet. I'm on the upswing, though. I can feel it.

By Saturday, I'm feeling pretty comfortable at Brayden's house. His mom hates me. I can tell. She kind of stares at me whenever I come over, like she's summing me up or something.

Then she puts on a fake smile and says, "more tutoring, honey?" like I'm anybody's honey.

"Yeah."

"He's been out running all morning. I think he's still in the shower."

Gag. I don't get people who run. Or do any sports. Sports are lame. Every time Brayden starts talking about basketball or lifting or any of that junk he does, I tune him out.

I stand there in the entrance hall waiting for her to tell me it's okay to go upstairs. She clearly doesn't want me in the same room as her, but I don't think she's eager to send me upstairs where I might run into a naked Brayden.

Finally, I walk up the stairs by myself, and she's too dumbfounded to call me back.

Once I'm up there, I realize I probably should have stayed downstairs, because his room is deserted, and I know I sure as hell would be pissed if someone snooped around in my stuff when I wasn't around. Not that it stops me from looking. I figure when I hear the bathroom door open, I can just rush back to the desk and pretend like I'm working or whatever.

All in all, his room's pretty typical for a guy. I find the posters of swimsuit models in his closet pretty quickly and roll my eyes. Every guy is a fucking pervert, even the nice ones. At least he has the decency to try to hide it. Jimmy had all his porn on his phone, not password protected, so sometimes when I unlocked his phone, I had to see it.

His closet is pretty mundane. Mostly just jeans and shirts. An old leather jacket is hanging in the back. I guess he wears that whenever his letter jacket doesn't cut it. And boy, he wears that damn letter jacket—blue and yellow—every day, all day long, to all of his classes and everything. Except gym. According to Jason, he puts it in his locker during gym.

Too bad. The leather is so much cooler.

I poke around all the stuff on his dresser. Video game controllers, cash just lying around, a Swiss Army knife with his name engraved on the side. More boy stuff, boring, but I run my fingers over everything. It's nice, sometimes, to touch things. For a second you can claim them for yourself. These are mine for now. And, I think next time he gets out his knife to cut something, he'll be touching where I touched, and he won't even know it. Like he's touching a part of me.

His laundry hamper is wedged between his dresser and the wall. It's piled pretty high and smells awful. Like, most people try to hide their dirty underwear a little, but his is just kind of thrown on top. He works out a lot, so there's a sweaty odor mingled with Febreze, which I can tell he basically just poured on top to try to mask the smell. Febreze has a very distinctive smell. You can tell right away when you walk into a room and someone uses it.

His mom comes in while I'm snooping, and I feel like a fucking criminal looking through all his stuff. She just forces a smile though and walks over to the dirty laundry pile, pulling the hamper out of the corner. That's when I see it.

A guitar.

A sleek, shiny acoustic guitar hidden behind that disgusting pile of underwear and sweaty gym socks. A real guitar, with steel strings and a pick wedged between them. It's a beauty. I can tell it's been played, because the varnish on the neck is worn where his hand has clearly rested. My fingers actually itch to hold it. To touch where he's touched.

As soon as Brayden's mom is gone, I grab it. Soft and hard at the same time. There are no words for the joy of an instrument in hand. You just feel like you can do anything, create anything. I pluck the strings softly. It's in tune which means he's played it recently.

Which means he's hiding it from me on purpose.

I turn the pick over in my fingers a few times. It's no drum set, but an instrument is an instrument. I haven't played in ten weeks, but who's counting? I strum a few basic chords. I have a good ear, not to brag or anything, but I can tell when I've got a good instrument in my hands. Some people skimp and buy cheap guitars, and that's a mistake. You can tell from the sound of them they're cheap. This one though, it's nice. It's got a real smooth sound, like butter.

Anyway, I keep on playing, and I guess I get caught up in it because I don't hear the shower stop, or the bathroom door open, or the footsteps down the hall.

But I do hear Brayden's voice.

"Put that down!" he growls, sounding downright scary. I practically jump out of my skin.

He's standing in the doorway with a towel wrapped around his waist, and water dripping down the sexiest set of abs I've ever seen in my life. I'm still clutching the guitar, and he looks like he's about to shit a brick or something.

"I'm sorry," I whisper, setting the guitar on the bed next to me.

"What are you even doing up here?"

"I was just—"

"Snooping," he accuses. Guilty.

I bite my lip and stare at the ground, but his voice softens as he continues. "Just step outside so I can get dressed, okay?"

I do, and he closes the door behind me. In the time it takes him to get dressed, I go from guilty to elated. When he opens the door again, I'm downright grinning.

I bounce into the room. "You play the guitar?"

He dodges the question. "Why were you going through my stuff?"

"I wasn't, just your mom came up to do your laundry." I snicker. "Your mom still does your laundry. That's kind of sad. You should do it yourself."

He glares at me.

"I just saw it," I say. "You should have hidden it better."

He picks it up off the bed, and I can tell by the way he cradles it in his arms, that he knows how to play. Like, really knows how to play. People who play around at playing instruments, they don't treat them the same. They don't love them like they ought to be loved.

He strokes the neck. "You didn't have to touch it."

Like I would ever hurt an instrument. Some things are fucking sacred. "You have to play for me," I say.

"No."

I open my mouth to argue, but he points at the desk. "Get your homework done. That's what you're here for." I turn around to give him my angriest glare, but he must be developing an immunity to it or something, because he just smirks back at me.

Fine, asshole.

I pull my book out of my bag and start crunching numbers. He wants me to work, I'll work, but dammit, I'm not leaving this house until I hear him play. Because, I'm starting to realize if no one's advertising for a new drummer, then I may have to put together my own band. And, I think I found my first member.

Thirty-One

Brayden

I have never seen Cynthia work faster than she does today. She finishes six assignments in the time it usually takes her to do two. I mean, she's still way behind, but she could totally catch up now if she tried.

At this point, I'm not even really tutoring her. Mostly, I just check over her work once she's done. She's smart. She just needs to focus better. That's been her problem the whole time.

She sits at the desk and twirls her drumstick in her right hand, and every time she finishes a problem, she taps the same little rhythm on the leg of my chair. I can almost do it with her, she's so predictable. It's kind of adorable though.

Of course, I know what she wants. She's being completely obvious about it. Between every assignment, she turns around in her chair and gives me a look. Now, she's tapping out her stupid rhythm about twice as often and when she looks at me, she's all shiny blue eyes and those lips, man, she pouts them out a little. I think she's doing it because she thinks that's what I'm into, helpless little girls.

When she finishes her last assignment, and our time is almost up, she turns around in her chair, ready to pout at me, but I stop her. "Knock it off, okay?"

"What?"

"That," I say, pointing at her face. "Right there, that look you get, because you want me to play for you. It's annoying."

Her face hardens immediately. Much better. "Fine," she says, slamming her textbook shut and shoving it in her bag.

I didn't even get to check the last assignment.

"You know, guys like you always think it's a piece of cake," she continues, her voice hot and angry. "I bet you learned three chords and thought you were Jimi Hendrix or something. You don't want to play because you know you're no good and you know I'll be able to tell. Not like every other girl out there who slobbers all over you just because you—"

"Shut up!"

Her mouth hangs open, but she stops talking. Her face is pure hard anger now. Anger, I can understand. Anger is how I'm used to seeing her.

I pick up my guitar. "One song. That's it."

That makes her smile. Cynthia smiles like no other girl I know. Most girls smile at me like they're trying to impress me. Like maybe if they show more teeth I'll buy them dinner or take them to the movies. Cynthia's smiles are tentative, nervous, like she thinks I'll attack her if she does it wrong, but she can't help it, because she's actually genuinely happy. It makes me feel pretty good that I made her happy.

Even if I am about to royally embarrass myself.

I shift on my bed and pluck the strings lightly to make sure they're in tune, then I glance at her. She nods in encouragement, but it's almost too encouraging. I close my eyes, take a deep breath... and play.

I get about three bars into the song when she stops me.

"*Stairway to Heaven?*"

"Uh, yeah?"

"If you're going to audition for a band—"

"I'm not auditioning for a band," I interrupt her.

She keeps talking over me. "Then, you shouldn't choose a song that's so recognizable. You have to hit every note perfect. It's a lot of pressure."

I gulp. "It wasn't until you said something."

Her eyes bore holes in me, and I feel my ears getting hot, like they always do when I'm embarrassed. I look down at my guitar.

Finally she speaks up. "I'm sorry. Keep going. It was good."

I start playing again. I actually get through the whole song, but I made a handful of mistakes along the way, and I had to slow down a bit a couple times. Every time I do, I can see Cynthia shift in her chair and her drumstick clinks against the leg, but her eyes never leave me. I don't think she even blinked. When I look up again, she's staring at me. Really staring at me. She's right. She's not like any girl I've ever met. None of them have ever looked at me like she does. With trouble in her eyes.

"I messed up." I say, just to say something.

"Everyone does, occasionally."

"Even you?"

Her lips tighten, and she stands up, so she's looking down at me from her measly height of five foot who knows what. Standing, I tower over her, but when I'm sitting, she has a couple inches on me. I feel like a child.

"Especially me," she says. "You're actually pretty good. If you practiced enough, you'd be really good."

I shrug. "My dad taught me to play. He's really into all that stuff from the sixties."

"Seventies."

"Huh?"

"*Stairway to Heaven* came out in the seventies." She takes a step closer to me. "Do you know any other songs? How long did it take you to learn that one? Can you sing while you play?"

The questions come so fast, and with each one, she steps a little closer to me, so she stops just inches from me. Too close. The air around me drips with essence of Cynthia.

"Um, yeah, I know a few others, I guess. I don't remember how long it took to learn them, and I have a terrible voice." I pause and grin up at her. "Not like yours."

She scoots another inch closer. Her knees are touching mine. "Play something else. I'll sing."

I shake my head. "The deal was one song."

"Brayden," her voice cracks. Her knuckles turn white, their grip on her drumsticks is so strong. She draws a shaky breath. "The only thing I want in the whole world is to play music. I can't do that without a band."

"No way."

"Look at me." It comes out like a whisper, and I do. Her eyes are swimming with tears, and oh God I have never seen Cynthia cry before. I've seen her pissed off, I've seen her wild, angry, ready to kill. But this? It's terrifying.

"There's a club in St. Paul called Grinders. Every year, they host Battle of the Bands." Every sentence is a struggle for her, a fight with the emotions welling up inside her. "Last year, the Stinks came in second place, but now they don't have me. They're going to fail." She hovers over me, and I can't look away. "I need to be there. I need to beat them. I need to show them that I am… important." A tear falls, plopping onto the smooth wood of my guitar, but neither of us moves to clean it off. "But," she continues, "I can't go there alone. No one pays money to watch a lone drummer, but with two people, I can make music."

"Cynthia…"

"All you have to do is learn a ten-minute set. Three songs. I'll write them. I'll teach you how to play them." Her voice grows stronger, almost frantic. "I'll find someone to do our sound mixing. I'll sing, I'll—"

"I can't!"

"Please, I'll do anything!"

"Anything?"

"What d'you want me to do? Have sex with you?"

"God, no!"

There's wet eyeliner running down her cheek, and she wipes a hand across her face, like a child, smearing black everywhere. She looks confused, and I start to realize that she's never known a guy who didn't want something like that from her. Boyfriends, band mates, whatever. She's had to buy her way in to their good graces, and now the kiss she planted on my lips last week feels tainted.

I set my guitar to the side and lean forward on my knees, hiding my face so I don't have to look at her. "Okay, here's the deal. You get at least a C on your semester final in Algebra, and I'll play with you."

She sinks back into the chair. Thank God, distance.

"You want me to pass some stupid test?" she whispers.

I yank her drumstick out of her hand and wave it in front of her face. "I want you to take something seriously besides this. I want you to realize how smart you actually are and apply yourself."

I drop the drumstick back on the desk, and she stares at it for a few seconds. Then, her hand crawls across the surface and folds around the familiar wood, and she nods. "Okay."

Thirty-Two

Jason

Normally, I navigate gym class alone. Brayden has a locker near mine now, but that doesn't make changing any easier. If anything, it's a thousand times harder. Jimmy's pretty annoyed by the whole thing, acting like it's some big imposition on him to have one of the jocks in our space. He dresses as fast as he can and hightails it out of there every day. Which is fine with me. Not like we're friends or anything. Once we get into the gymnasium, it's every man for himself. Brayden hangs with the jocks. The not-quite-jocks, not-quite-losers hang out together. And Jimmy and I refuse to hang out with each other.

Except, today, he's waiting for me outside the locker room. As soon as I start walking toward the gym, he falls into step next to me.

"What are you doing?"

He jams his hands into his hoodie pocket. "I need to ask you something."

"The answer is no." I try to pull ahead, but he speeds up to stick with me.

"You don't even know what I was going to ask."

"Doesn't matter," I say, "don't care."

"Look, can you just come by my house after school today?"

I stop walking. "If this is some stupid plan to get Cynthia back, forget it."

"It's not. I swear." He even holds up his right hand like he's in court or something. The idiot.

I stare him down, expecting him to come clean. "Fine, whatever, I'll do it." What have I got to lose anyway? More time with my parents? Yeah, I'll take this doofus over them any day. Which I guess is a testament to Jimmy's... something.

#

I am sorry to report that I still know how to get to Jimmy's house. I guess I'd hoped that during the three months since he and Cyn broke up, I would have completely wiped all essence of him from my memories, but sadly, that isn't the case. About twenty minutes after the last bell rang, I pull into his driveway.

He meets me at the door but doesn't invite me in. Never mind that it's December in Minnesota and I can feel my snot freezing to my upper lip. He steps onto the porch, and that's when I notice a black guitar bag slung over his shoulder.

"The band's coming over in a few, so we gotta make this quick," he says.

I snort. "The quicker the better, as far as I'm concerned."

He pulls the guitar off his shoulder and hands it to me. "Here."

"Gee thanks," I say with obvious sarcasm in my tone. "But I don't play."

"Not for you. For Cynthia."

"You're trying to buy her back?" I snap, shoving the guitar at him. "I told you. I'm not helping you."

"No, it's not that. I swear." He steps away, like he thinks I'm going to hit him or something. "Look, I bought that for her a while ago, when we were still together. I figured I'd give it to her for her birthday or Christmas or whatever, but then we broke up and... I dunno. I just don't really want it around anymore."

"So give it to Steve-O," I say, "Or Ray."

"Naw man, it's hers. It's all her. I saw it and I just knew it had to be hers." He rubs the back of his neck nervously. "You don't have to tell her it's from me, okay? You can pretend like you found it at a garage sale or something and got it for her. But it's her guitar."

Shit, he's really serious about this.

I nod. "Okay, I'll give it to her. No guarantee she won't smash it, but I'll give it to her."

"Thanks."

Jimmy turns to head back inside, but I call him back. "I'm not running any more messages between you okay? This is it. No more contact. You got me?"

"Yeah," he says sadly. "I got it."

Thirty-Three

Brayden

~~~~~~

Mark snaps his fingers in front of my face. "Dude, you're staring again."

I shake myself awake. "What? I was?"

"Yeah, same as yesterday, same as the day before. Every single day, there's Brayden, staring across the cafeteria at the druggies and the freaks, a little string of drool sliding out of the corner of his mouth."

I glare at him. "I wasn't staring."

"Uh huh," he says and glances across the cafeteria where sure enough, the druggies and freaks are huddled around Cynthia Marlow and whatever music video she's watching on her phone. Something fast and loud and screamy and full of pain. Like her.

I need to stop thinking about Cynthia. Because what we have is a business agreement, nothing more. I'm just teaching her Algebra so she doesn't flunk out of school. And I dunno, maybe we're starting a band? I figure I have about a 50/50 chance of actually having to follow through on that deal. I mean, can she really pull a C on the Algebra final? After months of never trying? Maybe.

I shake my head. Forget about her lip ring and the taste of cold metal when she kissed me. Was it really over a month ago? Her kiss is burned on

143
~~~~~~

my lips, ice and fire. Forget about the look in her eyes when she begged me to play guitar for her.

Forget it all.

Because Cynthia Marlow is trouble with a capital T. Everyone knows that. You'd have to be certifiably insane to want to risk being with a girl like Cynthia. Not to mention I have a girlfriend already. I have to remind myself more and more these days. It's weird. I spend hours with Angela, entire weekends, and I feel like I hardly know her compared to Cynthia. Not like Cynthia is opening up to me or anything about her life, because she's not, I just feel like I understand how all her pieces fit together. Jagged edges and all.

Or, maybe I just wish I did.

Mark chuckles and leans back in his chair. "You know, if Angela ever finds out you're stepping out on her, she's going to lose her shit."

"I'm not cheating on Angela."

"Whatever, man. I don't judge."

I turn to glare at him. "Cut it out, man. I'm not doing anything. I don't need you spreading stuff about me, okay?"

"Okay, shit man," he says. "You seem a little tense. Maybe you should."

"Screw you." I grab my tray and head for the trash, but not before shooting one last look at Cynthia's table. Her eyes are glued on me. No more music videos.

I guess I'm not the only one guilty of staring.

#

The last day of first semester is on a Tuesday, and it's a half day, so completely pointless. We go to each of our classes for about twenty minutes so our teachers can pass back our graded finals and tell us to stop acting like hooligans and be safe over the holidays. Like they're not all going to go home and drink a bottle of wine the second the bell rings.

Cynthia texted me almost as soon as school let up. All it said was "My house" then listed the address.

I stare at my phone for a solid minute before it registers. She must have passed her exam. I'm not surprised. I knew she could do it. I just wish I had told Angela about our agreement.

I take my time getting over there, swinging by my house to get my guitar, because I figure Cynthia wants me to bring it, even if she didn't specifically say so.

Then I drive on over. I don't start getting nervous until I'm standing on her front step. I haven't exactly been to her house before, unless you count driving her home after that dumb party. I don't know what to expect. There's a paper attached to the front door that reads:

Ring the bell and die a slow, painful death

It isn't in Cynthia's handwriting.

Instead, I try the handle. Unlocked. But do I dare enter? I guess I have to.

"Cynthia?" I call as I walk through the entryway, craning my neck right and left to look around. There are about a thousand family photos all long the front hallway. I guess I never figured Cynthia would come from a normal family, but they look pretty normal here. Cynthia at various stages of her life. Seven-year-old Cynthia with light brown hair in pigtails on a swing set. Thirteen-year-old Cynthia with braces, and not even bothering to hide them as she smiled for the camera. Cynthia with different adults, parents and grandparents, I assume. She looks so happy.

I hear her voice from down the hall. "Back here," and I follow it into a small yellow kitchen that is wall to wall covered in daisy decor. Daisies on the hand towels, daisies on the curtains, daisies on the plastic table cloth. Definitely weird. The last place I ever expected to find angry, tough as nails Cynthia is in a room adorned with flowers. And she's washing dishes, of all the crazy things.

She turns around when she hears me enter and wipes her hands on an apron—and honest to goodness apron—also covered in daisies. I burst out laughing, and her face sours.

"Shut up, I had to make lunch." She points to the stove where a pot of chili is bubbling. "Go for it, if you want."

I'm starving, but I don't move, because I'm also on a mission. "First thing's first," I say, "Did you pass your final?"

She bites her lip. "I had to get a 70, right?"

"Right."

"What if I got close?" she asks slowly.

I set my guitar down in the corner. "Then I would say that you're trying to cheat and leave."

"Oh." She looks down at her shoes. "What if I wasn't even that close? Like I was fifteen off or so?"

"Why are you wasting my time?" I turn to leave.

She grabs her bag off the chair and beats me to the doorway, pulling out her test and shoving it into my hands. I glance down.

"Holy cow, 83?" I ask, completely dumbfounded. She laughs and takes it back from me. Color me shocked, she actually looks halfway proud of herself. "So what now?" I ask.

"Now," she says, folding the exam and putting it in her back pocket, "now… we wake up my mom."

"Your mom's still asleep?"

She nods. "Yeah. She told me not to let her sleep past twelve, and well…" she points to the clock. 11:58. "Also, my drums are still locked up, so we need the key." She pours a bowl of chili and grabs a spoon from the drawer. My stomach growls audibly at that, and she gives me a look. "You can eat, Brayden. I promise it's not poisoned."

I'm already doing the calorie calculations in my head, because the smell coming from that pot of chili has me drooling. It's too cold to run outside, but we have a treadmill downstairs, and I could probably get a few miles in before bed if I tried.

I follow her out of the kitchen and up the stairs. "So is your mom like a stay-at-home mom or something?" I'm comparing her to mine, even though I know I shouldn't. My mom stays at home, and she definitely doesn't sleep until noon.

"No," Cynthia says over her shoulder. "She's a nurse at the hospital in St. Paul. She had like three back to back twelve-hour shifts this week, but today's her day off. She says I'm too loud, so she has to sleep when I'm at school." She stops at the last door on the left and knocks before entering. I opt for waiting outside because my parents would kill me if I let one of my classmates see them sleeping. I figure Cynthia's mom probably feels the same.

"Mom?" Cynthia says. Her voice sounds surprisingly calm and pleasant. "I made lunch."

There's some indistinct grunting, and I crane my neck out of curiosity. I can hear her shifting in her bed to sit up and a quiet. "Thanks, baby."

"I have a friend over."

Another grunt. "Jason?"

"No, someone else." There's a long pause, then Cynthia speaks again. "He plays guitar. We want to play."

Another long pause. "I'm not sure that's a good idea." Her mom sounds strained and worried.

"Mom," Cynthia says a bit more forceful than before, "no one from the band. He's different. He's been helping me with school and stuff." I hear some rustling. "Look." She must be showing her mom the test.

There's a minute of silence while her mom flips through the pages. "Did you cheat?"

I wince.

"No," Cynthia's voice pitches higher, "I told you I got a tutor! I studied!"

"Okay, I'm sorry." I can hear her looking through the test some more, checking over the work. Apparently, she's satisfied it's all truly Cynthia's. I hadn't even considered she might cheat. "So, you want the key to the basement?"

"No shit."

"This guitar player of yours, is he here?"

"He's in the hall."

"I want to meet him."

Cynthia hems a little. "Mom, you're still in your pajamas," she mumbles. I try not to laugh. Cynthia's embarrassed, it's kind of funny.

"Okay, okay." I hear the bed move and start to inch my way back to the stairs. "I'll get dressed, but I want to meet him. I'm serious. I get to meet all of your friends from now on."

I'm about halfway down the stairs when Cynthia bursts out of the room, mumbling angrily under her breath. She pushes past me and heads for the kitchen. I follow her, and as soon as we're alone, she rounds on me. "Okay, here's the deal. She'll be down in like five minutes and under no circumstances, NO circumstances," she repeats fiercely, "are you to imply that we are dating in any way."

"We're not dating."

"Yeah," she says, "well make sure she understands that you have never and will never have any sort of interest in doing anything like that with me."

I raise an eyebrow.

"Sex, Brayden! God!" she snaps, "you can't even give her the slightest hint that you want to do that at all, with me. Because if you do, she's going to boot your ass. She's really touchy after what happened with my last band. As far as she's concerned, we are just friends. Normal, not doing anything but playing music, friends."

"Okay." This whole speech is pretty presumptuous, if you ask me. She must think I'm just a walking erection, ready to blow at any moment. Like I'm the one who kissed her, and not the other way around.

Except, she's not even finished. "Also, you have to sound smart. The smarter you are, the better she likes you. The only reason Jason's allowed to come over so much is because he's like a genius or something, and he knows how to sell it."

I nod.

She keeps glaring at me for like an eternity, then bites her lower lip and turns to the cabinet to pull out more bowls. She unceremoniously scoops food into both of them and hands one to me. "Here. She's easier to fool if you're doing something."

She acts like her mom is a mind-reader or something.

My stomach lets out a depressing sounding growl right at that moment, and I flash back to my pitiful lunch. It was mostly celery. Cynthia sits at the table and pulls her feet up onto her chair, so one knee is situated just under her chin and her arms curl around it. Then she starts eating without looking at me.

I sit and take a bite.

First thought: Wow, this is spicy.

Second thought: And amazing.

"What's in this?"

"Secret recipe," she mutters to her bowl. "If I told you, I'd have to kill you."

I take another bite. "It's good."

She grunts in reply and keeps eating. She doesn't seem to realize that she's created culinary perfection. She doesn't appear to be tasting anything, just food in, breath, more food in.

I, on the other hand, intend to savor every bite. She's got the balance just right, chili powder and peppers and salt to cut the heat. My growling stomach is begging for more. When I finish my first bowl, I stand to get seconds. Which is when Mrs. Marlow walks in.

She stops in the door way, hands on her hips and looks me completely up and down. "Wow, Cyn. You don't normally like them so All-American. What happened?"

"Oh my god, Mom!"

I figure I should try to help. "We're just friends, Mrs. Marlow."

"Judy," she says with a bright smile. "So, my daughter says you're here to play band with her."

"We're not playing band," Cynthia grumbles, "we're forming a band."

I shrug. "She found out I play guitar and I got roped into it."

"Lucky you." She moves across the room to the fridge and leans over to dig out a pop. "So I hear I have you to thank for keeping her out of summer school?"

"I mostly just check over her work. It's not much."

Cynthia sits like a statue in her chair, breathing heavily through her nose and tapping her fingers on her knee.

Mrs. Marlow takes a sip from her pop. "And you're not sleeping with each other?" she asks in the tone of voice one might ask if you have a spare umbrella or if you've seen the latest football game.

"Mom!" Cynthia hisses.

At the same time I sputter, "No! No way. No… no ma'am."

I can't even look at anyone, so I just stare at my bowl of chili. I want to eat it, but I also feel like both of them are staring at me and I'll just embarrass myself.

"Okay then," her mom says with a smirk, "have at it." She pulls a set of keys out of her pocket and tosses them on the table.

Cynthia doesn't need to be told twice. She snatches the keys and darts out of the room like a runner off the blocks. For a half a second, I wonder if a gunshot has gone off. Then I shovel down as much food as I can, grab my guitar, and follow her.

By the time I get to the basement, Cynthia has already started. She's walking around her drums, tapping the skins with her finger to test the tension. She is completely in the zone, she doesn't even notice me standing there watching her put mute pads on everything and adjust the height of her stool. She swivels around a few times, then starts playing.

I use the time to look around the room. It's actually a pretty cool set up. The Stinks must have practiced here, because someone added soundproof padding on all of the walls and even on the back of the door. There are old amps stacked along one wall and an extremely dingy looking couch sagging next to the stairs with a granny-square blanket thrown over the back.

Cynthia stops playing, and when I turn back around, she's watching me.

"So," I ask nervously, "what do you want to do?"

Dumb question.

Thirty-Four

Cynthia

What do I want to do? I am going to kill him. What do I want to do? I think I've made it pretty abundantly clear, Brayden. I want to play. Really play. I want that feeling back when all the parts work together and it's not just noise anymore. It's music. Real music. The kind that turns me into a rock goddess. I've been wanting to play since the Stinks kicked me out and humiliated me and got my drumming privileges revoked. But now I'm back, baby, with sticks in hand and skins begging to be beaten.

It's not like I expected Brayden to be falling all over himself to start a band with me, but I guess I hoped. I mean, he has this whole, "I'm just fulfilling a promise, but I really hate being here" attitude about the whole thing that's making it hard for me to relax and just play.

I close my eyes to try to calm down, because I'm pretty sure our deal is null and void if I hit him with a drumstick. "What songs do you know? Don't say *Stairway to Heaven*, because I'm not playing that."

He unzips his guitar case, and I relax. At least he's getting his instrument out, finally. I've only been sitting back here, waiting to start for like five whole minutes, but by all means Brayden, take your time. I wonder if his coach ever threatens to beat him if he doesn't get changed for practice faster, because I sure as hell might.

When I open my eyes, he's holding his guitar, sans strap, on a propped up knee.

"You need a strap," I say. Not a question.

"I do?"

I drop my sticks on my stool and walk over to an old red tool shelf Ray found at a garage sale where the band used to keep spare picks and straps and sticks. All that stupid shit that breaks or gets lost a million times when you're going to gigs and coming home drunk or high. I toss him one of the old brown leather ones. Steve-O said it was too country for him and of course Jimmy and Ray, the great innovators, followed his lead and never used it again.

Brayden attaches the strap, loops it over his shoulders, then looks back at me. "What do you want to play?"

I smirk. "I'm guessing my repertoire is a little longer than yours, so you pick."

He shrugs. "I don't know."

It's like pulling fucking teeth. "Well," I say impatiently, "What's your favorite song?"

"Um, you know Radiohead?"

I burst out laughing. "Yeah, I know Radiohead."

"I need to hear it while I play along."

A true beginner. We've all been there. I pick up my phone. "What song you want?"

"*Creep?*"

I didn't expect that, some perfect jock with a thousand friends and a perfect life thinking that a song like *Creep* somehow relates to him. What the hell does he know about not fitting in, about feeling like something is just too pure and perfect for you?

I say as much, thinking he'll give some half-assed answer about hearing it on the radio, because even though Radiohead's got tons of good music out there, the radio only ever plays one song. Over and over and over again.

But he doesn't. Instead he looks down at the ground and says, "music belongs to everyone."

It floors me. Maybe he really does get it. Music and all. I pull out my phone and start swiping. I've got about every song I've ever heard downloaded on there, just a matter of finding it. Sure enough… here we go.

I grab the remote to turn on the Bluetooth speakers. "You ready?"

"I guess."

I press play and pick up my sticks.

Literally five seconds later, he stops strumming and looks at me. "I got off."

I pause the song. "What?"

"I got off. I missed a chord change and got off."

"So keep playing. Just jump back in."

He looks doubtful. "Can we just start back over?"

Ugh. "In a real gig, you can't just start over every time you make a mistake." But he doesn't say anything, just kind of shrugs, like I'm being mean or something. I sigh. "Fine, okay, we'll start over."

A couple tries later, and we finally make it all the way through. It's far from perfect, but still. Progress. Course, he's all ready to celebrate, like he thinks this is an accomplishment or something. He looks back at me grinning and I can't help but smile back. When it all comes together, there's nothing better. But we still have tons of work to do, and I'm not quitting until I get perfection. I move to click "play" again, and he groans.

"Can we take a break?"

"A break?"

"Just a few minutes? I could use some water."

I'm about ready to tell him to shove it, but then I remember I can't exactly alienate the only potential band member out there, so I just nod and stand up. "Yeah, I'll be right back."

When I get back from the kitchen, he's lounging on the couch, really making himself at home. "Here." I toss him a bottle and crack my own open, chugging down about a third of it, before setting it down. I pick up Brayden's guitar. "You mind?"

"Knock yourself out."

I grin and settle onto Steve-O's old stool, savoring the smooth wood in my hand, pick at the ready, for half a second, it's just me and this guitar. Then I start to play.

Nothing special. Just trying out a few things. I got to get songs written and fast, because I suspect it'll take Brayden a while to learn them, and even longer to make them perfect. I'm not holding back though, I'm not going to dumb down my writing just because he's inexperienced. He can learn it, but he'll need to work for it.

Plus it feels good to be writing again. I've been swimming in ideas lately, but with no instrument, it's hard to actually work any of them out.

I play for a while, with my back turned to Brayden, so I kind of forget he's there. I mean, I honestly just get a little lost in my own head. Anyway, I finish up what I'm doing, and spin back around, and I kid you not, he is staring at me.

Full on staring. Lips curled into a half-grin, brown eyes all soft and warm and intense all at once, and he's holding his open bottle of water halfway to his mouth, like he forgot it was there. What the hell?

I count to ten in my head and he doesn't blink, so I snap my fingers. "Hey! Stop staring, you freak."

He shakes his head, like he's coming out of a trance. "Huh? What?"

"Break time's over. Back to work."

#

I don't expect Jason to come over during Winter Break. For one, his parents are Nazis about the whole Christmas season. I said "Happy Holidays" to his dad once in tenth grade and was treated to a two-hour long monologue about the "true meaning of Christmas."

True meaning, my ass. Everyone knows Christmas was commandeered by the early Christians so they could trick pagans into converting. See, I pay attention in class occasionally. When it's interesting.

Anyway, he shows up at my house on Christmas Eve, of all the crazy days, so he must have come up with some good reason to get out of the usual brainwashing.

Mom has to let him in, because I'm down in the basement. Now that my drums are free, I basically spend every second down there.

I don't hear him at first, so he knocks on the wooden step behind him to make me look up. When I see what he brought with him, my jaw drops. Holy shit, it's like the universe is telling me I'm destined to win Battle of the Bands this year.

"Is that what I think it is?" I leap off the couch to examine it further, but as I approach, he holds the guitar away from me. I can see the familiar Fender script next to the pegs, and it is calling to me. It's a beauty. Not a cheapo-beginner guitar. This baby's seen things.

"Hang on," he says, "we need to talk first."

It's like he's never met me. Surely, he knows I have no problems tearing through him to get to that instrument.

"What?"

"Jimmy bought this for you."

Damn, the boy doesn't mince words, does he? There's not a lot to make me want to toss a perfectly good guitar out the window, but finding out my ex-boyfriend bought it for me? Yeah, that might do it.

My shoulders slump. "Oh."

"I've been debating for a couple weeks whether to even give it to you."

I glare.

"And, ultimately," he says dramatically, "I've decided to let you choose. Because honestly, it's a really nice guitar."

"No shit."

"And it'd be a shame to just get rid of it, you know?" He holds the guitar out to me, but now it looks like tainted goods. "Especially," he adds, "when the next great rock star is standing right in front of me. And though it pains me to admit this… Even Jimmy said so."

"He did?"

Jason shrugs. "I mean, he lacks my eloquence, of course, but he basically said that you were special and that he knew you were going places, and blah blah blah. Who cares? You have in front of you a free guitar, and a good one, no strings attached. I made sure."

Thirty-Five

Lindsey

Three times a year, our empty manor house is filled to the brim with family. Every one of my siblings return home, family in tow. Once in summer, again at Thanksgiving, and finally for two weeks every Christmas.

One would think it'd be chaos, five families under one roof, but it's not. Even the youngest grandchild—my six-month-old nephew, Andrew Haywood Banford—seems to know what is expected of him. Every second of every day is planned, from the multiple church services where we once again fill our pew and the one behind, to the charity galas and catered family brunches.

Precisely three days before Christmas, a professional photographer arrives to take the family portraits that will be displayed prominently in my father's office at the Capitol and my mother's in St. Paul's, not to mention used for various campaign advertisement in the coming months. It's an all day affair, with our outfits chosen by our mother, steamed and laid out by temporary staff. Every detail accounted for, chosen for me.

As a stylist curls my hair into ringlets, I think about Jason's suggestion to dye it, then imagine my mother's face if I were to show up to the photo session with Cynthia-esque blue.

I wouldn't live to see the New Year.

In the days leading up to Christmas, there are countless functions to attend, and even a few to host. In these, I can get lost in the crowd. And though I recognize the wealthy and powerful families I've known my whole life, I find myself looking at them through a different lens this year. As if seeing them through Charlotte's eyes or Harvey's. And when I think about all that is wasted on these functions while Harvey skips meals and works two jobs to help feed his younger brothers, I'm disgusted by what I see.

I don't want to be like these people.

On the morning after Christmas, my father finds me practicing Rachmaninoff at our upstairs piano, and he sits on the bench next to me.

"Are you hiding from your mother?"

My fingers come to a stop. "Of course not." I want to tell him that this is all too much, that it has always been too much. I am exhausted, not just from this week's obligations, but from all of them. Constantly smiling at things that don't make me happy. Constantly pretending.

To admit to these feelings is to admit to being less than. To not living up to the standard.

Instead, I return to playing, and he seems to understand.

He waits until the song has finished, then stands. "I've arranged for a short trip across the state over the next few days. Just your mother and me. And, I have informed your brothers and sisters, and Loretta, that you are to be allowed the freedom to come and go as you please."

The enormity of what he's said washes over me. Freedom, even just a few days of it. It's more than I've had for months. I jump up and wrap my arms around him, a display of affection rarely seen in the Banford home.

"Thank you," I say breathlessly, "thank you!"

He gives me a perfunctory pat on my back and leans away. "This is, of course, between the two of us. Don't tell your mother."

#

Almost as soon as my parents' car leaves the premises, I'm running up the stairs toward my bedroom to change into something casual. Jeans-level casual. I want to blend in. Only once I've pulled on my pea coat and wool cap, I realize that I have no idea where I'm going.

It's been so long since I've made my own plans, I've forgotten how.

Beth meets me in the foyer. "Where are you off to?"

"Dad said I could go," I say, but she holds up her hand.

"I wasn't trying to stop you," she says. "Just generally curious."

"Oh." I feel foolish. Even more so when I admit I don't know yet.

Beth gives me a little side hug. "Maybe you could call up a friend or something. Just try to have fun." With that, she's gone.

Call up a friend. Even more embarrassing than admitting I don't know where to go with my free time, is admitting I don't know who to call. My cellphone is filled with Student Council members or the children of wealthy donors. A handful of classmates from various projects or from church.

And Charlotte.

My finger hovers for a moment over her name, then I make the call.

She doesn't answer at first, in fact, I'm certain it will go to voicemail, then I hear her voice.

"Hello?"

"Hi, Charlotte," I say. "It's Lindsey."

"I know."

I try to ignore the annoyed tone in her voice. "Right, well, I was just wondering if you were busy today? I thought maybe we could go shopping or to the movies or something?"

"Um," she pauses for a moment, "I dunno."

"I can come pick you up."

"No!" she says quickly. "No, please don't… I mean, yeah I can meet you."

"Great!" I cringe. I sound way too excited. "Do you like rom-coms?"

"I guess…"

I put her on speakerphone so I can search movie listings, and pretty soon we've arranged a time to meet. "Looking forward to seeing you there!" I say.

"Right… You too," she says before saying bye and hanging up.

Thirty-Six

Charlotte

If you had told me a year ago I'd be spending my winter break hanging out with a blonde-haired, blue-eyed daughter of a wealthy Midwestern Senator, I would have laughed in your face.

And yet, here I am, sitting next to Lindsey Banford watching the previews leading up to a chick-flick that promises to be cringe-worthy in a thousand different ways. If the kids back home could see me now.

She looks perfect, as always, like a Barbie doll, fashionable and poised. I, on the other hand, barely threw on clean clothes before heading out the door. I didn't think I needed to dress to impress. Truth be told, I haven't for a while. Lindsey doesn't seem to mind though. She looks genuinely happy to see me when I show up, pulls me into an awkward hug and starts talking a mile a minute about how excited she is we're getting to hang out without worrying about schoolwork.

I try to muster up some enthusiasm but fall desperately short.

"Are you feeling okay?" she asks as she offers me some popcorn.

I take a handful to give myself time to come up with an answer. "It's been kind of a shitty week."

Her face falls. "Oh, I'm so sorry."

I shrug. "It's just the first Christmas since," I pause. Since my dad died. But

I don't want to talk about that, because I don't want to start crying. "Since we moved up here."

"Oh," Lindsey looks down. "Do you miss your friends?"

What friends? "Yeah, I guess."

She smiles indulgently. "You should give them a call. I bet they'd love to hear from you."

You can't call your dead dad, though. Luckily, the movie starts, and I'm saved trying to come up with something to say back.

#

Lindsey and I end up getting dinner after the movie, so I don't get home until around seven. It's pitch black outside, and Mom hasn't even left the porch light on, so I have to feel my way to the front door and into the house. When I get inside, I see why. She's exactly where I left her, staring blankly at the television. It doesn't look like she's eaten anything.

"Mom?" I say. "Are you okay?"

She glances over her shoulder at me, and I can see she's been crying. "How was the movies?" she asks, completely ignoring my question. "Did you have fun?"

"Yeah, I guess." Once I say it, I realize I did. I show her my to-go box of leftovers. "We got dinner already. But I can heat this up for you if you want."

She waves her hand. "No, that's fine."

I sit next to her on the couch, and scoot close to her. She's cold, and I grab a blanket to pull over the two of us.

"Winter here sucks," I say.

That's enough to make her smile. "Truth."

"It's so dry, and the snow is gross and hard to drive on," I keep going, "and you can't move in a winter coat. I feel like a big blob whenever I wear mine."

She laughs. "It's not so bad."

It is, but if I keep complaining, she'll think I'm trying to guilt her into moving back home. And even though once, I might have, I find I'm actually fine staying here. At least a little while longer.

She wraps her arm around my shoulders and kisses the top of my head. "I miss him too, baby."

Thirty-Seven

Cynthia

This guitar is so beautiful. It makes me want to cry. I spend nearly every second of Winter Break cradling it in my arms, tracing my fingers over its curves, trying to come up with a name for it. No, her. The drums are my first love, and they always will be, but this guitar, it's a close second.

I can't let myself get sentimental. Because from the moment Jason handed it to me, I knew my ownership was temporary. I have to pass it on. I'm a drummer, and I always will be.

Brayden's the guitar player.

He's busy most of the break, so we don't practice much. I sent him home with about a thousand pages of guitar tab to practice, mostly songs I know he's heard before, the classics, which he likes, punk for me. I plan on teaching him everything he ever wished he knew about the evolution of punk rock. Starting with The Ramones right up to present day. It's a crash course in raising musical hell, and I'm the teacher.

I'm still holding her when Brayden walks in, and his eyebrows skyrocket when he sees her.

"Where'd you get that?" he asks.

"It was a gift."

"Dang," he says, "Merry Christmas to you."

"Yeah, well," I stand up and hold the guitar out. "Merry Christmas to you, actually."

His mouth opens, then closes, and he shakes his head. "No, Cyn, I can't accept that."

Cyn. He called me Cyn.

I square my shoulders. "Hey Bob Dylan, time to give up acoustic and join the real rock 'n' rollers. We can't win Battle of the Bands unless we go electric, and this baby is damn near perfect." Then, for good measure, I stand up and practically push the guitar into his hands. "You better have been practicing."

Thirty-Eight

Brayden

Cynthia wasn't joking. The first thing she does after she hands me the Fender is peel her hoodie off so all she has on is a black tank top and some skin-tight black jeans, and I'm pretty sure she's not wearing a bra under there. I can't take my eyes off her. Any second now, she's going to jab me with a drumstick and call me a pervert, but I can see her nipples, and I'm about ninety-five percent sure they're pierced under there.

"Hey, asshole. Eyes up here."

She caught me. I shake my head to clear it. "Uh, sorry, um… I mean, aren't you cold?" It's January, and we're in the basement. Not exactly the warmest environment.

"You think I'm here to play around?" she asks, grabbing my acoustic guitar out of its case—without asking, of course—and strapping it over her shoulder. "We're here to work." She turns and grins. "Making music is a full body workout, and baby, I'm going to make you sweat."

I snort. "I run three to five miles every day, in any weather, plus I lift at school and have basketball practice for two hours after. I think I can handle whatever you throw my way."

"We'll see."

Then we're off. We warm up with The Ramones, which is good, because I picked up their style pretty quickly over the past few weeks. Course, she doesn't let up. If I start to slow down even a little, she slings the guitar onto her back, yanks a drumstick out of her black combat boot and starts pounding the beat out on her snare drum, all the while shouting at me to speed up.

"I can't," I pant after the third time. "It's too fast."

"Stop dropping the damn beat on every chord change!"

"I'm trying!" I say irritably.

"Not hard enough," she snaps back. "It's punk rock. Three chords played really fast. If you can't handle it, then get the hell out."

So I have to try again. And again after that. Until it's perfect. When I've mastered The Ramones, we tackle Dead Kennedys, Sex Pistols—whose name makes me uncomfortable—Joy Division, then finally, she hands me new tab, handwritten.

"What's this?"

"Our band's first song," she replies, pulling a couple of stools over so we can sit. "Watch me." Then she starts playing. We run through it real slow so I can learn all the parts. It's pretty straightforward, but I know she's going to expect me to play it faster, and without her help. But it's cool, learning something no one else has ever played. Just me and her.

When she gets into it, she forgets I'm there. Just starts playing on her own, humming a little. She pauses and pulls out her phone to type something up.

"What're you doing?"

"Writing lyrics," she mumbles without looking up. "Stop staring at me and keep playing."

I can't help it. I've developed a nasty staring habit. She's unlike anyone I've ever met. Mesmerizing.

When she's satisfied I can play it on my own, she moves to the drums, where she is undeniably in her element. "We'll play it at half speed at first, okay? Listen to my beat."

"Okay."

"And don't look at me." She points a drumstick at the opposite wall. "The audience is out there. You gotta play for them."

"There's no one there."

Her mouth hangs open and I'm pretty sure she wants to tell me I'm the world's biggest idiot, but instead she just taps her drumsticks together to set the beat and starts playing, so I have to scramble to finger the first chord and keep up.

By the time she lets me quit, it's dark outside. The tips of my fingers are sore, even though I already have callouses on them from before. I've never played this much at one time. My callouses need callouses. My legs hurt, and I've got sweat dripping down my back.

Cynthia doesn't look much better. Her black hair is slick with sweat, and her tank top is sticking to her in all the right places. She was right. This was a workout. I stumble over to the couch and collapse into it, exhausted.

Across the basement, Cynthia takes her time packing up, not really looking at me as she puts guitars back in cases and sorts through papers.

"Hey," I say, "come over here."

Her bright blue eyes find mine, and she pauses, bites her lip ring for a second, then walks over. "What?"

I hold out my hand, I don't even know what I'm doing, but she takes it, and I pull her closer. My heart is pounding in my chest. This is so wrong. I have a girlfriend. Why am I so obsessed with Cynthia?

And why do I want her to be obsessed with me?

Her knees bump mine, and she looks down at me, like she's not sure what I want. Hell, I'm not even sure what I want. So I just pull her even closer, until she sits on my lap, all dainty like how girls do, with her legs crossed, and she wraps her arms around my neck. Now she's hella close, and my body is basically on fire. A couple of hours ago, I was afraid it'd be too cold down here, but now this basement is an inferno.

Her fingers play with the short hairs on the back of my neck, and it's everything I can do not to pop a boner. Angela. Think about Angela. Angela? Angela who?

"I… uh…" I stumble over my words.

"Have a girlfriend," she finishes for me.

"Yeah."

She sits perfectly still, watching me, like she's holding her breath. Her mouth hangs slightly open and those lips. Those kissable lips. I want them.

"Did you tell your girlfriend that I kissed you?" she asks.

I choke. "No, no way. No.. no, nope, nope definitely not."

The corner of her lip curls. "You gonna tell her if I kiss you again?"

I reach up and trace my fingers along her face, drawing it to mine, until our lips are barely touching. "No."

Thirty-Nine

Cynthia

Three weeks of hardcore jamming, and we're actually starting to sound good.

Then Jason comes storming in, like he always does, ranting about his dad. When he sees us, he freezes on the bottom step, and we freeze too. Or rather, I do. Brayden's got his back to the door, so he doesn't know what's up. He continues on for about four bars before he realizes I'm not with him, then he drops off too and turns around.

"Oh," he says.

Jason gapes. "What's *he* doing here?"

"What's it look like?" I ask. I mean, it's pretty obvious. "We're starting a band."

Brayden ducks his head. He's a good player, but he's not in the head space yet. The we're-an-actual-band head space. He's going to need to find it before the auditions, or else we'll never have a chance.

Jason looks back and forth between us, first at Brayden, then at me. Like he's trying to put all the pieces together.

Then he pretty much floors me with four words. "Don't be stupid, Cyn."

"Hey!" Brayden says, "don't call her stupid." He looks at me. "You're not stupid."

Jason rolls his eyes. "Knight in shining armor, huh?"

Brayden opens his mouth to retort, but I interrupt him. "Shut up, both of you."

They continue to stare each other down, then Brayden scowls and turns away. "I'm gonna head out."

"Wait, you don't have to—"

"It's not a big deal," Brayden says, "seems like your friend needs you right now."

As soon as he's gone, Jason rounds on me. "This is a bad idea."

"You don't even know what I'm doing."

"I can guess." He puts on a fake thinking face and taps his chin sarcastically. "Let me see… You're thinking that you can start a band, get into Battle of the Bands, and show up Steve-O and his gang."

My face falls.

"I knew it!" Jason throws up his hands in exasperation. "God, Cyn, you don't know when to walk away, do you?" He flops onto my couch, and I go to stand in front of him, hands on my hips.

"You don't understand what he did to me."

He looks up at me, stares me straight in the eye. "Actually, I do." His expression softens. "As soon as I saw Julie's video, I knew. Which is why I think you should stay away from him."

I square my shoulders and put on the toughest face I can muster. "I won't get hurt again."

"Promise?"

"Yeah." I got him now. "You should come by, give us a listen. He's actually pretty good."

He snorts. "I think that whole jock look is going to mess with your punk vibe."

"I can work with it," I say as I sit on the couch next to him. "I mean, the school boy outfit worked for Angus Young, right?"

#

True to his word, Jason comes by for the next band practice. Brayden looks apprehensive, but I tell him it's okay. "He just wants to listen."

"Okay…" He doesn't sound convinced.

Jason sits through three songs. Nothing original, just a couple Joan Jett numbers. By the third one, he's leaning on his knees studying us so intently that even I feel a little nervous. Brayden's doing his best to ignore the eyes on him, but he keeps making careless mistakes, so I know he's got stage fright.

Great. Another thing to fix.

When we finish the third song, Jason stands up. "Okay, I've seen enough."

"And?"

"And," he sighs, "it's not going to work."

I scowl.

"I'm not trying to be mean, but c'mon Cyn. Two people don't make a band."

"Tell that to the White Stripes," I say.

"They broke up."

"But they were awesome. Also, the Dresden Dolls."

Jason rolls his eyes.

"Simon and Garfunkel," Brayden offers.

I grin at him. "The Black Keys, or Tenacious D."

His eyes find mine and it turns into a game. "Sonny and Cher."

"Twenty-One Pilots," I say, "even though they're just okay."

Brayden nods in agreement. "Daft Punk."

"Nice!" I say, "uh… Tegan and Sara!"

"Okay!" Jason snaps, "okay, I get it. But you're not them." He looks at Brayden. "Can you even sing?"

He shakes his head. "Definitely not."

"Well," Jason says, folding his arms, "Cyn, you're good, but you're not good enough to carry the lyrics and drum all on your own."

"Watch me."

"I did, just now," he says, "and you slowed down."

How dare he? I'm gonna kill him. I actually get up from my stool to do it, then Brayden says, "he's right. You did."

I sink back into my seat. "Fine, we need a singer."

"And bass," Jason adds. "Something to round out the sound."

I think of Jimmy and feel sick. "I'm not getting a bassist."

Jason rolls his eyes. "A keyboardist would do the trick." Then, it's like a light turns on in his brain. "You're in luck. I might just know someone."

Forty

Lindsey

Jason watches me for the entirety of Sunday morning service, his eyes following me from pew to piano and back with every hymn. I wish he'd stop. If I didn't know he was gay, I'd assume he wanted to ask me out.

After service lets out, he corners me at the coffee stand where I'm busy helping his mother pass out cookies, all under the watchful eye of my own mother who's schmoozing potential voters a few feet away.

"Hey," he says, "can we talk? You don't mind, Mom, right? Great." All of this comes out in a single breath. He grabs my wrist and drags me through the kitchen and out the back door.

"Ow, Jason!" I yank my arm free. "What are you doing?"

"I have a proposition for you."

This can only mean bad news.

"You see, Lindsey… I had you pegged the second I saw JJ's video."

"I'm out of here." I turn to go back inside, but Jason bars the door with his arm.

"Good girl like you, never gets in trouble. Youngest of five, always the pressure to be better than your siblings, to be perfect. Pressure get to be too much, huh? And you got the itch to do something bad."

My fingers twitch, and I narrow my eyes. "You don't know anything about me."

"Oh, yes I do," he says. "Your family has been coming to my dad's church since before I was born, and you know how he is. Trust me. I know what it's like to be a failure in your parents' eyes."

"I'm not a failure." Years of straight As prove that much.

"No," he agrees, "but you're not happy either."

I shiver, and not just from the Minnesotan winter.

"That's what I thought," he says with a smirk. "You need to live a little, break out of the oppression of your elders, explore your bad side."

"I can't. My mom has me on lockdown."

"Oh really?" The conspiratorial glint in his eye is positively blinding at this point. "Even if you were... say... studying AP Chem with the pastor's son three nights a week?"

"You want me to study AP Chem with you?" I ask stupidly.

He grins. "No. I want you to join a rock band with me."

#

"You're fucking with me." Cynthia stares at me with her arms crossed and a look of such disdain on her face, I'm a bit worried for my safety. If she murders me, how long before they find my body?

"Jason, this isn't funny," she continues. "You can't bring some tea-party princess into my basement and expect me to take you seriously."

"Give her a chance," Jason says. He shoots me a don't-mess-this-up look and points out the keyboard. "She plays for the church choir."

"This is rock 'n' roll, not angelic la-di-da."

Jason rolls his eyes. "Get off your soap box, Cyn. Basic chord structures haven't changed all that much in the last... I dunno... three hundred years or so. If you can have your pet prep then so can I."

"Hey!"

The deep voice startles me from behind, and I spin around to find...

"Brayden Matthews?" I am beyond shocked. "What are you doing here?"

He picks up a bright red electric guitar. "Fulfilling my end of a bargain."

"He means he lost a bet," Cyn says.

"A bet with whom?" I ask.

"With me," she replies. She spins a drumstick and settles onto a stool behind the drum set in the corner. "Fine. Let's see what you got, Blondie."

Jason stands behind the microphone and squares his shoulders before looking at me. "Well?"

"Um…" I look around at the three of them. "I'll do my best."

I've barely gotten positioned behind the keyboard when Cynthia stats tapping her drumsticks and counting off.

"Wait, what are we pla—"

Too late. The three of them are off and I'm scrambling to catch up. Brayden takes pity on me and starts shouting out chord names whenever he shifts. Chords, I can do. Before too long, I've picked up the pattern. It's not that hard after all. In fact, it's almost fun.

Cynthia pounds hard on the last few beats and the three of them end at the same time. I, however, stop a little late.

"Oops, oh, I'm so sorry!"

Cynthia snorts. "Don't be. It was your first time. That was…"

Here it is. I don't know why I care so much about her opinion, except I do. Maybe it's just that I need to be good at everything.

"Kinda awesome," she finishes.

My breath whooshes out of me. "Really?"

"Yeah. I can work with you."

Jason puts a hand to his ear. "Wait. What was that? Was that you admitting that I was right?"

"Don't push it asshole." She taps her drumsticks again. "From the top!"

Forty-One

Brayden

First Jason, now Lindsey. This is Cynthia's band, but I should have some say, right? With Jason in the room, I feel like I blend into the background. I tell myself to only worry about the music, but every time I sneak a peek at Cynthia, she's watching Jason. They have a secret best friend communication skill that must only appear in girls and gays because I know Mark and I don't laugh over nothing like they do.

By the end of our second week of practice, we're sounding great, but I haven't kissed Cynthia once. And my body's kind of missing it. I mean sure, I've made out with Angela, but Cynthia, she's something else. I can't even explain it.

So I come up with a plan.

When practice is over, I rest the guitar on its stand and slump onto the couch and pull out my iPhone to pretend to check messages or whatever. Then as I go to slide it into my back pocket, I slip it into the crack of the couch instead. No one will see it there. Phase one, complete.

After a while, we get bored with chatting, and Jason's dad expects him home at a certain time anyway. From what it sounds like, Lindsey's parents aren't much better. So the three of us go upstairs, leaving Cynthia behind with my acoustic guitar which she's basically claimed for herself. She's not ready to quit playing. Given the opportunity, I doubt she'd ever stop.

I wait until the three of us are already out the door, so there's no chance of them following me back inside, then fake searching my pockets.

"Shoot, I think I left my phone downstairs."

Jason's not fooled, but Lindsey looks concerned. "Do you want us to help you look for it?"

"Naw, it's cool. I got it." I hustle inside before they can argue.

Cynthia's mom looks up, but I just tell her I forgot something and she nods and goes back to watching TV.

Phase two, piece of cake.

I expect to hear music when I open the basement door, but it's quiet, and when I reach the bottom of the stairs, I see why. Cynthia's sitting on the couch, my phone in her hand, looking at me like she can't believe how stupid I am.

"Forget something?" she says as she stands up.

I chuckle and cross the room. "Yeah, must have slipped out of my pocket."

"Sure it did." Her voice full of fake disbelief.

When I go to grab it, she moves it out of my reach.

"Not so fast."

I can't help but grin. She wants to play. I can play. I got nowhere to be. "What'll it take to get my phone back?"

She bites her lip ring. Not nervous this time. Coy. "Just take it from me."

When I reach for it again, she laughs and scrambles up onto the couch, standing so she's the same height as me, and holds the phone above her head. I could reach it. Easily. I've got basketball player reach.

But I don't.

Instead I loop an arm around her waist and pull her close, kissing her hard. She laughs and kisses me back, her hand dropping to her side as she does. With my spare hand, I gently pry my phone from her fingers.

"Got it," I whisper into her lips.

"Guess you have to leave now."

I'm still holding her close, her body pressed against mine. I don't want to leave.

"Or not," I say.

Phase three: success.

#

My new Monday through Thursday schedule goes like this:

5:00 am: Wake up. Go running.

6:00 am: Return home, shower, get dressed, go to school early.

7:00 am: Scramble to finish homework that didn't get done last night. Feel guilty about not doing my homework earlier. Remember why I didn't get my homework done. Feel even more guilty.

7:30 am: Meet Angela at her locker. Apologize for not being able to hang with her the previous night. Remind her that I'm doing community service by helping Cynthia pass her classes. Attempt to avoid thinking about the cold metal taste of Cynthia's lip ring while apologizing.

8:00 am – 2:30 pm: School. Try to get all my homework done in class. Fail miserably. Try not to stare at Cynthia in the cafeteria. Fail miserably. Meet her in the hallway next to the boys' locker room.

2:30 pm – 4:00 pm: Basketball practice. Sneak time Angela who watches from the stands. Remind myself to be a better boyfriend.

4:00 pm – 5:00 pm: Go home, shower. Cologne, because I don't want to smell bad. Debate clothes for half an hour because I want Cynthia to think I'm cool, then I remember I'm not supposed to care about whether she thinks I'm cool. Race across town to Cynthia's house.

5:05 pm: Listen to Cynthia berate me for being late.

5:05 pm – 8:00 pm: Make music.

8:00 pm - ???: Make out with Cynthia. Drive home. Sneak inside so my parents don't yell at me for staying out all night. Masturbate furiously. Attempt mountain of homework, instead fall asleep at my desk.

Wake up. Repeat.

Cynthia is a drug. I've got my taste. Now I want more. All of it. I want to swim in an ocean of Cynthia. When I'm with Angela, I'm dreaming of Cynthia. When I'm talking to Angela on the phone, I'm scrolling through Cynthia's Instagram, I'm fingering her songs on my guitar, and I'm remembering the feel of her skin and the smell of her hair.

Addictive, drug-like Cynthia. I am walking through a haze. I'm barely awake. I almost dropped a barbell on Mark's foot the other day because I'm so tired. My grades are suffering. But at night, I have Cynthia straddling my lap, her fingers in my hair, her tongue inside my mouth. If Heaven is real, I'm pretty sure it's this.

If Hell is real, it's what Angela's going to put me through if she ever finds out I'm cheating on her. Angela, who has always been so perfect, so sweet. I'm the jerk who's ruining her life and she doesn't even know it yet. I know it's wrong. It is so wrong. But it feels… right.

Cynthia says it doesn't matter. It's just a game to her. Something to do to pass the time. What is it for me? I don't know. More action than I've ever gotten in my entire life, and we haven't even done anything but kiss. But man, the way Cynthia kisses. I want more.

Forty-Two

Jason

When second semester started, I told myself I wasn't going to take any more shit from the kids at school. Helps to have someone like Brayden watching out, even though I hate feeling like I need him. The locker room went from the most dangerous place on earth to just a normal locker room. Smells like shit and body spray, but relatively safe. Maybe it's because basketball season is in full swing and the guys can't risk getting kicked off the team. If that's the case, I need to figure out how to keep them off my back when the season ends and hunting season officially reopens.

Bathrooms, on the other hand, have been a bit of an issue. Even the losers act like I can't be trusted to take a leak without harassing someone. The homophobia is very real. So I've taken to trying to use the restroom during classes, when they're relatively empty. I just hope the teachers don't notice and start restricting my passes.

I raise my hand about ten minutes into my second to last class of the day.

"Yes, Jason?" Mr. Palmer has never looked so severe.

"Can I go to the bathroom?"

He tilts his head roughly twenty-three degrees to the left and says nothing.

"It's an emergency," I add hopefully.

He nods, but of course he doesn't look happy about it. I don't wait for him to change his mind, but dart for the door, clutching at my stomach. Alone in the hallway, I slow to a crawl savoring my time. I pass Darrell's class, because apparently I don't learn from my mistakes. When he glances up and makes eye contact with me, I scurry past the door. Not slick at all.

I turn into the boy's bathroom and head for the far urinal.

Twenty seconds later, I've barely yanked my zipper back up when a voice behind me makes me jump right out of my skin.

"You're not fooling anyone. You know that right?"

I turn around to find Darrell leaning against the sink, arms crossed over a near perfect chest.

I mirror him, keeping my distance. "Did you follow me in here?"

He smirks. "Maybe it's fate."

"Maybe you're stalking me." Or flirting with me, which would be worse. I think. I'm not sure. My eyes travel over his body, before I give my head a quick shake and look away.

Darrell saunters down the line of stalls, nudging each one open as he goes, making sure we're alone. By the time he reaches me, I'm grinning. I can't help it. We're alone, and he is within arm's reach, and… Freaking Leviticus verses run through my head, and I pull away.

He stops. "No one here actually believes you've been magically turned straight."

"Yeah, well the only person I need to convince is my dad."

He's inches away from me. I can feel the heat radiating off his body. He leans in so he can whisper in my ear. "Is it working?" His voice sends shivers down my spine. Good shivers. I definitely do not need this.

"According to him," I reply," the gay has been successfully prayed away."

"And according to you?"

I shudder. "I think you're trying to kill me."

"No, I'm trying to kiss you."

He moves to make good on his word, but I sidestep him, ducking past his outstretched arm. His head whips around, his eyes follow me, and they are filled with hurt.

"What's wrong with you?" he whispers.

"I can't, okay, Darrell?" I say. "It doesn't matter how much I want to—"

"So you do want to." He grins. Dammit.

I look away.

"I've tried texting you," he says. "No response."

"I blocked your number," I mumble.

"Why?"

I start laughing, only it comes out a coughing hack. "Did you forget JJ's video? Remember, the one where she outed me and completely failed to mention you were an equal participant?"

"Dude, keep your voice down."

My heartbeat starts pounding in my ears. Keep my voice down? After everything I've been through? "Do you know what my family's been like this year? The gay-conversion therapy? I'm doing manual labor at the church any chance he can get me, and reading books about God and sin and homosexuality. My mom swearing he does it because he loves me." I start to wash my hands, but I'm shaking so bad I can't grip the spigot. "Then your asshole friends broke into my locker during gym and pissed all over my clothes."

"What?"

"Don't act like you didn't know."

Darrell closes the distance between us. "I didn't. I swear. Coach made us run about a thousand suicides, but I didn't know it was because of you."

I close my eyes for a second, breathe through my nose.

"I'm sorry," he adds. "I'll leave you alone, if you want. For what it's worth though, I wasn't just messing around this summer. I really liked you. Or still like you, or something."

My eyes are still clamped shut, but I hear him move away, feel the absence of his body heat next to me.

"I like you, too," I say.

For a moment it's silent, and I think maybe I'm too late. Maybe he already left. Then, he chuckles. "That's good, right? Let's go out sometime."

I groan. "It's impossible."

"Well," he says, "if, for example, you told your dad you were asking a girl out, and instead hung out with me, do you know anyone who'd be cool covering for you?"

My jaw drops. "You do not learn, do you?"

"My mom says I'm incorrigible."

I sigh. "I might know someone, but…"

"But what?"

"But, it's January. Too cold for illicit midnight hookups at the park." As soon as the words leave my mouth, I realize that's why I've been mad at him. Because I actually like him, but last summer was just supposed to be fun. Something to pass the time. It wasn't supposed to mean anything. It didn't, until JJ released that video. This is for real, and it's unnerving.

He watches me, eyes narrowed slightly, like he's studying a particularly difficult math problem.

Then he says, "so, we go on an actual date."

Unbelievable!

"St. Paul is only thirty minutes away," he says. "We could have dinner, movie… whatever guys do when they're dating each other."

"Uh, musical theater, I'm pretty sure." I say, completely deadpan.

His nose wrinkles.

"That was sarcasm, Darrell."

"Oh thank God." He breathes a sigh of relief.

I look him straight in the eye. "You're serious?"

"Yes."

Trouble. Trouble. Alarm bells are going off in my head, but I push them aside. "Okay, it's a date."

"Awesome."

"And no more God talk, okay? I've had enough of him to last a lifetime."

Darrell laughs. "Deal."

#

Three days later, I pull into Cynthia's driveway, Lindsey in the seat next to me. "You sure you're cool with this?" I ask.

She gives me a look. "I said I was, and I am. You need to calm down."

"Just, you know if my dad finds out I'm lying to him—"

"I understand." Lindsey unbuckles her seatbelt and opens the car door, climbing out before I can hound her any more.

I rush out of the car after her, because I haven't exactly run this plan by Cynthia yet, and I'm pretty sure if Lindsey just appears at her front door, she might murder her or something. Luckily, Cynthia's mom opens the door.

She takes one look at Lindsey, then me, then jerks her head toward the stairs behind her. "In her bedroom."

"Thanks," I say, pulling Lindsey in behind me.

"When you get up there, tell her to turn the music down," Mrs. Marlow says. "I have a headache."

I don't need to, because when Cynthia opens the door and sees Lindsey, she does it herself, then flops onto the bed again, drumsticks tapping rhythms into the air in front of her. "What's she doing here?" she asks.

Lindsey stiffens next to me.

I sink onto the bed at her feet. "I have a date."

Cynthia grunts. She must think I mean with Lindsey.

"A real one, with a guy."

Her drumsticks slow to a stop and she lifts her eyes to meet mine, and hers are full of mischief. "Who?"

"Darrell."

Cynthia grins and nods toward Lindsey. "So what are you going to do with her? Let her come along in case Darrell decides to switch back to girls for a bit?"

I grit my teeth. "I was hoping she could hang with you."

She looks back and forth between Lindsey and me. "Why can't she just go to the mall and steal stuff?"

"Because if someone from my dad's church sees her, they might mention something, it could get back to," I pause, "him."

Cynthia looks past me at Lindsey, who has said nothing this entire exchange. "Do you actually want to hang out at my house all night?"

"Um, well, I'm sure we can find something to do," Lindsey says, "I can help you with your homework or something."

Cynthia raises an eyebrow. "I got it covered, Blondie."

"Cool," I say, "Well, I guess I'll—"

The doorbell cuts me off, and I grin in spite of myself. "He's here."

Cyn snickers. "Oooh, let's go give him the run down." She pushes me out her bedroom door and down the stairs. "Be back by eleven, and no funny business mister. And remember, Jason, if you order something expensive, you have to put out."

Behind us, Lindsey gasps.

"Kidding," Cyn says sarcastically before mouthing "Not kidding" at me.

I roll my eyes. "I'll be fine."

"Sure, sure. Call me if you need to be picked up or whatever."

"Right."

She pulls the door open, so Darrell's first glimpse into my personal life is of my five foot nothing menace of a best friend.

He gulps. "Uh, is Jason here?"

I wave from over Cynthia's shoulder. "Here."

She doesn't move out of the way. Instead, she jabs her drumstick at his chest. "If this is a trick and you and your friends beat him up, I will personally castrate every one of you and make a necklace out of your balls."

Darrell blinks. "Um… is that fashionable with your crowd?"

"Baby," she says with a toss of her head, "I am a trend setter. I will make it fashionable."

Forty-Three

Lindsey

Cynthia is less than enthused about my being at her house while Jason goes out with Darrell. I know, because she tells me. Except with words more along the lines of, "don't expect me to entertain you, Blondie."

I suppose I should be hurt, but I'm not. I've been hanging with Cynthia and her friends long enough to know that "Blondie" is more a term of endearment than anything else.

At least, I hope it is.

For a long time, we just stand in her foyer not speaking. I'm too polite to play on my phone or anything. She's not polite enough to care. I let out a bored sigh, and she glares at me.

"Alright," she says, "let's go."

"Go where?" I follow her down the hall. "Did I do something wrong?"

"No," she hollers over her shoulder as she wrenches open the basement door, "but while you're here, let's practice." She disappears into the basement.

I stop at the top of the stairs. "Practice?"

"Yeah, I got a couple song ideas I want to try out. C'mon!"

I have no choice. When I get down there, she's already got Brayden's guitar strapped on.

"Aren't you playing the drums?" I ask.

"Naw, I can play the guitar too." She strums a few chords to make her point. "They haven't invented an instrument I can't pick up."

I don't know what to say to this. I guess I look kind of silly, because she gives me a sardonic little wink and nods toward the keyboard.

"Follow along, okay?"

I nod and scamper around the keyboard to get set up. Cynthia barely lets me turn the instrument on before she starts playing, nodding at me as she does, and I can barely manage to pick up her chords and play along. She's right. She can play. As soon as I've got the chord structure down, she starts playing around with riffs, testing out melodies with the guitar.

We start and stop a lot. More than when we're playing as a group. She keeps dropping out randomly and writing things down on the paper in front of her, and I drop out with her, until she looks up and brushes sweat-soaked hair off her forehead.

"Keep playing."

We lock eyes, and I nod. "Yeah, okay."

"I'm gonna start singing." She swings the guitar to hang on her back and starts unplugging amps and moving them around, plugging new cords in. She knows what she's doing, which is good, because I'm certain I don't. I just watch for a while, but then she snaps without even looking up. "Keep playing!"

"Okay, okay!"

Something happens. She steps up to the mic, pulling her guitar back in front of her as she starts playing, and suddenly the random chords and riffs we've been playing become music. Real music.

She keeps glancing down at the paper in front of her to remember what she's written. She starts and stops over again, testing out different phrasing, then slams her pick down on the stool. "Yes, got it!"

Grinning, she spins around to face me. "We got it!"

I get the feeling I'm supposed to be as excited as she is. "We do?"

"Fuck yeah, we do!" The way she looks, so happy. It feels like we're more than just strangers in a band together. It almost feels like—

"Don't move," she says, pointing at me, "don't move a muscle. We have to record it. Right now, before I forget. Shit." She scurries around the room. "Steve-O used to handle all this stuff." I watch her dig around in an old tool chest, looking for something.

"Can I help?"

"No, I'm telling you, don't move. If you move… it's like… stuff like this, it comes and it goes, and if I don't hang on to it, I might lose it." Through all of this, she digs around in equipment, until she pulls out a beat-up old laptop. "Aha! Got it."

She opens it up and starts typing, fingers clicking over keys. "C'mon baby, work for me…"

For a second, it looks like it might, then the screen goes black.

"Well, fuck."

"Can you fix it?"

She shoots me a look. "Do I look like a computer nerd to you?"

I blink. "Maybe we could record on our phones or something?"

But she shakes her head. "No, sound quality isn't good enough. Plus you can't manipulate it. We need real sound editing software, which this piece of junk has." She smacks the side of her computer. "But it's just not working."

"I might, um…" I look down at my hands.

"Might what?" Her eyes light up. "Do you know someone who can help?"

"Maybe?"

"Spit it out! Is that a yes or a no?"

I take a deep breath. "Well, um, you know Charlotte, from the, um… the video?"

"Yeah?"

"She's really good with computers."

Cynthia starts to laugh and runs her fingers through her short hair. "God, that stupid video." She puts her hands on her hips and paces around the room, then flops onto the couch and looks at me. "Well?"

"Well, what?"

"Call her!"

Forty-Four

Charlotte

"This computer sucks." I don't mince my words. "Where did you even get it?" Never in a million years would I have expected to be in Cynthia Marlow's living room. And to have Lindsey invite me over? Never in a billion years. Yet, here I am, trying to revive the world's saddest laptop.

Cynthia scowls. "Thrift store," she says.

My eyebrows skyrocket. I'm not saying you can't find hardware at a thrift store, but you have to know what you're looking at. And you have to know how to piece things together. I built a desktop from scratch with garage sale finds, but I know what I'm doing. Cynthia obviously doesn't.

"Can you fix it?" Lindsey asks tentatively.

I burst out laughing. "No. This mess is beyond fixing. I could probably salvage some parts, but..." My voice falters when I see Cynthia's face. "What do you need it for?"

Lindsey and Cynthia exchange looks, then Cynthia answers. "Recording and sound mixing mostly."

"Like, music?"

"Yeah."

Cynthia, I get, but Lindsey? She's not exactly the type. She looks at me so earnestly though, and Cynthia looks like all of her hopes and dreams depend on the health of this laptop.

I sigh and pull my own laptop out of my bag. "What software are you using?"

Cynthia tells me. "But it's kind of expensive."

"Sure it is," I say, my fingers flying over the keys. "If you go the legal route."

Pretty soon I've found a backdoor in and started the download. I set my computer on Cynthia's coffee table and lean back on her sofa. "So, you two are starting a band or something?"

Cynthia grunts as an answer.

Lindsey, on the other hand, is bursting with excitement. "Yes! It's been amazing! There's four of us and we're actually quite good, and it's so much fun, Charlotte!" She catches Cynthia's eye and goes silent. "Well, I've only been a member for about a month," she finishes lamely.

Interesting.

For several very long, very uncomfortable seconds, Cynthia stares me down, then I guess she decides I'm okay and says, "you'll need to learn how to work a soundboard."

"Huh?"

"You're in, right?" she asks. "You got the computer, the software. All you need now is a soundboard. C'mon, I'll show you."

Just like that, I became the sound mixer for Cynthia's band.

Forty-Five

Brayden

I decide to spend all weekend with Angie, mostly because I feel bad about kissing Cynthia. Again. Multiple times. A lot actually. Dang it. It has to stop. I need to focus on my actual girlfriend, and not my… whatever you'd call Cynthia. Hook up?

Plus, Valentine's Day is coming up. I feel like I have to make it extra special.

Angie and I settle into the couch in her parents' finished basement, a much more comfortable and warm set up than Cynthia's cold and dingy band space. But this basement lacks character. It could be any suburbanite's basement. Plain off-white walls, artfully decorated with mass printed "art." A beige couch, and a giant flat screen TV which is already starting to play the opening sequence for one of Angie's cheesy rom-coms.

Ugh.

I recognize the song playing in the opening scene though. The band played around with it last week, trying to add it to the repertoire. As Cyn says, it's good to know some covers. People like that. I smile at the thought we'll ever actually play shows. We haven't even auditioned for Battle of the Bands yet.

"What?" Angie's voice interrupts my thoughts.

"What what?" I ask

"Why are you smiling?"

"Oh, uh… I like this song."

She gives me a look like I'm being silly, then settles against me and grabs some popcorn from the bowl in my lap.

"Want some?" she asks.

I shake my head. "No, I'm good."

We spend the first half of the movie like this, her snuggled against my side, snacking until the popcorn is gone, her eyes fixed on the screen. She laughs at all the jokes, coos at all the sappy parts, asks me if I think something that happened is so sweet?

"Huh? Oh, yeah."

She looks up at me. "Are you even watching?"

"Not really," I say apologetically. "Sorry."

She grabs the remote and turns the movie off. "We don't have to watch this if you're not into it."

I shrug. "Whatever you want."

She sighs, clearly annoyed. "What do you want?"

I consider the question carefully, then set the empty bowl onto the floor next to my feet. "Come here." I pull her closer and press my lips to hers. We've been together for almost a year, but lately it seems like we never make out. Just quick little kisses when we say goodbye. I open her lips with mine and slide my tongue into her mouth.

She pulls away. "My parents are upstairs."

"Yeah, but they never come down here." I kiss her again. This time, she doesn't stop me. Quite the opposite, she presses closer to me, her arms looping around my neck, drawing me in.

I let go of all thought and let instinct take over. My hand creeps up from her hips, stops to rest on her left boob and miraculously, she doesn't stop me.

Yes. This is what I need in order to get Cynthia out of my head. I lean over Angie, laying her back on the couch, hovering over her. Oh God this feels so good. I imagine us together, letting our hormones take over. I start wondering if I have a condom, because this could be it, when I finally—

"Ow!" Angie pushes me away. "You bit me!"

"What? No I didn't."

"Yes, you did," she cries. She touches her bottom lip tenderly and shows me the tiniest droplet of blood on her fingertips. "Look!"

I think about how Cynthia's teeth feel on my lips, my neck, my earlobes. Delightful. My body responds to the idea like any guy's would, and Angie feels the movement.

"Get off of me!"

I do, trying awkwardly to hide the changed topography of my sweatpants. "Angie, I'm sorry. I just got carried away."

She scoots away from me. "What has gotten into you lately?"

"Nothing," I say way to quickly. "What do you mean?"

She makes a list on her fingers. "You're always busy, we hardly talk anymore, then you come over here and act like a complete animal."

An animal? "Angie, c'mon."

"Maybe you should go home."

I open my mouth to argue. To tell her I had planned to spend the whole day with her and I didn't mean to hurt her, but she's not in the mood and I guess I'm not either.

I sigh. "Okay, yeah. I'll go." I stop at the basement steps. "I'll see you Monday, right?"

She nods. "Course."

I get in my truck and start to drive home, but then I remember my mom's not expecting me until tonight. I have an entire day to waste. So I turn the opposite direction and head to Cynthia's place instead.

#

Cynthia answers the door, which I'm sort of surprised about, until she says her dad is out on a job and her mom's upstairs asleep. Leaving Cynthia alone.

She looks me up and down from the doorway. "I thought you were Jason."

"Nope."

"What're you doing here?"

I haven't come up with a good excuse. "Uh, well I guess I thought…"

She raises an eyebrow.

"Maybe we could work on band stuff?" It sounds so lame.

She backs away from the doorway to let me in and smirks knowingly. "Uh huh."

I follow her down the normal path, halfway down the front hallway, through the doorway leading down to hell or paradise. Or, her basement.

There are papers strewn all over the floor, and my acoustic guitar resting on the couch, where I suppose she had been working when I rang the bell. I pick up a piece of paper. "What are you working on?" Looks like words and guitar tab.

She snatches the paper out of my hand. "Don't touch that! I have a system."

"A system?" If her system involves making it look like a tornado tore through the basement, then I guess I believe her.

"Yeah," she says, putting the paper back where I found it. "I'm working on some new music. For the band."

"Oh, cool. Let's play it."

She scowls. "It's not ready."

I sit down on the couch. "Well, maybe I can help."

It takes some convincing, but she finally agrees, handing me the acoustic guitar, then looping the red electric over her shoulder before settling on a stool directly across from me. She nods her head to set the time, then we start to play. I follow along with her fingerings, then start to improvise my own. We run through her song a few times, then I ask her if she wants to sing.

She shakes her head. "Lyrics aren't any good yet. They gotta come to me, you know?"

Not really.

"What's it about?"

She doesn't answer at first.

"Cyn?"

"Life," she says softly.

I look down. "Oh, sorry."

"Just, I don't know," she mutters, then grabs a paper off the floor and pulls a pencil out from her behind her ear. "You know, like how the way people screw you, you know? Like the way they pretend to be your friends, pretend to care about you or whatever, then toss you aside the second they can't use you anymore. And not just that." She's not looking at me, too busy scribbling away on the paper while she mutters. "But they have to go out of their way to make you look bad, make you out to be something you're not." She falls silent.

"So it's about your band." Her head snaps up. "I mean, your old band. Not us. Not—" God, I'd almost rather be getting emasculated by Angela right now than see her angry eyes. "Sorry."

"Stop apologizing."

"Okay, sorry, I mean…"

She fiddles with her lip ring, then the corners of her mouth twitch. "It's fine. I'm just in a mood today." Then she grabs a handful of papers and plops down onto the couch next to me. "Here, look."

I start reading, but I'm not sure what I'm looking at. Not really. Scribbled lyrics, more crossed out than actually written. But I start to see the pattern of it, after a while, and it's, "wow."

"Really?"

"Yeah, I mean. I'm not the expert, but I like it. I mean I like what you have so far. It's poetic. It's got soul."

She looks so happy, like maybe I've just given her the best praise she's heard in her entire life, so I hand the papers back to her, just to break her gaze. "When did you learn how to do all this?"

"All what?" she asks.

I gesture at the basement. "This, music. The drums, the guitar, writing it? I mean, no one else at our school can do this. Not like you can. And like… it's this hidden talent. Like, no one even knows you got this in you, Cyn. Not really."

She shrugs. "I don't know. My dad bought me a drum kit for my eighth birthday, mostly just for fun, you know? But once I started, I just couldn't stop. Then the guitar, well I figured I should probably pick it up, you know?

So I started learning it in middle school." She looks down. "How about you?"

"Well, I guess for the longest time, it seemed like playing guitar was the only thing my dad and I had in common. We used to just sit around, listening to his old records, and play along. It was nice, but," I pause and rub the back of my neck. "We're both too busy these days. So…" There's a lot that I'm not saying, that I'm not even sure how to put into words.

"Yeah."

A thought occurs to me. "Did you ever write anything for the Stinks?"

That pisses her off. She huffs and glares at the wall. "Yeah, I wrote a lot of stuff for them. Then, they kicked me and Steve-O made a big deal about how my songs are the band's property, not mine. So…"

That sucks. I can't even imagine. I'm not creative like she is, I don't make anything. But if I did? I sure as hell wouldn't want some loser stealing it from me and pretending it's his own.

When I catch her eye, she's staring at me. Not really angry or sad or anything. More like she's just studying me, trying to figure me out. I guess I'm trying to figure her out too.

"I can head home, if you want," I say.

She shakes her head. "No," she says, "stay."

Forty-Six

Cynthia

In the basement, Brayden is mine. He plays for me, and when the rest of the band has left, he stays with me. Every night a little longer. We don't talk about it, this thing that we're doing. I'm not even sure how to put it into words. It's not sex, because we haven't done that. But it's definitely not romance either.

If anything, it's exploration. We explore each other. We dive deep into the oceans of each other and with each dive, we discover something new. Sometimes it's silly, like the spot on my inner thigh that is so ticklish I burst out laughing every time he touches me there. Sometimes we're deep diving, finding treasures in the darkest pits of our souls. Sometimes, we don't kiss at all or touch. Sometimes we just talk.

Every evening he spends in my basement, I know I'm being sucked deeper into something treacherous. This isn't mild flirting anymore. It runs deeper. I've started to depend on these evenings. I think about them all day, and from what I see in his eyes when we glimpse each other in the hallway, Brayden thinks about them too.

Our basement. Our couch.

We've taken to sneaking moments together at school. It's dangerous here. We could be seen. I watch him from my locker, as he jokes with his friends.

I catch him staring at me in the cafeteria, his girlfriend sitting beside him, oblivious to his transgressions. After lunch, I walk with Jason to the boy's locker room, pretending I'm there for him, the best friend who's got nothing better to do.

But, I'm not there for Jason. Not anymore.

I'm there for Brayden. For the glance he sends my way when he's talking to that idiot friend of his, and for the smile he shoots at me when no one's looking.

And on days when we're really lucky. When everyone else has already gone into the locker room, and the bell rings, and it's just the two of us.

Those days are the best.

The hallway where I met Jimmy to fight is now the hallway where Brayden and I test the limits of our secret. We kiss.

Not like the basement kisses which survive on adrenaline and music. These are so sweet and innocent. Moments of pleasure in the middle of my dreary day, and they hold promise of everything that will come later in the night. Here, he treats me like a lady. He tucks my hair behind my ears, and I turn into one of those sappy romantic girls. He presses his lips to mine, just enough so I know he's really there, not enough to make me lose control.

Then he reminds me to get to class so I don't get marked tardy, and I spend the rest of the day dreaming of him.

Forty-Seven

Lindsey

Band practice is my favorite part of the day. It's silly, because I've never been interested in music before, beyond what my parents required. Piano lessons and recitals, playing for the church. Maybe it's the fact I have a choice here that makes it so much more fun. Or maybe it's the energy of it. All five of us are so different, but when we come together, it's magical.

There's a reverberation in the air when a song ends that is so lovely and final, it makes you want to hold your breath as long as you can so you don't scare it away. Like when I watch the deer who come into our backyard from my bedroom window. I'm so far away, I can't possibly scare them, but I stand still and silent while they nibble berries from the bushes. Here, in Cynthia's basement, we freeze, waiting for the sound waves to dissipate.

Rumble

My stomach grumbles audibly and everyone in the room looks at me.

"Oh my gosh," I say quickly, "I am so sorry. That is so embarrassing."

Cynthia laughs. "Relax, Blondie. You're allowed to be hungry."

Now that she says it, I realize just how hungry I am. I forget about everything else when we're playing, but now I'm positively aching with hunger. I check my watch. 8:24. I've played for three and half hours? It felt like nothing.

Brayden asks the question I'm too scared to. "Are we done for the night?"

"Yeah, I guess," Cynthia concedes.

He pulls his guitar off and rests it on the stand before flopping onto the couch. "You guys want to order pizza?"

Everyone goes awkwardly silent. Jason turns toward Cynthia to avoid the tension, but she has her eyes trained on Brayden.

"Like you would actually eat it," Charlotte says. She has a bluntness that I admire, but could never actually manage myself.

Brayden looks taken aback. "I eat."

"Celery and cottage cheese don't count as a meal."

Charlotte's not backing down, and Brayden knows it.

"I'll eat a slice of pizza," he says, "I promise."

She grins and looks at the rest of the group, clearly expecting praise. It's the first time anyone's ever mentioned Brayden's eating problem. We all know about it. We've all seen him checking calories on packaging and skipping meals. But now it's out in the open, and we're all uncomfortable.

I clear my throat. "I can buy it if you want."

"Free food," Cynthia says, stretching as she scoots around her drum set. "Hell yeah. I want Hawaiian."

Jason groans. "No pineapple, Cyn."

"It's good!"

"It's gross."

I pull out my phone. "I'll get one Hawaiian and one…" I look around the room.

"I'm a vegetarian," Charlotte says.

"I'll eat veggie," Brayden puts in. I can already see him justifying pizza in his head if it's covered in low calorie vegetables.

"Jason?" I ask.

"Veggie's fine with me."

I nod. "I don't mind pineapple, so I'll eat Cynthia's as well." I put in the order with the credit card I have stored on my phone. Hopefully my parents don't wonder why Jason and I needed two whole pizzas for an AP study session. I can think of a lie on my way home.

Cynthia sits on the couch next to Brayden. Close. Really close. Hmm. Charlotte sees it too. She and I exchange knowing looks. There's something there that they're not telling us. I feel bad for Angie, but a good politician knows how to stay out of high-emotion situations.

I shrug.

"So," Jason says as he meanders over to where Cynthia is sitting and not so subtly encourages her to scoot away from Brayden a bit, "how's life everyone?" He's been in a much better mood lately, and I suspect it has to do with Darrell and their secret relationship. I've been sworn to secrecy, so I definitely don't bring it up.

Brayden raises an eyebrow at him over the top of Cynthia's head. "You're joking, right?"

Jason shrugs. "I dunno, I guess. It's a little weird though, right? The five of us working together? All of us from the video."

"Except Harvey," Cynthia reminds him.

"Right, where is Harvey these days?"

Cynthia shrugs. "Same old same old, I think. Trying to earn money any way he can."

"Illegally," I mutter without thinking.

"Excuse me?" Cynthia snaps.

"I'm sorry," I stutter, "I-I didn't mean…"

But before Cynthia can go crazy, Charlotte steps in. "Did you know his dad left right after his youngest brother was born? And his sister has diabetes."

"Really?"

"Yeah. His mom works like three jobs just to pay rent and bills and try to afford insulin. Harvey has to work to help out. He doesn't have any other options."

"But why can't he do something legal?"

"Because the sort of jobs that hire high schoolers don't exactly pay a ton of money. And politicians like *your dad* are too busy bending over backwards to make corporations happy, they don't really who on the bottom rung of the ladder gets hurt." Charlotte shrugs. "Just saying, don't judge. Especially if you've never had to scrounge for enough money to buy groceries."

I fall silent, playing with the hem of my skirt from where I sit on the floor. I want to defend my dad, to tell her that she's got it all wrong, but how many fundraisers have I been to where my dad promised businessmen he would keep their interests in mind on the Senate floor? How many people like Harvey or Charlotte does he talk to? Not enough, and only during election years. It makes me feel ashamed.

"I'm sorry," I whisper. "I didn't know."

For a moment, no one says anything, then Brayden says, "that's the thing, isn't it? Everyone's got something going on."

"You never know what's happening backstage," Cynthia puts in.

"Or off the court."

I think about my parents and all their rigid rules about who I can talk to, what I can say, where I can go, how I have to look. To everyone at my school, I'm a spoiled rich girl.

"I'm not like my dad," I say. "Or my mom, or any of them. Or I mean... I don't want to be like them."

Charlotte reaches over and squeezes my hand. "You're not like them."

I smile weakly.

"I'd love to see your parents' faces if they found you here," Jason says, barely containing a chuckle.

"My parents?" I say, "what about yours!"

He goes pale. "Ugh, let's not even talk about them."

"Why?" Brayden asks. "What's wrong with them?"

"Everything," Jason mutters. His voice is quiet and scared, and he shrinks into himself so he looks nearly as small as Cynthia, which is saying something.

Cynthia leans across the couch and gives him a side hug. "Fuck them. They suck. They don't deserve you."

Brayden, realizing he messed up, tries to backtrack. "Hey, do you guys ever wonder how JJ found out your secrets?"

"Nope," Cynthia says, "I already know. She was sleeping with my boyfriend." She pauses. "Ex-boyfriend."

"And good riddance to him," Jason adds.

Charlotte shrugs. "She caught me and Mr. DuPont in the Chick-Emporium parking lot after my shift. I didn't really think it was anything, until the video came out. I have no idea why she was there."

"To keep tabs on Harvey?" I suggest.

"Maybe."

"Who do you think blabbed about you?" Jason asks, leaning around Cynthia to direct his question to Brayden.

"I don't know, that's the thing." He rubs the back of his neck. "It's not like I hang out with my friends talking about *not* having sex. Kind of the opposite of normal locker room talk, ya know? Angie and I talked about it."

At his girlfriend's name, Cynthia shifts in her seat, putting a bit more space between her and Brayden.

"But, she wouldn't tell."

No one meets his eyes. The fact is, lots of people talk to JJ. You give her dirt on someone else to keep her off your back. I've done my fair share of it over the past few years. I'm not proud, but I had an image to maintain. Now, that image doesn't feel important anymore.

"She might have just overheard Angie talking about it to one of her friends," I suggest. "JJ's like that. Eavesdropping. She's always been that way."

"The question isn't how she discovered our secrets," Jason says, "it's why she exposed them."

No one answers. Each of us mulling over the question on our own, trying to figure out what we've ever done to make JJ want to hurt us. The thing is, I can't come up with a thing. I've never been friends with JJ, but I've never been her enemy either. Barely acquaintances. So why would she want to hurt me?

Cynthia breaks the silence. "Some people are just assholes. They don't need a reason for it."

It's not a satisfactory answer, but before we can think of something better, the doorbell rings above us.

"Got it," Cynthia says, bounding up the stairs. I have only a moment to marvel at her endless supply of energy before she's back in the group, two pizza boxes and a stack of paper plates in her arms. "Dig in," she says as she unceremoniously drops the boxes onto the floor next to me.

Everyone lunges forward, grabbing plates and slices, and when it's all settled, we're pleasantly surprised to find Brayden's taken not one, but two large pieces onto his plate. He doesn't even hesitate as he takes his first bite.

Forty-Eight

Cynthia

The drive to the audition is tense. Somehow the five of us manage to cram into Brayden's pick-up truck, all of our equipment in the back. Lindsey sits up front with Brayden while Charlotte, Jason and I squeeze into the back. The only reason she got the good seat is because I'm so small. I'm practically on top of Jason's lap how it is. Not cool.

We don't say a word the thirty minutes it takes to get to Grinders. Everyone's too nervous. I need them to be their best. We get one song to impress Rod, the owner of Grinders, and if we fail. That's it. We're done.

When we get to Grinders, it is empty. Too empty. I twirl my drumstick as I make my way to where Rod sits at a table, staring at me with fuck-me eyes. Pervert.

"Hey," I say as I stop in front of his table and bend over to sign in. "Where is everyone?"

"Band before you canceled. Lead singer issues."

I chuckle. "Drama queens."

I assume he recognizes me, because the Stinks played this venue at least a dozen times before I got kicked. Pretty good gig. I bet they still play it.

He leans around me to watch my band mates setting up. "New crew huh? What happened with the Stinks?"

"They kicked me out."

"Oh yeah?"

I shrug. "Apparently I can be a real ball buster."

Rod snorts and flips through the sheets of paper on his clipboard. About two-thirds down the second page, I catch the Stinks' name, already highlighted, which means they got pushed through to performance night without having to audition. Which is bullshit, if you ask me, considering they have a new drummer and all.

He lifts the next sheet. "What do you call yourselves?"

"Sick as Cyn."

Someone drops a cymbal behind me and it clatters to the floor. I turn around to see Brayden frozen behind the drum set, deer in headlights, the cymbal at his feet. I mouth the words "I will kill you," then turn back to Rod.

"C-Y-N," I say, "not S-I-N."

"Cute."

Wait until he finds out where I got the name. Thank you, Steve-O, for writing a song about what a whore I am, because it made naming my new band super easy.

He jots the name down. "Whenever you're ready."

It takes us a few more minutes to set up, and Rod taps his fingers impatiently. This is part of the audition. We have to prove we can set up and break down quickly between acts, so the audience doesn't get bored, but we're scrambling. We don't have the practice.

Finally, we're ready. I sit at my stool and take several deep breaths, trying to calm down. Trying not to think about how if this fails, it's all over for me. No Battle. No revenge. No watching Steve-O's life fall to pieces while I skyrocket to greatness. I guess I'm a little nervous, too.

Then, I close my eyes and count us off, tapping my sticks together to set the beat. For a millisecond, there's silence, then we play.

One song. That's the rules. So I chose the one we're most consistent at, even if it's not my best writing. Brayden has a little solo moment during the bridge, which he slams. Jason nails the lyrics, of course, putting every ounce of anger he has toward his dad into his performance. Him, I don't need to worry about. Lindsey may look cute, but she's actually rocking on the keyboard, pounding out chords and ostinato rhythms to provide the emphasis needed to carry Brayden's guitar playing.

And me? Well, I fucking rock.

When the song ends, we look out at Rod, who's leaning back in his chair, stroking his beard like a movie villain or something.

"You took a long time setting up."

I stand up and come round to the front of my drums. "I know, but we can do it. We'll practice. Get it down smooth."

"Get yourself a roadie or two, so your guitar player doesn't have to do all the heavy lifting." He eyes Brayden's arms under the slightly too tight shirt I made him wear.

I nod. "We will."

He watches me for a while longer, debating. Taking too long to debate. I chew on my lip ring hard enough to make it hurt. I hate waiting.

"Alright," he says, "you're in." He takes his highlighter and swipes it across our names. "I'll email you the details later this week."

I grin, and Jason lets out a whoop of delight. Even Lindsey looks pretty damn pleased.

But Brayden...

Brayden grabs me and lifts me off my feet, pulling me into a tight hug as he sweeps me around in a circle. It's total fairy tale princess garbage, but it's fun too. He's excited, which makes me happier than anything.

When he sets me down, we hold each other's gaze for a moment, then turn to see all three of our band mates staring at us with jaws dropped.

"Um..." I start to say, but Jason interrupts.

"When did that happen?"

Forty-Nine

Brayden

After that Battle of the Bands audition, Cynthia tells the other three to beat it. She's not even playing it cool. She just says that the two of us will unpack and gives them a look like she will kill them if they argue.

As soon as they're gone, she is all over me. And I want it. Bad. With her.

We keep eyeing each other as we pass on the stairs carrying drum cases. Her eyes on my biceps, my chest, once we pass, my butt. I mean, I assume it is. I guess I don't know for sure. I'm checking hers out. That's for sure. Her butt, her boobs, her lips, and those blue eyes. Oh man, I'm here for it. I'm Pavlov's dog. I am drooling for this girl.

She makes a real show of unloading the drums, checking each one, while I'm waiting for her on the couch, bursting out of my jeans for her. Come on Cynthia, screw those drums, come to me. I need you. I need this. I need her body in my arms right now.

I've been horny before. I'm a guy, right? This is so far beyond horny. She is a mind-altering drug, and I'm pretty sure she knows it. I keep telling myself I have a girlfriend, then Cynthia bends over, and her skirt rides up, and my mind goes blank. Angela? Angela, who?

I can't wait any longer.

I cross the room and stop her, pull her away from her cymbals, and thread my fingers through her hair, pulling her lips to mine.

Oh sweet God, this is it. Then she laughs. "It's performing."

"What is?"

"It's the adrenaline, pumping through your veins." She lifts my hand, traces the veins in my wrist. "Can't you feel it?"

"No," I say. "All I feel is you." God that sounds corny. She's going to tear me to pieces for that.

Only she doesn't, so I guess she feels it too. She presses against me, leaning up on her toes to stretch that tiny frame of hers up until our lips meet again. This is it. This is happening. It has to happen. I can't wait a second longer.

She takes control, pulling me by the shirt to the couch, pushing me down and climbing on top of me. Her fingers make quick work of the buttons on my shirt, ripping it open like I'm Clark Kent or something, only instead of a big red S, I just have skin and muscle and bone. Any other time, I'd be embarrassed, ashamed, but with her? No. Never.

Her body slides over mine, her lips on my skin, my mouth, my neck. Her teeth sink into my earlobe, and it should hurt. It does hurt, but it feels good, and I groan and grip her hips tighter, pulling her close to me. Cynthia, Cynthia, oh my God, Cynthia. I don't even know if I'm saying it aloud, or if it's in my head, but it doesn't matter either way, because she responds all the same.

I pull her shirt over her head, then roll on top of her, pinning her beneath my body. For a second, she's into it. I know she's into it, because her back arches, and her hips wiggle beneath me, and she lets out a little whimpering moan. She is hot molten metal in my arms, fluid and untouchable.

Then I get burned.

Her soft lips wrapped in steel wrench away from me. Her fingers, which had clutched at my shoulders only seconds ago, now push me away. Gone is the arching back and wiggling hips.

"Get off, get off of me!" Her body is rigid, her voice shrill, panicked.

I scramble to the other side of the couch. The second she's free, she gasps for air, then curls into herself and bursts into tears so unexpected and violent they could only be hers.

"I'm sorry," she chokes out.

"It's okay."

"I'm sorry." She hides her eyes with her hand. "I'm sorry. I'm sorry."

"It's okay." I breathe the words rather than say them. They rush out of me faster than I can think. "It's okay. I get it."

"You get it," she scoffs, her voice cracking with the tears. "Fuck you. You don't get anything."

"Cyn…" I reach out to her, but she tenses, cringing away. My hand falls to my lap.

Her fingers dig through her hair. "Oh God. Oh shit."

I know I should be annoyed that we're not having sex, because that's obviously where this was going, but I honestly don't care. She won't look at me, and that's way worse.

I should say something, I just don't know what. Something so she knows I'm not mad. She sits doubled over, fingers threaded through black hair, face hidden in her knees. I clear my throat, and she jumps about a mile and glares at me. My first taste of her gaze and it's angry and hurt, and I don't know what I've done wrong.

"Sorry," I mumble. She looks away again. "Uh, Cyn?"

Her shoulder lifts a fraction of an inch then falls, so I assume she's listening.

"Remember how back in October, I caught you and Jimmy fighting in the hallway next to the boy's locker room?"

Silence.

"Uh, well…" This is hard. So hard. But I can't hide it anymore. "I um, I listened in on your conversation."

Her head snaps up.

"I wasn't trying to spy or anything, honest. I just wanted to make sure he didn't hurt you. I swear. Then you told him all that stuff about Steve-O and about how he—"

"Get out," she hisses. Her eyes are wide and frantic.

"What?"

Her whole body starts shaking, her fingernails are digging into her temples, leaving angry red marks on the side of her face. "Oh my God," she cries, "You have to go. I can't be around you. Just get the hell out of here!"

She grips her hair, and I'm afraid she's going to pull it out, but she's right. I have to go. I can't stay here.

I stand up. She looks so small curled up on the couch like that.

"I'm sorry."

Then I beat it.

#

I skip basketball practice on Monday and get to Cynthia's house almost on hour early, way before any of the rest of the band. I want to make sure she's okay. After Saturday and the audition. I dunno. I messed up, and I have to make it right.

When I get there, she's already in the basement, cradling my guitar in her lap, strumming something I've never heard before. Something so perfectly her.

"That's cool," I say.

She jumps. "Shit, you scared me."

"Sorry."

She checks her phone. "Why are you here so early?"

"I wanted to talk."

"About what?" She's not looking at me.

"Cyn, c'mon." I sit on the couch next to her. Not quite touching, but she immediately scoots away. "About what happened Saturday night. I just wanna—"

"Forget about it." She stands up quickly and walks away. "It's not a big deal."

"Yeah, it is. It is a big deal." I try to follow her but she keeps backing away from me. It's like after everything we've gone through together, she's a stranger again. It hurts. Why does it hurt so much?

"I didn't mean to hurt you," I say stupidly. "I wouldn't do that."

"Yeah, you gotta protect that nice guy image."

"That's not it and you know it." I can't believe how badly this is going. "Cynthia, I care about you."

Her eyes find mine and her expression is stone cold. It's not mad or hurt or angry. It's nothing. Nothing is worse. I almost wish she was mad. We're trapped in a staring contest, and she would never back down. Never. So I do. I sink into the couch and lean forward with my elbows on my knees, like how I do in the locker room, planning strategy with my team. Across the room, she leans on the wall next to the stairs, arms crossed, teeth working her lip ring furiously. Ready to run for it if things get too tough.

"You know my dad used to be this big track star back in high school?" I say. "Got his name in the paper, competed all over the country. It was kind of a big deal. Then, his sophomore year in college, he tore some ligament, and he was done."

"Why are you—"

I cut her off. "Just let me explain, okay? You saw my photo at my house, the old me, how I used to be kind of chubby, right?" I sneak a glance at her, and she shakes her head disbelieving. "Yeah, I was. So imagine this dynamic okay. My dad goes from star athlete to college nobody in a matter of days, marries my mom who is an amazing cook and who's always pushing double helpings on everyone at the table. Dad gains weight, and every year he's further from his idea of perfection. He's bitter, right?

"Then, I come along. And all I'm everything he hates about himself. I'm chubby and quiet. I like video games and playing guitar." I stop and rub my neck. It's weird how I never thought about these things until this year, until Cynthia. "I was a disappointment."

"Brayden..."

Our eyes meet.

"He never said anything. Not to me at least. He was a good dad. We used to be really close. I never would have known, except the summer after seventh grade, his company had this huge picnic. Like, everyone was there. Families we'd never met before. They had games, sports tournaments, races, you name it.

"I was old enough to hang out on my own. I played a little bit, but I didn't know anyone, and I was shy."

Cynthia grins, like she can't believe I was ever shy.

"And, of course, I ate. Who's gonna turn down free burgers and chips and potato salad, right?" I close my eyes, reliving this moment like I've done a thousand times over the past few years. "I was leaving with my second plate of food when I overhear my dad chatting with some of his coworkers. They're around the corner of the building, and they can't see me. They're just hanging out, talking about their kids. So-and-so is doing this, so-and-so won that. And my dad, he gets this tone of voice that's so… hurt, and he says 'The only thing Brayden's winning is an eating contest.'"

Cynthia's jaw drops. I get it. Mine did too, back then. Because what kind of parent thinks that sort of stuff about their own kid? Let alone says it.

I rush through the rest of the story, because it still hurts.

"All his friends started laughing while I just stood there with my food, listening and feeling like I wanted to disappear."

Cynthia moves across the basement and stands in front of me. Her knee-high black boots toe to toe with my Jordan's.

I take a deep breath. "Eventually, they walked off, but I couldn't eat. I was too humiliated. I just dumped all that food in the trash. And now… I dunno. I guess I just keep hearing his voice in my head, every meal, every day." I sigh and look at her. "I've never told anyone that."

The truth is, eating anything anymore is hard. I can't go back to being that kid. I'm terrified all the time that I'll do one thing wrong, and I'm back to where I was five years ago. But with Cynthia, I'm not scared at all.

I'm still staring at the toes of my shoes when I feel Cynthia's fingers comb gently through my hair and trace down the back of my neck. I look up, and she climbs onto the couch next to me, wraps her arms around my shoulders, and burrows her face into my neck.

"Steve-O used to send me back to his place to order food after gigs, while the rest of the band packed up." She pauses, takes a breath, "One time, I get there, and I wasn't alone. It was like he was waiting for me. Like he knew I was coming."

She goes silent for a moment. Breathing against my neck.

"I tried to fight, but I just… couldn't. Then that video came out and it all clicked. Steve-O… the drugs… the band… all of it."

She falls silent, and I hug her body to me, holding her close, afraid she'll fly away again at the slightest provocation. I'm sitting so still. Little Cynthia. She's like a bird, all fragile bones and razor-sharp claws. When she finally pulls out of our embrace, my shirt is smudged with her black eyeliner.

Fifty

Charlotte

I've been working with the band for about six weeks now, and it has been eye-opening. I never knew anything about music until this. Now, I'm fiddling around with sound-mixing software like it's a real studio or something. It's been nice, watching them evolve. Back in February, they were kind of a mess. I mean, they could play the music, but it was a little rough.

Now? They are a well-oiled machine. Getting into Battle of the Bands helped. Cynthia has unstoppable drive, and it is infectious. All of us feel it, even me.

They wrap up the last song and Jason literally collapses on the floor. "Please, Cyn. Can we be done?"

She throws a drumstick at him, but it's just a joke. She's not aiming to hurt. "Wimp."

"I'm tired too," Brayden says, and Lindsey nods along.

"Okay, okay." She stands up and stretches, her tank top lifting so everyone can see her belly button, then she tosses her leftover drumstick on top of her snare and comes out from behind the drum set. "We're sounding really good."

"Good enough to win?" Lindsey asks.

"Maybe."

Jason sits up on the floor. "We're still short a song."

"I'm working on it," Cynthia says.

"Who's our biggest threat, you think?" Brayden asks as he sets the guitar on its stand and walks over to the couch.

Jason and Cynthia exchange looks.

"Honestly?" she says, "The Stinks."

Awkward silence. Everyone avoids looking at each other. Brayden leans his head on the back of the couch.

Then he speaks. "You know what we do on the basketball team?"

"Here we go," Cynthia says sarcastically. "Sports metaphors."

"Right before a big game, like the championship game two weeks ago? We study the other team. Literally sit in the locker room, watching videos studying. You know why?"

Cynthia rolls her eyes.

"Why?" Jason asks.

"We learn their weaknesses," he says, "so we know how to attack."

That gets Cynthia's attention.

"So what's the Stinks' biggest weakness?"

"Shitty drummer," she says with a smirk.

"Be serious, Cyn."

She stands up and paces around the room, her hands clasped behind her head. "Steve-O."

"Really?"

"He's an addict, he's always low on money. He's got a bad temper. He used to take it out on me, but I'm gone. So who's taking the brunt of it? Ray? Jimmy? The new guy? Maybe all of them. Maybe… we put a little pressure on him, get him really stressed out. Maybe the band starts to fall apart?"

Jason's lip curls. "Whatcha thinkin', Cyn?"

Her head swivels to me. "Charlotte? You think you could hack into JJ's YouTube account?"

I consider. It'd take some work, but I think I could manage. I start to nod. "Yeah. I think I can."

"Great," she says, "so here's the plan."

Fifty-One

Jason

⚜

"Getting into Battle of the Bands is a great and all, but what we really need is a chance to psyche the Stinks out," Cynthia says as she leans over the cafeteria table, her mouth full of half-chewed food, to show Harvey and Lindsey possible band logos.

Harvey rolls his eyes and goes back to his lunch. It's chicken nugget day, and he's got double because Charlotte doesn't eat meat.

"What?" Cynthia turns to Harvey, "Got something to say?"

He shakes his head. "No ma'am."

"That's what I thought."

Harvey's not much of a talker, but he says a lot without saying anything. If that makes any sense. His "no ma'am" translated easily to the rest of us into, "you're in over your head. Don't get too confident. You need to play it safe."

Basically, everything I've been trying to tell Cynthia for weeks.

The band has basically taken over his cafeteria table. First me and Cynthia, then Lindsey, and now Charlotte. The only member not present is Brayden, who still sits with the basketball team across the cafeteria. No one talks about his absence, because no one wants to admit that it kind of hurts that he still chooses them over us.

Darrell sitting next to Mark hurts worse though. We've been on enough dates that I guess I can call him my boyfriend? Maybe? We haven't really discussed labels.

There's one label I know he doesn't want. And that's "gay." Hence the pretending we don't know each other at school, and him still buddies with the guy who bullied me all first semester.

Charlotte's perpetually nervous voice interrupts my train of thought. "Don't we um… need someone help us move equipment around? That's what the guy at the audition said. Maybe Harvey could…" She glances nervously at Cynthia.

"You gonna pay me?" Harvey asks.

Cynthia sighs. "There's a $1,000 grand prize."

"If you win," Harvey cuts in.

"*When* we win," Cynthia retorts, "we'll split the earnings."

"A thousand dollars isn't divisible by six people, Cyn." I say.

"Thanks, Brainiac," she says, "we'll figure it out."

Harvey does a few quick calculations in his head, trying to decide if just over $150 is worth it. Then he shrugs. "Fine, I'm in."

"Anyway," Cynthia says pointedly, "back to the discussion at hand. We gotta get inside Steve-O's head."

"My birthday is in a few weeks," Lindsey says. "Maybe I could throw a party and we could play?"

"Why would Steve-O come to your party?"

Lindsey looks crestfallen. "What if… I hired him to play, but after his set, we went on…"

"And proved that we're better," Cynthia finishes with a grin. "Yes!"

I look back at Brayden's table, carefully avoiding Darrell's eyes as I do. "You think you can convince Mr. Man over there that he wants to be seen in public jamming with us losers?"

Everyone's shoulders slump at the same time, but Cynthia's got wheels turning in her head. I can tell. She gets a conniving gleam in her eye.

"Maybe," she says, "we don't need the whole band."

#

Darrell and I have been dating on the DL for about six weeks now, and we're getting pretty good at it. The key, apparently, was introducing him to my parents as my super cool, totally manly straight new friend. He's the guy my dad wishes I was. Total jock, chick magnet, which is actually kind of annoying, his parents are doctors, and he's a Christian. He is above suspicion in my father's eyes.

I, however, am not. The first time Darrell came over to my house, Dad pulled me into his study and treated me to a long lecture about perversion and homosexuals preying on good, upstanding boys, and how dangerous my sins were.

Kind of hilarious, considering Darrell came onto me.

On my way home from mandatory youth group, my phone dings with a new message from Darrel. They all are. We send about a trillion texts a day, we've become one of *those* couples. We've even got a code. When he asks if I want to come over and shoot hoops, he means do I want to make out in his bedroom. Do I have the notes from AP History? That means do I want to order pizza?

I check my phone than change course, heading to Darrell's house instead of my own. Thank that non-existent god my dad is always raving about that they finally let up on my prison sentence. Having a new best friend has done wonders for me.

Still, I better check in.

Mom picks up on the second ring. Phew. She's a thousand times easier to convince that Dad.

"Hey," I say, "so Darrell has a Biology project due tomorrow, and he wants to know if I can help him with some of the research. It okay if I go over there for a couple hours?"

There's a pause of silence, a long pause. "I don't know, honey, your dad…"

I force a smile. If I sound irritated, there's no way I'll be allowed to go. "It's no big deal. He's just not quite getting the Punnett square thing. Genetics, you know?" That thing that gave me Dad's green eyes, Mom's dark hair, and some unknown relative's homosexuality.

Mom sighs. "That's fine. Do you think you'll be home for dinner?"

"Uh, I dunno. I can always grab something on the way home."

"I suppose…"

I can feel the question on her lips. Moms know things. I get the feeling she suspects Darrell and I are more than friends. But if she says something, it's all but admitting that Dad's methods aren't working. Not even she's willing to risk that.

Still, I should throw her a bone. "I might call Lindsey and see if she wants get dinner with me."

"Oh, that'd be fine then."

We hang up. I don't feel good about this. Lying to my dad is a necessity. Lying to my mom feels like real betrayal. Course, the second Darrell opens the door, I forget all about my guilt. He cups my jaw in his hands and kisses me. Hard. Like, backs me into the wall hard. My fingers dance over his chest, gripping his shirt even as I pull myself free. "Where are your parents?"

"Working late at the hospital."

"Excellent."

I all but run upstairs, and Darrell is right behind me.

I don't have a long list of people I've kissed. Cynthia because you gotta learn on someone. A couple of pecks exchanged with unsuspecting girls during my denial phase in late middle school. Those were gross.

But Darrell is the only guy I've kissed. Ever. And it is like lightning. Hot and fast and dangerous. We stumble into his room and onto his bed, and in a second, he is all over me. His body pressed against mine, his lips on my lips, I could do this all day. I kind of get it now, why some couples spend the entire school day making out at their lockers. If I could get away with it, I'd do this all day too.

He grinds his hips against me and lets out a groan. I groan right along with him. I am on edge, I am on fire, I'm about to explode. I'm TNT, dynamite. And he knows it. His hand fumbles with the zipper on my jeans, loosening them so I burst through, not sexy at all. Just a hard as rock dick poking through the gap in my boxers. I'm not sure whether I should be mortified or grateful.

He glances down, taking it all in, death or glory.

"I've never had sex with a dude before," he says.

I suppose that's supposed to make me feel good, but it doesn't. "Is that why you asked me over?" The still-very-horny voice in my mind is screaming at me to shut up, but it's too late. I've decided to pick this fight. Right here. Right now.

Darrell rolls off of me, flopping onto his back on the bed next to me. Even that is sexy. I could shut up right now, and lose my virginity, and everything would be okay. But then tomorrow at school? I'd feel like shit as he ignored me in the hallway.

I climb off of his bed and stuff myself back into my jeans. "So, you've had sex with girls?"

"Well, yeah," he says, like it's obvious, "a few."

"Do you pretend like they don't exist too?" It's a completely unfair question, but too late. It's out there.

He sits up. "We agreed to keep this secret. Because of your dad."

"Yeah, my dad," I snap, "not your stupid homophobic friends."

He looks up at me, eyes narrowed. "Seriously?"

"It just kind of sucks seeing my boyfriend hanging out with the guys who bullied me. And oh great, it stopped this semester, but honestly. I think Brayden did more than you ever did." I cross my arms, glaring at him. "Do they even know you're bi?"

"Boyfriend?"

It's like he didn't even hear anything after that word. The question hangs in the air, all it takes is one of us to answer it.

Darrell hunches over his knees, talking to the floor, not me. "I've been friends with Mark since we were kids."

And just like that, I know. He's not giving up his friends for me. I don't even want him to. I'd never give up Cyn for him. But now that it's been said, I can't un-hear it. It feels like we're in the exact same place we were last summer. Two dudes hooking up. Not boyfriends. Not dating.

"I should go home," I say, grabbing my shirt off his floor. "I'll see you at school." I don't wait around for a response.

Fifty-Two

Lindsey

P arties in the Banford house are typically planned affairs, with caterers and curated guest lists and a strict dress code. Every birthday party of my life, I've dressed in clothes my mother picked out, smiled politely and made courteous but dull conversation with the sons and daughters of donors and other politicians.

This birthday party? If my parents knew, they would lose their minds. There would be long family discussions about PR and how will my misbehavior affects my father's political standing. Discussions not unlike those centered around my pilfering ways, though I imagine these would be much worse.

My only hope is that the band will help me get everything back in order before Mom and Dad return from their yearly trip to Europe. It only hurts a little when I think that this year, they planned it during my birthday.

Paying off Loretta was far easier than I expected. She put up a small fight, but I think in her heart, she likes that I'm not as uptight as my mother. I gave her an extra $200 on top of her normal wages to take the week off. On her way out the door, she patted me on the shoulder, reminded me not to completely destroy the house, and suggested that a little rebellion might be the healthiest thing that has ever happened to me.

We scheduled the party for Friday night, giving us all of Saturday and Sunday to clean up. Cynthia and Harvey arrive an hour before the show begins. When I let them in, they stop in the foyer and gape at their surroundings.

"Is something wrong?" I ask.

Cynthia, with guitar case and a dress bag slung over her shoulder, spins a drumstick in her hand. "Wow."

"It's just so… so…" Harvey breaks off, shrugging and staring at his feet.

"Big," Cynthia finishes for him. "Like shit, I knew you were rich Lindsey, but I didn't know anyone actually lived like," she gestures around her, "this!"

My cheeks burn. "What do you mean? This is normal."

"No," she says with a choked back laugh, "this is not how normal people live. Believe me. The sweeping staircase, the fine china and fresh bouquets in every room? Not normal. The baby grand piano in the whatever sort of room that's supposed to be."

"Parlor."

"Parlor," she says. "Not normal. Do you have a butler?"

I think of Loretta. "Well, we have a—"

"Not normal," she interrupts.

I go silent.

"Hey, it's cool. Just, we're surprised. Right Harvey?"

Harvey shrugs.

I play with my hair. "Maybe, we should start setting up?"

Cynthia nods. Back to business. She starts directing Harvey and me around like she owns the place. I lead her through room after room, and she points and directs. "Stage over there. Start moving the furniture to the walls. That way if people want to dance, they can. You're gonna wanna hide all the breakable stuff. Put it somewhere no one would go. Better yet, if you have a room that locks, put it there."

I rush around each room gathering up vases and photo frames to store in my father's study, while Harvey and Cynthia lift furniture. At some point, she finds my parents' liquor cabinet and chuckles. "Not even locked."

"They'll notice if anything goes missing."

She raises an eyebrow. "Trust me, Blondie. I know what I'm doing." With that, she grabs several bottles of hard liquor, a large punch bowl from my mother's pantry, and starts pouring. And pouring. And pouring. My eyes go wide.

"Harvey?" she asks when she's done. "Care to try?"

He dips a finger and pops it in his mouth. "Tastes like cleaning solution."

"Perfect!" She grins at me, and hands me a half empty bottle. "Start filling with water. I'm going upstairs to change." She unzips her dress bag to reveal a dress I loaned her earlier this week. Or what's left of that dress. I'm glad it's not one of my favorites, because it is near unrecognizable at this point. With a wink, she disappears up the sweeping staircase which is, I suppose, not normal.

#

It doesn't take long for the house to fill up with students from my school. People I've spoken to over the years, campaigned to for school president, but never really gotten to know. In fact, the only people I really feel like I know in the crowd are the band members. But I feel odd, hanging out with Harvey and Jason all night. The Stinks have started their set, which takes away any pressure to entertain. I wander around the house, watching my classmates dance, lounge on the couches, drink out of plastic cups. They're all so happy with their friends. But I'm alone.

Charlotte looks just as awkward as I feel, where she stands near a bookshelf in the corner of the family room, so I make my way over to her.

"Hey,"

She smiles as soon as she sees me and pulls me into a hug. "Hey, happy birthday."

"Thanks," I say. Hugging is not something Banfords do regularly. This unexpected display of affection throws me off balance, but only for a moment.

She pulls a small box out of her pocket. "Here, I got you something."

"Charlotte, you didn't have to." But she insists. I take the box. "Well, thank you."

"It's really stupid, you don't have to open it or anything—"

I pull off the lid and grin. "Is this what I think it is?"

She nods. "The shade of lipstick you got caught stealing in JJ's video. The resolution on the video was just good enough I was able to zoom in and catch the name."

"Wow, impressive."

A proud smirk crosses her face. "I hope you like it."

I hold up the tube. "Scarlet Seductress. My mom would die if she saw me wearing it." We trade conspiratorial looks, and I pop off the lid, twist the tube, and carefully apply a layer of deep red lipstick. "What she doesn't know won't kill her."

Fifty-Three

Brayden

The Stinks finish their set with *Sick as Cyn*, and silence falls over the crowd. What applause they earn is scattered, almost bored sounding. Not the thunderous cheering they had back when Cyn was playing with them.

Everyone falls into conversation, ignoring the band as they rest guitars on stands, turn amps off, chug water from bottles on the floor next to them, and saunter off the stage, which now sits empty, a wasteland of dashed musical dreams.

Talking fills the void, it's loud and excited. The promise of summer around the corner keeps us alive and happy. We forget all about the empty stage.

Angela leans closer to me, as if sensing my urge to sneak away, to do something bad and wrong. I keep glancing over the top of the crowd—the joy of being tall—for Cynthia's black and blue hair, but she's nowhere in sight. So I stick close to Angie, my arm around her shoulders, the image of perfection.

Then sound blares out of the speakers, the opening chords to *Cherry Bomb*, loud and angry, and like one, all the heads in the room whip back to the stage, eyes glued to the cherry bomb herself.

Cynthia Marlow.

No wonder I couldn't find her.

She's dressed in what I can only assume is one of Lindsey's cast-off housewife dresses, only it's been slashed, shredded, held together with safety pins and rendered indecent. Cynthia's thin, pale legs extend below a frayed hem.

But that's not all. In her arms is a cherry red electric guitar. *My* cherry red electric guitar. And she is rocking out in all the best ways, God, I can feel my blood pressure skyrocketing just looking at her. Shit.

She leans into the mic and screams the lyrics. She's trouble, she's the girl next door, she's a wild girl and she wants everyone to know it. During the bridge, she shreds, really shreds that axe, better than I ever could.

When the final chord fades, the room erupts into applause, far more excited for her than they were for The Stinks, and she eats it up. She clutches the microphone in her hands and grins. "Happy to see me, huh?"

Someone whoops from the back of the room and she winks. "That's right baby, it's me. Sick as Cyn in the flesh, ready to teach you fine folks what real music sounds like. Normally, it's considered bad form to show up the headliners, but between you and me, their lead singer is a dick." The crowd laughs.

Then she's off again, shifting between chords with ease and singing into the microphone like a real rock star. That's what she is. A star. Bright blue, burning hot, like her eyes, we're all struck blind by her light. She navigates the stage like she was born and raised up there. When she spins, her skirt flares and the whole crowd gets a glimpse of milky white thigh, and I feel jealousy brewing in my gut.

Cyn plays her own song:

> *"You might have heard a rumor 'bout a friend of mine*
> *Something 'bout a guy and a bag of pills*
> *And what she's willing to do to catch those thrills*
> *Well I'm here to set the record straight*
> *Not up for debate*
> *It isn't true, not like you think*

Truth is, she was on the brink
Of fame and fortune and a lifetime of everything she could ever want, ever need
But the man at her back was filled with greed
He couldn't let her win
So with a few careless words, he sold her into sin.
Sick as Sin
Sick as Sin
Cynthia."

Not just any song. Her song. It's all anger and revenge. We've worked it to perfection, or at least I thought we did. She makes those runs look too damn easy, and I find myself fingering along, trying to keep up, at least until Angela notices and raises an eyebrow at me.

I shrug sheepishly. "Just playing around." I don't think she believes me.

"You might have heard a rumor 'bout this guy I met.
Slinging dope just to pay the rent
You think he's shit 'cuz he doesn't look like you
Long hair, and he don't care
About the things you do.
He's got worries, stories, a weight on his shoulder
Feels like the world
And it's never going away.
Every day
He's getting older.
He's a middle-aged teen, working double just to make ends meet
So he had to do a few things he's not proud of
Just to get by
But he's an honest guy.
Yeah he's an honest guy.

Realization dawns on the crowd, and Angie turns to me. "Is she going to sing about everyone from that video?"

I shrug. "How would I know?"

"What's she going to say about you?"

"Nothing." That's a lie. I have a verse in this song. We all do. Knowing what's coming makes my palms sweat, but if I wipe them on my pants, Angela will know I'm nervous. I force a chuckle. "I mean, what does she know about me anyway?"

Angela's eyes narrow. "You spend a lot of time with her."

"Tutoring," I remind her. "Math. It's nothing."

Cynthia continues to sing:

You might have heard a rumor 'bout a friend of mine
He was caught making out with another guy.
Not like there's anything wrong with that.
And that's a fact.
It's the 21st fucking century, and some people still think it's a crime to fall in love.
To feel this way.
Their hearts are filled with hate.
Their minds are small.
Their boxes confining.
Some people spend their entire lives toeing the line
Refusing to see themselves as they truly are,
Refusing to love and accept what's in their hearts
But baby, you're perfect just the way you are.
Yeah, you're perfect just as you are.

I catch Darrell's eye as Cynthia finishes this verse and he shifts uncomfortably and looks around the room. Which I get. Then, he surprises me. His gaze lands on Jason, hanging with Lindsey and Charlotte across the room, and he slips backward, out of our group of friends, and starts walking toward them.

Good for him. I wish I had guts like that.

You might have heard something 'bout a girl I know

Slipping trinkets into her purse when no one's watching her
You might think damn, that girl has it all
Why's she need to steal from the shopping mall?
Sure she has a lot,
Big house, nice car
Everything's designer
But what you don't see is the one thing she ain't never had
Control
Over her life
Her future
She never had a choice, everything's been planned since before she was born
Now she's tired and alone
Desperate to feel anything
Anything

Then, she surprises me. After Lindsey, she finishes the song with a flourish, wild strumming the guitar. When she's done, she pants and grins at the crowd. "You like that? It's called *Six Secrets.*" The crowd cheers. "And that's not the only thing I'm working on. Cynthia Marlow is making a comeback, full force! You ready to hear some real music?"

More cheers.

"I said," she screams into the microphone, "are you ready to hear some REAL MUSIC?"

Before we can respond, she's launched into another song. A song everyone recognizes, because the Stinks performed it just fifteen minutes earlier. *Fire Flight.* Only with Cynthia jamming out, it sounds a million times better. Steve-O may know the lyrics, Ray may know the chords, but Cynthia has the heart and soul to land it pitch perfect. Which she does.

When she's finished she grips the microphone like she's holding on for dear life. I can see her knuckles turning white from where I stand on the opposite side of the room. And I can hear the tension in her voice.

"That's my song," she whispers. "My song. Anyone else wants to play it, they're gonna have to go through me. Okay? That doesn't belong to the

Stinks anymore. You hear me, Steve-O, wherever you are? Fuck you. You can push me around, you can let your drug dealer rape me, you can kick me out of the band and tell everyone I'm a slut, but you cannot take my music."

Her accusation hangs over the entire room, which went from cheering to horribly silent in seconds. We all heard it. People start to look away, uncomfortable. No one wants to come to a party and hear about their classmate getting raped. Even I'm uncomfortable.

But I'm not looking away.

She looks coldly out at the crowd. For the first time since she took center stage, she looks like her normal, scary, hard as stone self, but it's different. There's no more pain or fear anymore in those eyes. Just redemption.

Fifty-Four

Jason

D amn, she's good. She hooked every person at that party with her music, got them to pay attention, then she dropped a bomb on them. I love her. My crazy best friend. I fucking love her.

She's a natural performer. She really is. She got her speech out, made everyone in the room as uncomfortable is humanly possible, waited the exact right amount of time, then starts playing again. Green Day this time. *Still Breathing.* Smart to insert another cover after two original songs. Keeps the crowd interested. It's a damn appropriate song too. She's still here, still breathing, fighting for what she deserves.

It's fast and over quickly, and after finishing and dropping a sarcastic as hell curtsy for the crowd, she turns toward the stairs, but someone from the back of the room shouts "ENCORE" and more voices join in.

"More!"

"Do another!"

At first, she plays coy, like people do. "That's all I have prepared…"

But Brayden shouts "Bullshit!" from where he's hanging with his girlfriend who looks positively venomous, and the entire room bursts into laughter, so none of them see the bitten lip ring, the held back smile that she shoots across the room at him.

Then, of all people, Ray pipes up. "I'll play for you!"

"Not a chance, baby," she says, "I got brass in pocket."

"What's that mean?" someone asks.

"She's gotta have some of your attention!" I shout.

"Give it to me!" She screams, as she starts playing. "Last song, then I'm done. It's a party, I wanna have some fun! Oh, and happy birthday, Lindsey!" Next to me, Lindsey hides her face in her hands, her ears turn bright pink.

Maybe our classmates expected something fast and fun, like what she'd been playing all night, but that's not what they get. She tosses her bangs out of her eyes and leans close to the mic.

At first, I can't place the song. Because it's so not Cyn. But Lindsey whispers the title next to me, half amused, half in awe.

"*Illicit Affairs*," Lindsey whispers, half-amused, half in awe. "She's a total Swiftie!"

"No, she's not," I say quickly. "She's playing to the crowd."

But it's not just that. It's the way she sings it, raw and beautiful. A song like this, something slow and haunting, really brings out all the good qualities in her voice. She's made it punk rock, added some guitar riffs, nothing too showy, and she's looking right at Brayden. The message couldn't be clearer. She loves him, and she's sick of hiding it. My eyes never leave her, so I don't notice when Darrell comes up behind me and slides his hand into mine.

I know it's his just by the feel. Dry, but warm, strong. I've held his hand dozens of times over the past two months, but never in this town in front of these people.

"Aren't you worried what your friends will say?" I mutter under my breath, not even turning to look at him.

"No."

He pulls me closer to him. No one looking at us could think we're just friends. Then, he kisses me.

"I don't care about them," he whispers. "Let's get out of here." "After Cynthia's done."

He squeezes my hand in agreement, then pulls it loose so he can drape his arm over my shoulders, and in spite of myself, I turn to look at

Darrell's friends. Mark makes eye contact with me, then glances at Darrell at my side, and slowly but surely, his mediocre mind pieces the puzzle together. With gritted teeth, he offers a begrudging nod, then looks away.

I let out my breath in a relieved *whoosh*.

Fifty-Five

Cynthia

As soon as I whisper the last line into the microphone, the room erupts into applause. I'm not gonna lie, it feels fucking good. You can live off applause, man. I bow elaborately, then jump off the stage, where I'm immediately swarmed by my classmates. No more liar, cheater, whore here. Everyone wants a piece of me tonight. Too bad, boys, because I got my sights set on one guy, and one guy only. My eyes catch his in passing and I flick them up at the ceiling, praying he reads my mind. *"Meet me upstairs."* Brayden has to know I sang that song for him. All I gotta do is make it upstairs, and he'll find me. I know he will.

I wind my way through the crowd and up the stairs, past other couples in various states of sexual exploration. I'll be one of them soon. As soon as Brayden ditches the Barbie and finds me. I lean over the banister on the top landing, to look down into the living room, trying to catch sight of him. But he's nowhere. I crane my neck.

Five minutes go by. Still no Brayden. I debate going downstairs to find him, but then what? I can't go up to him and his girlfriend and demand he come upstairs with me. I have to wait for him.

Six… Seven… Then I see him. Arm around Angela's shoulders, letter jacket on as he walks out the front door. My chest goes tight. I am so stupid.

"That was some performance."

I just about jump out of my skin, then turn around to find Jimmy. Just my shitty luck.

"Don't start with me," I say, "I'm not in the mood."

"No, I mean it. You were good. You've always been good."

"Thanks." I glance back at the crowd below.

Jimmy steps closer. "Steve-O's gonna kill you though."

"I don't care."

He chuckles. "So… what're you doing upstairs? Waiting for someone?" His voice is suggestive, almost teasing. He knows me too well.

I look away.

"Did he show?" he asks, even though the answer is obvious.

Hard to hide my disappointment there. I clamp my lip ring between my teeth before I remember that Brayden always teases me about that, my tell. Why I can never play poker.

Jimmy recognizes it too. He smirks and starts walking down the hall, toward the bedrooms. "C'mon Cyn."

Still no sign of Brayden. I guess maybe I'd hoped he would return, but no. He's long gone. It hurts, but he chose Angela over me. He doesn't want me.

But someone else does.

I follow Jimmy down the hall as he tries every door. The bedrooms are all locked, but not the bathroom. He takes the lead, locking the door behind us, lifting me onto the counter, looping a finger around the waistband of my underwear and sliding it down. Between each step, a pause, like he expects me to fight him. But I don't.

"The second I saw you out there with my guitar," he says, "I knew you were back. My Cynthia. I knew you wouldn't stay down and out for long."

"Really?" I whisper.

"Yeah." He steps closer to me, resting his hands on my thighs. His lips find mine, and he kisses me slowly, patiently. Better than he used to. He tastes like beer, no surprise there. But what is surprising is how nice he's being.

Last summer, it was all grabbing and pushing around and walking the fine line between fighting and fucking, and I didn't know what was what.

Now, I dunno, it's like he actually cares about me. Even as he deepens the kiss, wraps and arm around my waist to pull me closer to him, it still feels… different.

Almost kind of sweet.

So when he fumbles in his back pocket for a second, and his hand returns to mine so I can feel the familiar foil wrapper, a part of me thinks… why not? I meet his eyes and give a slight nod, then look away. I don't need to see this. I stare at the floral wallpaper over his shoulder as he goes about his business, kissing my neck, holding me closer, tensing, then relaxing. He nuzzles my neck while I study paper botany, and I know I should feel something. Anything.

But I don't.

Mostly I just wish he'd hurry up and get it over with.

When he's done, he tosses the slimy condom into the toilet and zips up his fly.

"I really missed you, Cyn."

I hate him, but I don't feel angry. I just feel sick. I'm not sure my voice even works anymore. I close my eyes and nod, choking out a barely audible "okay."

"I have to play our second set, but can we talk after?"

"Okay."

I am barely keeping it together. Every cell in my body is about explode and if he doesn't get out of the bathroom soon, I might start crying or screaming or throwing up. Or all three.

"Hey," he says, rubbing my thigh. I flinch, but he doesn't notice. "I'll talk to Steve-O. If you apologize about today, I bet he'll let you back in the band."

"Okay," I choke.

He kisses me again and opens the door. "This is good, Cyn. You and me." He smiles back at me. "Sometimes it's just meant to be, you know?"

I nod.

As soon as he's gone, I race to the toilet, doubling over and emptying my stomach. His used condom floats in the water, bobbing between chunks of chips and salsa in a pool of vodka.

Fifty-Six

Charlotte

As soon as Cynthia steps off the stage, my work begins. I stop recording on my phone, grab my laptop bag and head to the study in the back of Lindsey's house, the key Lindsey gave me for the door in my pocket.

I hacked into JJ's YouTube a week ago, but I've been laying low so she wouldn't know I was there. Tonight, all that changes. I get right to work editing the video of Cyn playing. It doesn't take much. I figure all I need to do is add some writing, lose some of the miscellaneous applause from the crowd, and it's ready to go.

Then I log in. First thing first, I change the password and recovery email. As far as I'm concerned, JJ lost the right to this channel months ago. She'll have a hell of a time trying to get back in. Once that's done, I start uploading the video. It takes a while, and while it loads I do what I always do when computers are being too slow. I chew my fingernails until the ping on my laptop tells me it's ready to go.

One quick view to make sure everything is perfect. I smile with satisfaction at Cynthia. She's got presence. The crowd loves her.

At the end of the video, my writing pops up.

Want More?

**See Sick As Cyn live at the Annual Battle of the Bands
Grinders - April 27 - 8 pm**

Followed by the logo Cynthia came up with back in February. One more click and it's been shared with everyone on JJ's subscription list. My work here is done.

#

When I make it back to the party, I slip the key to the study into Lindsey's hand and whisper, "done," before heading to the nearest couch.

By this time tomorrow, everyone in school will know that Cynthia is playing Battle of the Bands next month. They just won't know who else will be there. Nothing left to do but enjoy the party. Harvey hangs with me for a while, then goes out back to smoke, leaving me alone.

So I do what I always do. I check my phone. Social media is a bust. Nothing but party pictures. I check my school email. Still no college news. Then, my secret email. The one only Mr. DuPont knows about. It's been empty except for spam for months but it's habit. I have to check it.

I glance over my shoulder then type my password.

One new email.

Oh my god.

It's from an address I don't recognize, but it can only be one person. Mr. DuPont.

He emailed me. He's been gone for months. I don't even know where. Mom never let me watch the news about him. Sure, I heard things in the bathrooms at school. Talks about plea bargains, girls calling him a creep, saying he'll get what he deserves in prison. If he even goes to prison.

I stare at the email for what feels like a million years. Should I open it? Maybe. I don't know. My finger hovers over the link.

It's him. Mr. DuPont. The one who started it all. The video. The secrets. My friends.

I have friends. Real friends. For the first time since I moved here. After that video came out, I thought I'd never make friends, but Lindsey likes me, and Cynthia let me into her band, and Harvey's pretty cool. I'm happier now than I ever was with Mr. DuPont.

It's a freeing realization, but one I can't savor, because even before I hit the delete button Cynthia barrels into me. Tears are streaming down her face, black eyeliner going everywhere, and she has a faint smell of vomit about her that turns my stomach.

"Cynthia, what—"

She clutches my arm. "Where's Jason? I need him."

"He left with Darrell a while ago."

She covers her mouth and lets out a choking sob. "Oh god, oh god, I need to get out of here."

"Why, what's wrong?"

She won't tell me. Or can't. She just looks all around the room, desperately. Then the music starts up again, which can only mean the Stinks are playing again.

"Oh god." She stumbles and almost falls over. "I can't be here."

She's in a bad way. I stand and loop my arm around her waist to keep her upright. "It's okay. I'll drive you home."

"My guitar—"

"I'll go get it. Just go outside, okay? I'll take care of everything."

She nods. "Okay."

I guide her toward the door and into the cool fresh air. "You wait here. I'll be right back."

It doesn't take much to sneak into the main room where the Stinks are busy playing their second set. No one's really paying much attention to them, because well, they're just not as good as Cynthia. No one pays any attention to me either.

A few minutes later, I deposit Cynthia and her guitar in the back seat of my car and we're off. The whole ride home, she just clutches her guitar and whimpers that she's sorry. Over and over again. "I'm sorry. I'm sorry"

Honestly, I don't mind driving her home. It's better than being at the party. When we get to her house, I climb out of the car and walk her up to the front door.

"You don't have to come in."

"I don't mind." Gives me something to do. I do the whole friend thing, like you see in the movies. Walking her up to her room, helping her get out of that trampy dress of hers and into some pajamas. I even help her clean the makeup off her face while she sits on the toilet looking lost and scared. When I'm finished, I help her into bed, then climb in with her.

She leans against me and whispers, "thanks" into my shoulder.

"Don't mention it." I smooth the hair down on the back of her neck, and she starts to cry again. "What happened?" I ask.

"I messed up."

"No, Cyn. You were amazing up there. You're a rock star, you really are."

"No," she whispers. "I'm not. I'm just a fuck up. That's all I'll ever be."

Fifty-Seven

Jason

Darrell and I practically fall over each other as we race across Lindsey's lawn to get to his car. His hands are on my hips, his feet tripping mine up, we stop in front of a group hanging by the front gate and he pulls me close, kisses me. Who cares who sees?

When he pulls away, I can't help but laugh. "You are officially out."

He grins. "Guess so."

"What a way to do it."

He leans around me to push the gate open. "Better or worse than a YouTube video?"

Better. So much better.

We breathe for the first time in his car. Still high on endorphins. I glance at him, and he is giddy, staring at everything and nothing. His hand finds mine.

"Where to?" he asks.

"Your place?"

"Can't," he says, "my parents have friends over."

For a second, I debate Cynthia's house, but her mom is probably still up, and I'd have to explain Darrell to her. My house is definitely out, which doesn't leave a lot of options.

"The park?" I ask.

He smirks and starts his car. "Sure thing."

I can't stop smiling. Every time I glance at Darrell, I grin like a fool. This must be what happiness feels like. Darrell parks in the back parking lot, far from any playground equipment. Not that it matters, it's late, the park is closed, and there are no kids in sight. Just me, Darrell, and his spacious backseat.

My fingers fumble with the buttons on his shirt, but when I finally yank it off his shoulders, I find abs for days. Swoon. For a moment, we're a mess of limbs in a cramped space, but soon enough, we find our rhythm. I forget everything outside this car. All I know is his body is warm, his mouth crashes into mine, and it is everything.

He finds my belt, then my fly, then his mouth leaves mine, ventures lower and oh my god. I am pretty sure this is what death feels like. I am going to die right now. I can't focus on anything but this feeling right now.

Then the door behind me opens. I fall back and come face to face with my dad in all his fury.

Yup, I died. Now I'm in Hell.

My blood runs cold. Dad grabs my upper arm and yanks me out of the car. I crash to the pavement, and even as he drags me stumbling across the parking lot, all I can think about is how my obituary will read that I died because of a blow job.

He throws me into his car, gets behind the wheel and peels out of the lot before I've even pulled my jeans up.

"Dad…" I start, but he holds up his hand and I shut up.

"When we get home," is all he says.

Which gives me three minutes and forty-six seconds to contemplate my death. At home, my mom watches in nervous silence as I am dragged through the living room and into Dad's office.

"Start praying."

Prayer is about the last thing on my mind. His belt clangs as he unbuckles it, and I hear the familiar *fwap* as he pulls it through his belt loops, and still the only words coming out of my mouth are "holy shit, holy shit, holy shit."

My dad, the ex-Marine. He's huge and strong and mean. He came back from the Middle East when I was five with muscles on top of muscles and a mission to make the whole world his version of Christian. Which, if you actually read the Bible, and I have about a thousand times, would probably make Jesus projectile vomit all over the place.

I, on the other hand, am and have always been and probably will always be a wimp. I'm scared out of my mind around him. Hell, I've been eighteen for months, and I'm still living with him.

"Leviticus!" he says. I wish he'd yell. The quiet in his voice is like the calm before the storm.

My whole body starts shaking. "Dad, please."

"Say it." His voice is fire and brimstone. When he raises his arm, his belt jangles, and I know what's coming next.

"Th-th-thou shalt n-not lie with… with…"

A crash behind me interrupts the verse and I turn around in time to see Darrell and Dad scrambling against each other against his bookshelf. Dad may be strong, but Darrell is young and fast, and after a scuffle that sends most of his books flying, he has Dad pinned to the ground, his knee wedged into Dad's shoulder blades.

"Pack a bag," he pants.

"What?" I am so stupid. I just stare at him.

"You're leaving. Tonight."

Leaving.

I've thought about leaving practically every fucking day since ninth grade. But what was the point? He would just drag me back, and it'd be so much worse.

Darrell doesn't think like that. He sees a problem and the obvious solution, and he's not going to wait for permission. I race to my room and start shoving anything I can think of into my backpack, underwear, socks, a handful of T-shirts. It's bulging when I finally zip it up. Then I come back to Dad's study.

"I'm ready."

Darrell climbs off my dad and comes to stand next to me.

Dad doesn't even get up. Just glares at me from the floor, not quite looking me in the eye.

His lip curls. "Don't come back."

Darrell pushes me out the door and down the hall. "Do you want to say bye to your mom?"

"No."

"Okay." He leads me out the front door and back to his car, which is good, because I'm still in such a state of shock, I can barely move except to do what he tells me to do. I sit in the passenger seat and clutch my bag to my chest while Darrell runs around the car to climb into the driver's seat.

"You okay?"

"Did you follow me home?" I ask stupidly.

His hand falls onto my arm and I tense.

"I didn't know it was that bad," he says. "I swear, I didn't know."

I pinch my eyes shut. "Can we just go?"

By the time we reach Darrell's house, I'm a little more lucid. But now I'm dreading a whole other parental confrontation. Luckily, Darrel handles it, starting with the drive over when he calls his parents to ask if I can spend the night. Just like that. Not technically a lie. Not the whole truth.

Their party is still underway when we arrive, but it's not really a party like I'd normally think of one, so much as a gathering of a few couple friends to drink beer and play board games. Adulthood. Kill me now.

I wait in the living room while Darrell goes into the dining room and interrupts their game. I can't really hear what they're saying, and my imagination is running wild with all the possible outcomes. What happens if both Darrell and I get kicked out of our houses? Cynthia's parents will take me, but Darrell? I'm not so sure.

A few minutes later he comes back, with his mom on his heels. Her jaw drops when she sees me, so I guess I've got some pretty bruises to show off at school on Monday.

"What happened?"

"Jason's parents kicked him out," Darrell says.

"Why?"

Darrell makes brief eye contact with me before saying, "because he's gay. He's my boyfriend."

His mom glances at him, then at me, then she nods. "Oh, I see."

"Yeah."

"Well then," she says, switching into doctor mode, pure business, "take your friend upstairs and get him cleaned up, and get some rest. We can talk in the morning." She turns away to return to her game then pauses and looks back at us. "Separate rooms."

Fifty-Eight

Cynthia

I wake up with the world's worst headache and the weight of another person in my bed. Charlotte. That's right. She gave me a ride home last night, and apparently, she stayed.

When I groan, she rolls over to face me. "How are you feeling?" she asks.

"What's the worst adjective you can think of?"

She smiles softly. "That bad, huh?"

She doesn't even know the worst of it. I've done a lot of bad things in my life, but sleeping with Jimmy probably takes the cake. I start to sit up and she shifts over to give me room. When I curl over myself to hide my face in my knees, she asks if I'm going to throw up.

"No."

"Did something happen last night?" She is so earnest, like she really cares. I don't deserve that.

I nod.

"Do you want to talk about it?"

No, no way. Not with her. I want it to go away. All of last night. From the point I stepped on that stage and everything after. I want it to just disappear.

"I can help," she offers.

I cringe. Nothing she can do makes up for the fact that I am a terrible human being. Everything is wrong, and Charlotte, as nice as she's being, needs to go. There is only one person I can talk to and that's Jason.

Charlotte shimmies out of bed and stretches. "I guess I should go home." She says it like a question, all uncertain and nervous. What she really wants is to stay, to be invited into the hell hole I've dug for myself. But no, this is my penance and I get to serve it alone.

"I'll see you at school on Monday," she says, "I guess."

"Yeah."

"Hey, Cynthia?"

I grunt to show I'm listening.

"Whatever happened, it's going to be okay, you know that? I mean, you can come back from it. Look at me after what happened with Mr. DuPont."

"Mr. DuPont," I repeat. "Did you know it was wrong when you were in it?"

Charlotte stays silent and I look up to find her chewing her thumb nail.

"Sorry," I say.

"No, it's okay," she says. "I knew it was bad, but I didn't realize how good he was at manipulating me until it was all over."

Now I feel like shit. "Yeah, I know how that goes."

And just like that, she sees an opening. "He emailed me last night."

I look up. "Oh yeah? What'd he say?"

She keeps chewing on her nail. "I don't know. I deleted it. I don't want anything to do with him anymore." It sounds like she's waking up from a dream. "What you said in your song last night? About me, about all of us. It was true. What he did was wrong. I don't want to be a part of that anymore."

Then, because I'm stupid and sentimental on top of being the world's biggest mess, I slide out of bed and give her a hug. She looks like she needs it just as bad as me.

When we're done acting like girls, she wipes her eyes and says she's got to go home, and I follow her downstairs, because I'm starving and I need caffeine and aspirin. But when she opens the door to leave, Jason is standing on the other side and if anything, he looks worse than me.

I push Charlotte out of the way and launch into his arms. "What are you doing here?"

"Ah well…" He glances nervously at Charlotte, then over his shoulder at Darrell who is leaning against my porch railing. "My parents kicked me out. Or I ran away. It was all a blur."

"His dad's a psycho," Darrell adds from behind him.

"No shit," I say.

Charlotte clears her throat. "I think that's insulting to people who suffer from real psychosis."

I roll my eyes. "Whatever, his dad's a mean, angry fuck. Is that better?"

"I guess."

I pull Jason inside, and the other two come along for the ride. If anything can make me stop worrying about Jimmy and Brayden and my big mistake, it's Jason who doesn't and has never deserved any of the crap that has been poured onto him by his parents.

We sit at the kitchen table, all four of us, while Jason tells us everything that happened. From him and Darrell leaving the party, to getting caught by his dad, to spending the night at Darrell's house.

"It was stupid," he finishes. "I don't know what I was thinking."

Not as stupid as what I did last night. I have zero room to judge.

"The important thing is that you're safe," Charlotte says kindly.

"Homeless, you mean."

I raise an eyebrow. "Come on, Jason. Don't be stupid. You're going to live here, with me."

"What about your mom?"

"Are you kidding?" I say. "My mom loves you. You're smart and helpful and gay, so she doesn't have to worry about pregnancy. It's the perfect adopted son trifecta, as far as she's concerned."

"Well, at least someone appreciates it." Then, he started crying. Like really crying. Head on the table, soul bared to the world crying.

I leap out of my chair and hug him. "It's going to be okay," I promise, sounding just like Charlotte did a few minutes ago. I kiss the top of his head, and he just starts crying harder.

He mumbles something, and I have to ask what he said.

"Why can't I just be normal?"

His fucking dad. This is all his fault. I hate his dad so much. I've never hated anyone in the world as much as I've hated Jason's dad. Not even Jimmy or Steve-O or even his dealer. At least they make sense in their warped ways. This is just senseless, making someone like Jason feel like this over nothing.

I lift his chin and make him look at me. "Because no one is normal." I glance at Darrell and Charlotte for confirmation, and they nod in agreement. "Because you're fucking perfect the way you are."

Fifty-Nine

Jason

Cynthia's phone rings non-stop all Sunday morning, and she won't
answer it. It feels weird, not being at church all day, but freeing
as well. I'm almost giddy with the extra time. When Cyn's mom
wakes up, she explains why I'm moving in, and just as predicted, all she does
is give a shrug, say "whatever" and tell me to sleep in the guest room.

In all the drama of being a newly emancipated man, I forget to check in
with Cynthia about how the rest of her night went after I left. She's not
offering any details. Either way, I find out plenty the next day at lunch,
when Jimmy plops himself down right next to Cynthia at our table and puts
his arm around her shoulders.

"Hey, Cyn," he says, "I tried to call you, but—"

She pushes his arm off her shoulders. "Leave me alone."

Jimmy? How did Jimmy get back in the picture? My mouth hangs open
like an idiot. Across the table, Harvey doesn't look much better.

"We need to talk," Jimmy continues. God dammit, his hand is on her leg.
Get your disgusting hand off my best friend's leg.

"We're not getting back together," she says. "We don't need to talk."

He stares at her like she's speaking a foreign language.

Then, she drops her voice and leans into him, but I still catch what she says. "I just wanted to get laid. You were convenient. That's it. It didn't mean anything."

Now I know I look like an idiot, because I know my girl did not sleep with that asshole. No way. She wouldn't do that. Except… the way he's looking at her, his hand on her leg, I think maybe she did.

He glares for a solid minute, then stands up, calls her a "dumb slut" and storms away.

Then, silence, which I break.

"You had sex with Jimmy."

"Jason, don't start…"

"I can't believe you. You had sex with Jimmy!" I hiss between my teeth. "Are you insane?"

Harvey glances back and forth between us, then I guess decides this conversation is too much for him, because he grabs his lunch and hightails it across the cafeteria to where Lindsey is sitting with Charlotte and a group of Student Council members.

Cynthia hangs her head, biting hard on her lip ring to keep from crying.

"What were you thinking?"

"I wasn't," she sobs, "I was upset and drunk and it just kind of happened and now…" she glances over her shoulder at where Brayden is sitting. He offers a half smile, then turns back to his friends.

"How long do you figure before he finds out?" she whispers.

"Well," I say, "my guess is Jimmy, using whatever tiny speck of decency he has left in his body, wanted to talk to you before he bragged to the whole school."

She draws a shaky breath and shrinks into herself.

I continue. "But, now that you've shot him down…" I fake check an invisible watch. "We have PE together, so you have until we get to the locker room to tell Brayden yourself, or else he's going to find out the hard way. About ten minutes."

Sixty

Cynthia

Ten minutes. Ten minutes until everything falls apart. No more Brayden. No more band. No more Battle of the Bands. No more music. No more laughter. No more making out on the couch with him.

Ten minutes and it will all be gone.

I have to tell him. It's the right thing to do. I can't let Brayden find out from Jimmy. It's bad enough what I've done, but if he hears it from Jimmy, I'm dead.

I follow Jason down to the gymnasium from the cafeteria and wait around in the hallway for Brayden. Jimmy gives me a death glare as he walks toward us, but Jason stays right with me the whole time. He stares Jimmy down until he's disappeared into the locker room.

I don't deserve his friendship. I'm a monster.

Brayden comes walking down the hall with a whole group of basketball players, laughing with them about something. Boy stuff, probably. The rest of them disappear into the locker room, so it's just Brayden, me, and Jason in the hall. He glances around to make sure the coast is clear, then ducks into the side hallway with me. As soon as we're alone, he leans over and kisses me.

"Hey," he whispers.

I open my mouth to speak, but no words come out. Jason's no help. When I look to him, he just shakes his head and walks into the locker room.

Brayden runs his fingers through my hair. "Are you okay?"

I close my eyes. Is it so wrong? To savor these last few moments of something good? I'm only human. It's like the last bite of a birthday cake, when you know in a second or two, the celebration will be over and you'll wake up just Cynthia again. You chew slowly, mull the crumbs around in your mouth, and try to make it last.

I shake my head. No. I'm not okay. Far from it.

The bell rings, and I jump.

He laughs. "You're late for class."

I force myself to open my eyes, to face this like a woman and not run away.

"What's wrong?" he asks. "You're crying." He reaches up to wipe my eye, but I back away. "If it's about Saturday, look, Cyn, I'm sorry, I just," he pauses, glances around, then leans closer. "I don't want it to be like that. It means something. I don't want it to feel like we just got drunk at some party and hooked up. You're too special for that."

"Stop," I gasp. I can't take it anymore. He's too nice, too good for me. Jason was right all along. I don't deserve someone like him. "I had sex with Jimmy." Every word hurts.

He steps back. Gone the fingers in my hair, his hand in mine. Gone the warmth and strength, the presence I have come to love so much.

I force myself to look at him. He deserves that much. But his face reveals nothing. It's blank. Not like a poker face, studied calm to hide everything inside. His is the blank of someone so shocked by what he's just heard that he can't even comprehend it.

He sucks in a low breath. "When?"

My lip trembles. "At the party. After you left."

"Oh." He stares at the wall, and not at me. Time is frozen. We're standing in the hallway alone, and for a moment it feels like this isn't even real. It's like I'm watching a movie. Girl meets boy. Girl falls for boy. Girl sleeps with someone else. This can't be real.

"I'm sorry," I whisper.

He shoulders his bag and turns away, heading to the locker room without another word.

I can't go back to class. Instead, I race to my locker, grab my backpack, then sign myself out with some stupid excuse.

When I get home, I burst through the door, scaring my mom who is plodding around in her pajamas. "What are you doing home?" she asks, but I don't answer. I dart up the stairs, lock myself into my bedroom, and blast music as loud as I can.

Sixty-One

Brayden

I hate Jimmy. I hate everything about him. I hate his stupid spiked hair which he dyes bright red. Red like the color of my guitar. Red like a sunset. Red like the color I keep seeing right now. I hate the stupid gauged earrings in his ears. I hate his septum piercing. I hate the way he talks. Every word out of his mouth sounds like nails on a chalkboard. I want to kill him. I want to maim him. I want to watch him suffer. I want to wrap my hands around his throat and watch the life leave his eyes.

I hate him.

Even worse, I hate Cynthia. Everything everyone always said about her. True. The girl I thought I knew. A lie. She's been pretending this whole time to be something she thought I wanted. My face is red hot, just thinking about her. I did want her. I still do, but she never cared about me. How could she, then go and do that?

When I get to the locker room, Jason is already dressed. I can see from his face that he knows exactly what Cynthia just told me.

Then I see him.

Jimmy.

The asshole.

Everything goes red.

Next thing I know, Mark is holding my arms behind my back, pinning me down on the bench, and Jason is holding Jimmy back against the opposite locker. His nose is bleeding heavily and he's shouting incoherently and pointing at me over Jason's shoulder. I clench my fists as hard as I can and yank out of Mark's grasp, then pummel my locker until it is completely obliterated and hangs loosely on its hinges.

"I don't ever want to see your face again," I snarl at Jimmy.

He shoves Jason off. "Lay off the steroids, asshole," he says as he storms out of the room.

Our row of lockers goes silent. Mark looks back and forth between me and the locker, mutters, "shit, man" then stalks off. I gasp for breath and run my fingers through my hair, trying to calm down. Anything to make the ringing in my ears disappear.

Jason stands back, his eyes wide. Like he doesn't even recognize me. I get it. I've never lost my temper like this before.

I take a deep breath. "I'm not going to go off on you, okay?"

"Right," he says. "I'm gonna head to class."

"Whatever."

My hands won't stop shaking. Adrenaline is pumping through my veins. I think I'm going to throw up. I don't go to PE. I just sit there in the locker room for the entire class period trying not to think about Cynthia with Jimmy. But you know how it is, when you try not to think about something, that's all you end up thinking about. I'm going crazy thinking about it.

When the bell rings, I escape upstairs to AP Chemistry. Jason comes in a few minutes after me, but he's smart. He doesn't try to talk to me. Good, because when I look at his face, I see Cynthia laughing with him, her head leaning on his shoulder, kissing him on the cheek. Her chaste little friendship kisses.

Angela sits on the stool next to me and drums her fingers on the lab table. "Why do you look like that?"

"Like what?"

"Like someone else."

I groan. "I'm sorry, I think I just have some sort of stomach bug. Puked all over the boys' locker room last hour."

Her face switches to concerned so fast. "Are you okay? Do you need to go home?"

"I just want to get through the day."

She lays a hand on my arm. "Anything I can do? I can bring over some soup tonight. We could stay in, watch a movie?"

I smile. "Yeah, that'd be nice. Six-thirty?"

"Perfect."

#

Muscle memory is a beautiful thing. It's how athletes operate. How gymnasts stick their landings over and over. How quarterbacks throw perfect passes. How I can make free throw after free throw when I'm shooting hoops.

Not so great when I end up standing on Cynthia's front porch about twenty minutes after school lets out. I don't even think about it anymore. I'm more used to driving to her place than I am to my own at this point.

Still, I'm here, so I might as well go inside. Her mom is sitting on the couch watching some awful HGTV show. She glances up when she sees me. "Hey Brayden. Cyn's feeling a little under the weather today. Up in her room. You're welcome to go see her."

Under the weather. Seems like that's going around.

I climb the stairs toward her room, stopping when I see the door closed. I try the handle. Locked.

"Jason?" I hear her ask. Her voice sounds heavy, dull, like she's been crying.

"No," I say. "It's me."

Her bed squeaks, there's some rummaging around, then the music stops playing. She opens the door, and her face is definitely red from crying.

"I didn't think you were coming."

I grit my teeth. "A deal's a deal. I said I'd play Battle of the Bands with you, and I plan on following through."

"You don't have to."

"Yeah, well," I sound so cold. "My mom says a person's only as good as their word. So I kind of do."

That hurts her. Good. I wanted it to.

"Okay," she says weakly.

"But I'm leaving at six. I have plans."

I turn and walk down the stairs so I don't have to look at her face. She follows. I figured she would. Music is the only thing she cares about.

Sixty-Two

Jason

I'm not an expert on hell or eternal damnation or anything, but I'm pretty sure if it exists, it'd be this band practice. Awkward doesn't even begin to cover it. Brayden and Cyn won't even talk to each other. Cyn keeps casting pitiful glances at him, but he's giving her the total cold shoulder. No words, no looks. Nothing. He's here to play guitar and nothing else.

Tense.

Everyone feels it. Charlotte's chewed through half her fingernails while she watches us. Harvey's pretending he doesn't notice, but he's been staring at a blank phone screen for five solid minutes.

Lindsey, of course, is flitting around trying to fix everything. Talking a million words a minute every time we finish a song. "Was that okay? Do you want me to embellish that run a little? Did you like what I did during the bridge? Should I take notes? Does anyone want anything to eat? You know, I think we sounded pretty good there actually. Don't you?"

She's delusional.

At exactly 6 o'clock, Brayden's Apple watch buzzes and he lifts the cherry red guitar off his shoulders. Mid-song and everything.

"I promised Angie I'd meet her at 6:30," he says to the wall.

Everyone looks at Cyn. She's the boss after all. Everyone except Brayden. The look she gives the back of his head speaks volumes. Pain, anger. Love, hate.

She looks ready to chuck a drumstick at his head. I gotta say. Brayden's got balls.

Lindsey looks to me for help, but no way I'm wading into these dangerous waters.

Brayden, meanwhile, packs up his things: guitar picks and handwritten tab. He rests the guitar, Cyn's guitar, on its stand then slings his bag over his broad shoulders.

In a desperate attempt, Cyn tries to save face. "Yeah, that's probably a good stopping place." She sounds ridiculous, but nobody laughs.

With a satisfied nod, he says, "I'll be here tomorrow" then climbs the stairs. No bye or anything.

And just like that, Brayden's set the new practice schedule. We used to play as long as it felt right, until my throat was sore and Cynthia's hands blistered. Now, it's 4 to 6 sharp.

For a moment, the basement is silent, eerie, cold. Lindsey shivers. Cynthia cowers. Charlotte keeps gnawing on her nails. She'll be down to the cuticles soon.

Harvey speaks up. "You guys kinda sucked."

"Harvey!" Lindsey gasps.

He gives Lindsey an apologetic shrug. "Sorry, but I mean, someone had to say it. You all are playing in the same room, but you're not playing together."

I hate to admit it, but he's right.

Lindsey clears her throat. "Um, maybe we should go."

Cynthia says nothing. Her eyes are fixed on Brayden's empty spot.

"Yeah, okay, um Harvey," Lindsey says, "do you want to get some dinner?"

"Sure."

"Charlotte?"

Charlotte shakes her head. "I have homework."

"Oh, okay." Lindsey looks at me.

But I shake my head. "I live here now, remember?"

"Oh, yeah." She's spinning out of control, unsure how to fix this. I've spent enough time with Lindsey now to know that she can't handle not having control. I need to get rid of the three of them. I'm not sure how much longer Cyn can hold off. She will absolutely kill me if I let everyone see her cry.

I gesture toward the door with my head and mouth, "get out while you can," and Lindsey does. The three of them rush through packing up and hurry up the steps. The door slams, and Cynthia slumps on her stool.

"Oh god," she sobs.

"Hey, Cyn, it's okay," I say. I walk over to her and kneel down to face her, rubbing her arm like a total weirdo. "It'll be okay."

"No," she says, "no. This isn't going to work. I should just break up the band."

Which is what I told her months ago. Give up before she looks like a fool trying to beat bands who've been around way longer. But now? Now that she's basically promised Steve-O she's coming for him? After we've all worked so hard? I can't let it end like this. I can't let Jimmy and Steve-O beat her like this.

"You know," I say, "*Rumours* is widely considered Fleetwood Mac's best album."

"So?"

"So, they wrote it when they were all pissed at each other and broken-hearted and all. They just locked themselves up and churned out the best music they could write."

She looks at me, tears still swimming in her eyes.

"Some of the best music out there was written from a broken heart." I stand up. "So you better get writing."

#

Alone in my room that night, I call Darrell. It still feels weird to have a boyfriend I can actually call on the phone and do all those sappy romance movie things with. I tell him everything about the band. Cynthia and Brayden starting it, me and Lindsey joining up, the Battle of the Bands

263

audition.

"Wait, seriously?" he says. "That's where Brayden's been hanging out all this time?"

"Yeah…"

I know I probably shouldn't, but I tell him about Cynthia and Brayden hooking up for the past few months, but now they're fighting.

"It's a complete mess, man."

He gives a low whistle. "Wow. And he's been telling everyone he's been tutoring her."

I sigh. "Can we talk about something else?"

"Sure," he says, "so do I get to come watch you perform?"

"Oh god," I say, rolling my eyes.

"Hey, I've never dated a verifiable rock star before."

"And you still haven't." I slump against the wall. "If you come early, you can help us set up the stage. The more hands the better."

"Deal," he says.

I smile in spite of myself. Yeah, it definitely feels good having a boyfriend I can talk to. I could get used to this.

Sixty-Three

Cynthia

When the music comes to me—and it does—I can't control it. It takes over. There's no point in fighting it. Which is why for the third night in a row, I'm still awake at half past two, surrounded by guitar tab, sheet music, and a lukewarm pot of coffee on the floor next to me. I ditched the coffee cups long ago. Easier to drink straight from the pot.

I cradle Brayden's acoustic guitar, the last piece of him I can still halfway claim. I grip the neck he's held, I finger the frets he's touched. It's almost like touching him.

Almost.

When I play through what I've written, mumbling the words as I go, I know for a fact, this is the best thing I've ever written. Maybe the best thing I'll ever write. It doesn't matter. After Battle of the Bands, music as I know it is over. I'll never be able to find another band like this one. My band. I almost get it, why Steve-O was so protective of his band back in August when he booted me. Because it's different, creating it yourself, building it up, watching it grow, flourish. Die.

Yes, it's over after this. No one wants the drummer taking over. It's either my band or no band. So it feels good, ending on this song. Jason was right.

I took my pain and I wrote it in, and it's good. Really good.

And today after school, I'm sharing it with the band. If we close our set with this piece, we can win. I know we can win.

#

School goes by in a blur. I fall asleep during history. I barely have time to collapse into my seat next to Harvey before my head hits the desk. The next thing I know he's shaking my shoulder and telling me class is over.

I blink slowly and wipe drool from my mouth. "What?"

"Late night, huh?"

"I think I nodded off around three."

"Wow."

"I don't suppose you have anything in your locker to get me through the rest of the day?" I hate asking, but desperate times.

He gives me a look that fills me with regret. Such venom. "Go to the gas station and buy a Monster. I'm out of the business. For good this time."

I try to force my face into something resembling a supportive smile, but I can't smile anymore. "That's really great, Harvey. Good for you."

He shrugs and follows me into the hall. "Sure, really great. I work two jobs and survive off of school lunches and barely any sleep. But at least I'm out from under his thumb, you know?"

Yeah, I do know.

"What're you even doing?" he asks.

Harvesting my broken heart for my art? "Writing new music," I say. "Winning is the only thing I have left these days."

It really is. Jason's got big college plans, so he'll be gone in just a few months. Not me. My grades have plummeted now that Brayden's not checking my homework. I figure after Battle of the Bands, I'll try to find some job, maybe sell the drums. Get rid of all the evidence of my failure as a human being. Become another mindless worker ant.

Until then, I'll keep playing.

I chug a couple energy drinks on the way home from school. They give me jitters and sit heavy in my stomach, but at least my eyes are open. I sit on the stool in front of the microphone, three stacks of sheet music ready on my lap, and wait for the band to arrive. My leg shakes in anticipation and nerves, until Jason teases me from the couch and I force myself to sit still. Lindsey shows first, of course, and I hand her the top stack.

"What's this?"

"New music."

She grins. "Cool!" Within seconds, she's set up at the keyboard and trying it out.

Charlotte rolls in a few minutes later, reminds us that Harvey's working, which I already knew, and sets up her laptop. I hand her a stack of papers. "I'd like us to run through it a few times before we record. But I want it down before we leave tonight."

"No problem." She settles onto a chair near Lindsey and connects her laptop to the keyboard, already squinting at her screen.

Now, we just need Brayden. I don't bother hiding my nerves while we wait. And wait. And wait. Then the basement door opens above us, and my heart jumps to my throat. I close my eyes, take a deep breath, and stand right as his foot lands on the bottom step.

"Good," I say in what I hope is an authoritative voice. "Everyone's here. We can start." I hold the last stack of papers out to Brayden without looking at him, and when I feel them leave my fingers, I turn toward the microphone, lowering it to my height.

Brayden stares at me. "Why aren't you on the drums?"

I've been steeling myself for this all day. "I'm singing this one."

Silence.

"We don't need drums for this one. Lindsey can provide the beat," I glance quickly at Brayden then duck my head. "You play guitar. I sing. Jason, well, um… Jason…"

"Shakes a tambourine and looks pretty," he chimes in, saving my ass from having to explain that I had forgotten about him.

I nod. "Let's get started."

I make Lindsey and Brayden play it on their own a few times through, me tapping beats on one of my toms until they get in sync. By their fourth go through, they can do it without me.

By the fifth one, I'm ready to sing.

"Charlotte, record this time, okay?"

She types furiously on her computer, then gives me a thumbs up. Brayden starts up with the guitar melody, Lindsey joins in with some punchy chords, and I grip the mic and sing.

Used to be, I could read you like a book, with a look
And I knew what it took to make you smile.
Now the only look you toss my way
Is full of hurt and dismay
But baby, you gotta know, I'm feeling it too.
I would rip my heart out and give it to you
When you surround me, I can't breathe. I can't breathe
But you're gonna do what you wanna do.
Again and again, hell so am I
I refuse to admit this is goodbye.
Baby, I still think of you, every second of every day
I want you. I need you.
And I'm hoping you do too
Cuz I'd rip my heart out and give it to you.
I'd do anything you wanted me to
When you surround me, I can't breathe. I can't breathe.
You got what you got and so did I
But I refuse to admit this is goodbye
This can't be goodbye
I don't know if I'm weak or I'm stronger with you.
I don't know if I'm lost or if I've been found by you.
All I know is I don't want it to end. Didn't mean to push you away
So baby, kiss me again.
Didn't mean to push you away.
And I refuse to admit this is goodbye.
Don't let this be goodbye.

The final chords fade into silence which stretches way too long. Then Charlotte clicks her mouse, leans back in her chair and says, "wow" in a tone of voice I can't quite figure out.

"What?"

Jason chuckles. "Damn, I wish someone would write me a song like that."

I look over my shoulder at Lindsey, because I absolutely cannot look at Brayden. She nods encouragingly. "It's really good."

Brayden says nothing, but I can hear him shuffling around with things. I force myself to turn his way.

"What did you think?"

He looks furious, eyebrows knit, jaw clenched, and his grip on the neck of his instrument is terrifying.

"It's your band, Cynthia," he says. "Just tell me what to play, and I'll play it. But don't ask my opinion."

Like a fucking stab to the heart. It takes me a moment to process, but when I do, I give him a curt nod and turn away. "Okay."

Sixty-Four

Brayden

Getting out of band practice the Friday before Battle was kind of tricky. Ever since she slept with Jimmy, Cynthia has been on a rampage. Then she wrote a love song for him? Trey! Whatever. I can't think about it, because if I do, I won't stop. I still can't believe I let her worm her way into my life, just to go and do something like that. It's better to focus on Angela, on what's right with my life.

It's Angela's and my anniversary, and really at this point, I'll take any excuse not to have to play that damn song. Bad enough she's trying to get him back, but do I need to witness it?

Cynthia lost her mind when I ditched, but it is what it is. I need to recommit to Angie, which means I'm going all out for this anniversary. A nice dinner at Chez Louis's which I totally can't afford. I even got her a necklace, a gold chain with a little gold heart on it, with her birthstone. I'm trying. Really, I am.

It's April, but the weather is still cool, so I grab my leather jacket on my way out, pulling it over a button down that feels a little looser than normal. Good. I was gaining weight when I was eating at Cynthia's house. That's all over, and I'm back to regimenting calories like my life depends on it.

Angela meets me at the door, sliding out of her house before I can even ring the doorbell.

"You look nice," I say, but it sounds awkward, like this is a first date not an anniversary.

Angie mumbles a "thanks" and walks ahead of me to my truck, completely ignoring the arm I held out for her.

Great.

I have my work cut out for me. Not that I'm complaining, it's my own fault. I've been ignoring her, pushing her aside in lieu of the other girl who was not worth it. That's okay. It's over. I'm focused on Angie. I'm going to make this work.

I hope.

The hostess at the restaurant leads us all the way to the back of the restaurant to a little two-seater with a white fabric table cloth and candles and a real red rose in a glass vase. Very fancy. I pull out Angela's chair for her then sit across the table and smile. "Happy anniversary."

"Hmm," she says, forcing a half smile.

I open my menu. "What do you want to eat? Order anything. I've got some money saved up."

"Honestly," she says, "I'm not all that hungry."

My heart drops to my stomach. "Oh." I start fidgeting with my napkin. "I guess we could just go to the movies or something." I say lamely. I'm a little annoyed because it was pretty hard to even get a reservation to this place and now it's all going to waste.

I open my mouth to say something, but Angela cuts me off. "Brayden, we need to talk."

Oh no. I can't even play dumb. I know what this talk is about. Sure, Angie's my first ever girlfriend, but I know the talk.

She takes a deep breath. "You're cheating on me."

Can't deny that.

"With Cynthia Marlow of all the people," she finishes.

I can't even look at her. It's awful to hear it aloud, like until this moment, it wasn't exactly real, or it was someone else doing it and I was just observing. But no. I am culpable. I am guilty. I am…

"I'm sorry," I whisper, sneaking a glance at her face for the first time all night. It crumples. Maybe she didn't really believe it either. "It's over, though, I swear. It was a mistake. It was stupid. But she's hooked up with Jimmy, and I'm with you and—"

"Did you have sex with her?"

"No!"

She looks down. "Did you want to?"

I sigh. "Yes."

"So why didn't you?"

My mind flashes back to that night with at Lindsey's house. I knew what Cynthia wanted. I knew she expected me to meet her upstairs. But I didn't go. So she met someone else instead. Why didn't I go? Why?

"Because I didn't want it to be tainted," I say, "by you." I am such an asshole. There is literally no way to say this without hurting her, and I am hurting her. So badly. But it's the truth. The real reason I didn't meet Cynthia.

A tear slides down her cheek, then another, and she stares at her lap.

"This doesn't have to be the end for us," I say. I'm reduced to begging.

"Yes," she says, standing up. "It does." She walks around the table and leans over, kissing me on the cheek. "I can't be with someone who's in love with someone else."

In love with someone else.

"I can drive you home." I'm desperate to prolong the inevitable.

"My mom's picking me up. She should be waiting outside already."

If anything, it hurts worse that she had this planned out so carefully. How long has she known and waited to confront me? To make sure we're somewhere public so it can't be dragged out.

There's nothing left to do except nod and say goodbye and try not to look devastated as she winds her way through the other tables of happy couples who no doubt know exactly what just went down at our table. Once she's gone, I fish the necklace out of my pocket. I am so stupid. Did I really thinking a trinket could somehow salvage what I had spent months destroying? So stupid.

"Sir." The waiter has shown up, hovers over my shoulder. "Is the young lady returning?"

"No," I mumble.

"Are you dining with us tonight?"

My fingers close over the gold chain. "No."

"Then, I'm afraid I'm going to have to ask you to leave."

I nod numbly. "Right."

I wasn't going to eat anyway.

#

I thought the break up was bad. I didn't anticipate going back to school on Monday. Good-bye popularity. Angela must have spent all weekend on the phone with her friends, because every girl in the school is giving me the stink eye.

Mark catches me at my locker, giving me a bro-hug and jabbing me in the ribs. "Brayden, my man! Who knew you had it in you?"

"Don't tell me—"

"Angie told Rosa, who's best friends with Stephanie who came over to my house yesterday for a little physical education, if you know what I mean."

I groan. "Everyone knows what you mean."

He throws an arm around my shoulders. "Putting it to the rocker chick. Nice. Is she a freak in bed?"

"Stop it."

"Lighten up, man. You're a free agent now! Single and ready to—"

I shake his arm off. "Could you just cut it out? Not everyone's on the constant look out for their next hook up, okay? Do you know how dumb you sound?"

He holds up his hands in mock surrender. "Okay, okay. I thought you'd be excited or something, now that you don't have that frigid bitch on your back the whole time."

"Well, I'm not," I say. "I'm not excited. I hurt a lot people I care about because I couldn't be honest with myself. Not exactly the highlight of my year."

I turn to head to class and come eye to eye with Jason, who's standing at Darrell's locker, clearly broken off mid-conversation so he can watch me. The look on his face makes me want to throw up. Pure disgust. And the thing is, I'm disgusted with me too.

Sixty-Five

Cynthia

We take two cars into St Paul. No one wants to be trapped in a small space with both Brayden and me. I get it. Thirty minutes of awkward silence is good for no one. So we pack my drums, Lindsey's keyboard, his guitar, and all the amps into the bed of his truck and Charlotte and Harvey climb in with him while I try not to burn with jealousy that I'm not the one squeezed up next to him.

The rest of us pile into Lindsey's car, a real luxury vehicle, way nicer than anything I've ever driven. Darrell sits up front with her, leaving Jason and me together in the back.

He immediately pulls out his phone and passes me an earbud. That boy knows me too well. Mind numbing music to get me through this drive. I pull out my sticks and start to play on the back of Darrell's seat. From the way he keeps shifting in his seat, I can tell I'm bugging him, but he doesn't complain. Even Lindsey stops herself from reprimanding me. This is my night. I need to get into the zone.

When we arrive, I hope out of the car before she even slows to a complete stop. "I'll go sign us in."

The show starts in thirty minutes, but all the bands have to sign in before they open the doors to the public. Once we're signed in, we can start unloading and what not. Plus, I wanna see when we're scheduled to hit the stage. The later the better. The audience doesn't really start to fill up until eight-thirty, and by nine, they've had a drink or two in them.

I keep an eye out for the Stinks as I elbow my way through the crowd. Not that I'm scared of them or anything, I just don't feel like getting into it with Steve-O. Or Jimmy. I definitely do not want to see Jimmy.

There's a twenty-something girl with gauged ears and purple braids standing near the front holding a clipboard, and I make a beeline for her.

"Is this where the band sign in?"

"You betcha," she says. No amount of hardware on her face can take away that Minnesotan accent. She sounds like my mom. "Your name?"

"Cynthia Marlow," I say. "Sick as Cyn's the band."

"Cool name." She makes a check mark about three-fourths of the way down the list. "Gotcha signed in. You go on at 10:15."

Awesome. The show ends at eleven. We got a good slot. Everyone knows they pack the last few slots with bands who actually have a chance of winning.

"Thanks," I say, "Uh, have most of the bands shown up already?"

She glances at her list. "Still missing a few. Not too many."

"Great. Thanks." I head back out the door to help unload. The thing about Battle of the Bands—this is my third year after all—is that backstage is total chaos. The audience has no idea, because it just looks like one act after another on stage, but behind the scenes… basically twenty bands all trying to squeeze into a space designed for two or three. The best they can do is stake out a place to dump their crap, then take rotations with the gang to see who's gonna watch it while everyone else escapes outside for fresh air or into the audience to watch the show.

There's not much floor space left to claim, so I haul ass to Brayden's truck so we can get a move on. Brayden and Lindsey found a couple of parking spots a few blocks over. That's another thing. Parking downtown is a pain. We don't have that problem at home. We leave Lindsey with the rest of the gear and everyone else grabs and instrument or amp and starts hiking back to the venue.

We drop everything off in the best spot we can find, then Brayden says, "Cynthia, you stay here. We'll get the rest."

"I can carry my own drums."

"It's better if you stay." His tone leaves no room for argument. I can't even think of a good comeback.

I sink onto my stool. "Fine."

As soon as they're out the door, I start thinking of all the nasty things I could have said back at him for bossing me around. I'm so busy being mad at Brayden, that I don't even notice Steve-O and his band walk in. But they notice me.

"So you actually showed up."

I look up. Steve-O towers over me, arms crossed, flanked by Jimmy, Ray, the new drummer and… him. I force myself to keep my eyes on Steve-O's face.

"Yup."

"Do you even have a band? Or are you just going to go out there and make an idiot of yourself alone?"

I stand up, which is dumb because I barely come up to his chin. Still, I gather up every ounce of tough in my body. "I have a band."

He fakes looking around, like he's searching for someone in a crowd. "Oh really? Where?"

I open my mouth to speak, but Brayden's voice cuts in first. "Is there a problem?"

He fills the door frame, the heavy keyboard under his arm like it weighs nothing. His eyes meet Steve-O's and he stalks across the room, sets the keyboard down behind me, then stands right next to me and folds his arms, sending ripples through his biceps. I can feel the heat radiating off of him.

Steve-O doesn't even bat an eye. "Nope. No problem. Just catching up with an old friend." His eyes flicker to mine and they are filled to the brim with malice.

"You've caught up," Brayden says, "Now get lost."

"Sure thing… bro." Steve-O looks back at me. "Good luck. You're gonna need it." Then he strides away followed by the rest of the Stinks. I clench my jaw and hold my breath as they pass. One—two—three—four—then *he* stops, looks me over from head to toe and back up, real slow and says, "Looking good, Cyn."

I freeze. I can't think. My mind goes blank, my fingers and toes go numb. There's ringing in my ears, and I can't see anything. I can't feel anything. Until Brayden's hand brushes my elbow.

"Are you okay?"

"I need some air."

Then, I run for the exit.

#

Brayden finds me about twenty minutes later, sitting on the back of his truck, my feet dangling over the pavement. He sits down right next to me—close enough that I can smell his cologne—and doesn't say anything. Just sits there. Long enough for things to feel weird.

"Who's watching our stuff?" I ask.

"Everybody else," he replies. "If I didn't know any better, I'd think they didn't want to be around us right now."

I snicker, and stare at the ground. "You don't have to check up on me, okay?"

I feel him shrug next to me, but he doesn't leave. Just kind of sits there, staring out over the road in front of us. The wind blows through the parking lot, rippling my hair, and I pull my coat a little tighter. It's spring, but it's still Minnesota. Sometimes our state doesn't get the memo.

Still, silence. I don't even know why he's still here. Like he wants me to say something, but I don't know what to say. Except that I'm sorry. But I can't open that wound right now. Not before we go on stage. Maybe after. I can do it after. So I just join him in silent staring.

We watch the clouds roll past the buildings and the cars drive up and down the street looking for parking. We watch people climb out of cars, looking like they're heading straight for Grinders, dressed for a night of music. Our potential audience members.

I clear my throat, and he jumps.

"Sorry, uh, do you know what time it is?"

He checks his phone. "Quarter to eight. What time do we go on?"

"Ten-fifteen." I tuck a loose hair behind my ear and turn my head away from him. "Uh, is um, Angela coming?"

"No. We broke up."

"Oh," I say. "I'm sorry."

"Don't be." He slides off the truck bed to stand up, then holds a hand out to help me down. "It was my fault."

I look at his hand for a second, then slide mine into it. We haven't touched in so long. Not since, well, since before Lindsey's birthday party. But it feels right. I search his face for any sort of clue that he feels it too, but he's got his poker face on.

"You know," he says, as we start walking back to the club. "Steve-O's scared of you."

"No he's not."

"Yeah, he is. I told you, it's a classic sports move. Intimidate the opposition to throw them off their game." He gives me a knowing look. "He knows you can beat him, so he's trying to scare you. He's trying to make you mess up."

I square my shoulders,

"But," Brayden continues, "the Cynthia Marlow I know would never let some jerk intimidate her like that. The Cynthia Marlow I know would channel all that rage into something pretty spectacular."

I can't help it. I smile, and look up at him. And I'm pretty sure I see him smile too.

Sixty-Six

Charlotte

Nerves. That's all we are. Seven people, standing in a row, waiting for our name to be called. Seven separate bundles of uncontrollable nerves. Lindsey, for once, has nothing to say. She paces back and forth and practices piano runs on her legs. Jason rocks back and forth on the balls of his feet, stretching up tall, then shrinking down into himself, Darrell hovering next to him with his hand on his shoulder. Brayden's gone green and sick looking. And Cynthia. She stands stock still, her eyes never leaving the stage. The stage Harvey, Darrell, and I set, every piece of equipment exactly to Cynthia's demanding specifications.

I perch behind the soundboard, ready. We wait. All of Cynthia's talk about stage presence and attitude has flown right out of our minds. Back here, we are just kids. Do we even belong here?

The bar manager's voice pumps through the microphone. "And now... feast your eyes and ears on stage one for Minnesota's newest up and coming band.... Sick as Cyn!"

Cynthia glances over her shoulder at the rest of us, nods once, then runs onto stage. The other three have no choice but to follow.

I immediately start adjusting controls on my board, bringing up lights and turning on amps. A single spotlight lands on each of them. For a second, it's calm, quiet, then Cynthia lifts her sticks above her head and counts them off.

The set becomes a whirlwind of sound and motion. I have no time to think. I just do. All of us do.

Brayden shreds his way through each song, keeping perfect time with Cynthia's maniacal beat, all the while, Jason belts lyrics into the mic. His voice, her words. But it's a shared feeling. All of us felt it this year. Loss, pain, anger, hatred. JJ took something from all of us. Jason's safety. Cynthia's power. Lindsey's control. But she changed us. For the better, I think.

Harvey sits shoulder to shoulder with me, helping me with the switches. Partners at work once again. His ear is better. He listens for anything that needs a boost here, toned down there. We bring Lindsey's keyboard solo to full volume as she and Cynthia trade jabbing rhythms.

When it's all over, when Cynthia's final song, her song, the one she wrote over the past three weeks, falls silent, Harvey claps me on the shoulder. And we share a knowing grin. Jason shouts something into the mic, a sassy goodbye only he could deliver, and the crowd goes wild, cheering, clapping. Hooting and hollering. And in the chaos, the band comes rushing back stage, a tidal wave of sweaty bodies, high on adrenaline and applause. It crashes into Harvey and me, and for a second, I see nothing, hear nothing. There is just the press of flesh on flesh, as we hold each other in our exhilaration.

JJ took Mr. DuPont from me. But that loss was trivial, so pointless. I can see that now. He was nothing. Less than nothing. He was negative. He took things from me.

The negative of a negative is a positive. And that's what this is. Positive. Exactly what I needed.

One final tearful squeeze, and we pull away, looking around. Cynthia sees it first. A cherry red guitar, leaning all alone in the corner next to my laptop.

"Where's Brayden?"

Sixty-Seven

Cynthia

There is nothing like it. Being on stage in front of a crowd you can't see because the lights in your face are so bright. Everything is just white light and noise. It's magic. From where I sit in the back, I can see Jason strutting around like the next Freddy Mercury, Brayden stoically running through riff after riff. He's improved so much. I did that.

And whatever happens, I'm proud.

At this point, everything comes like second nature. Me pounding on the drums through our first two song. My body knows what to do, so I don't have to think. I just do it.

When the second song ends, the crowd is wild, full of energy and adrenaline. I hear Darrell whoop from backstage, and even though I know that's for Jason, it feels like it's for me as well. Now it's my song. Jason hands me his mic and sits on my stool and I creep out from behind my drums.

All my life I've felt small and insignificant, but the real power of rock'n'roll is that even the smallest person becomes a god in the spotlight. I don't want to be a god though. I just want to be with Brayden.

And that's what I put into this performance. All of my love. For him.

When it's over, he disappears.

Sixty-Eight

Jason

"He's gone," Charlotte says.

"No shit," Cynthia snaps, "where'd he go?"

Lindsey pulls away from our group hug. "His jacket's gone."

That letter jacket of his. He never goes anywhere without it. Which means…

"I'll uh… go break the stage," Harvey mutters. Darrell and Lindsey are hot on his heels to help. Charlotte backs away slowly, all nervous like, then darts after them.

So it's just Cynthia and me.

"Cyn," I start to say, but she cuts me off.

"Shut up, okay. Just shut up. I can't…" She grips her hair, "I don't want to hear it right now."

I nod hurriedly. "Okay."

She stares at the backdoor for a while longer, her shoulders slumped, then tosses her hair and turns toward the stage. "We should probably help with the equipment."

Cynthia doesn't say anything as we pack up her drum set, or haul amps backstage. When all the equipment is crammed into our small corner of the backstage, she sits on the largest amp and pulls out her phone. I don't ask if she's texting him. Her thumbs fly over the screen. Then she stares. And stares. And stares.

Nothing happens.

There are only two acts after us, and we spend the time hovered around our corner, not talking about the missing elephant in the room.

For my part. I'm pissed. He ditched us. He didn't even see the whole night through.

Harvey clears his throat when the final act ends. "Uh, how are we gonna get all this stuff home?"

Cynthia glares daggers at him, but he's used to her temper. He just shrugs. "I mean, we kinda need his truck."

Cynthia goes back to scowling at her phone.

"We'll figure it out," Lindsey says. "We can call an Uber or something." None of us remind her that an Uber all the way home is gonna be more than we can afford.

The last band crowds off the stage, and all of the contenders cram into the space and wait in tense silence for the votes to be calculated. I glance over where the Stinks are huddled together and catch Steve-O's eyes. He pantomimes something despicable, then mouth's the words "you're going down." I look away. Honestly, I think we have as good a chance as anyone. We played our hearts out. But that's not all that matters. It's like Cynthia says. It's working the crowd. Every person in the audience gets a vote. You need to make the audience love you.

The speakers crackle, and everyone's ears perk up. Cynthia's hand finds mine and grips it so hard her fingernails are digging into my skin, but I don't tell her to let go.

"Alright ladies and gents, the moment you've been waiting for. The votes have been tallied, and we'd like to invite our top three bands on stage. Please join me up here…. The Stinks!"

I groan, and I'm not the only one. Behind me, Darrell swears under his breath.

"The Misplaced Modifiers!" Reggie continues, "And last, but not least…. Sick as Cyn!"

"Oh my God," Lindsey whispers, "I can't believe it."

I chuckle. "I can. C'mon" I have to practically drag Cynthia out there. She's in a state of shock. Too much going on in her head right now. The audience cheers us as we take our place on stage. The lights beat down on us, and sweat gathers on my upper lip.

I give Cynthia's hand a squeeze. "I'm here, Cyn."

"I know."

The anticipation is killing us. Reggie knows how to play it up too. He gives this whole speech about the history of his club and how this is the fifteenth Battle of the Bands they've hosted, thanking his sponsors and blah blah blah.

"And now, without further ado…" he glances over his shoulder at all three bands on the stage with him. "In third place…"

I swear, everyone on stage actually leans a little closer to him. Cynthia's grip tightens.

"The Misplaced Modifiers!"

The band on our right looks disappointed, but still, there are smiles and hugs. Third place ain't something to sneeze at. It still takes a lot of talent to get there. And venues notice. They'll get plenty of gigs from this.

Of course, this only leaves two of us on stage. The Stinks and us. This is it. Everything Cynthia's been fighting for since September. Moment of truth. All the clichés. She looks over at her former band. We all do. And they stare at us. Seven people trading cold hard looks. Looks that could kill.

We have to win. We have to. Cynthia won't be able to take losing to them. Again. And honestly. She doesn't deserve to. She's got the talent. She's got the drive. She's the one who's going to keep fighting day after day to make it in this business. The Stinks? They're falling apart at the seams as it is. Yelling at their useless drummer, taking pills to stay awake, pills to go to sleep. Steve-O doesn't know which way is up half the time. They're nothing next to Cynthia.

I hope the audience saw that.

Reggie clears his throat into the microphone. "In first place, and winner of the $1000 grand prize is…"

Seconds tick by. My lungs hurt from holding my breath.

"Sick as Cyn!"

Cyn lets out long breath, doubling over so her hands on her knees. Like she ran a marathon or something. "We did it."

Sixty-Nine

Cynthia

Everything is chaos. We're swarmed where we stand. Musicians, audience members, roadies—everyone surges forward to get a piece of us. And my short ass, I can't see a thing. Just smoke and bodies. The noise is deafening. Jason grips my wrist and pulls me through the crush back stage where, if anything, things are worse.

Everyone's shouting questions and encouragements faster than I can keep up. Cameras flash. Reporters? Maybe. I can barely breathe.

Jason takes care of everything. "Hey guys, back up would ya? Give her some space!"

"You heard the man." Darrell steps in, his arm around Jason's shoulders. "Back it up."

"How do you feel?" someone shouts.

"Pretty fucking awesome," I gasp. "And… tired." Everyone laughs.

"What are you going to do now?"

"More of this, I hope, but um…" I pause and look around. Brayden's gone. This isn't the win I wanted. "Uh, I have to go. Sorry."

I push my way through the crowd to where we left the equipment but it's gone.

I whirl around. "Where are my drums?"

Charlotte comes running, skidding to a halt a foot away from me. "Brayden loaded up his truck. He packed up while you were on stage waiting for the winner to be announced."

I gape at her.

"He just left," she finishes.

"Where'd he go?"

She points at the back door, and I take off running. Someone tries to grab me for another interview, but I don't have the time. It may already be too late. I burst through the exit in time to see Brayden lift the back of his truck bed and slam it shut. He turns, his back to me, to get into the driver's seat.

"Wait!" I shout. "Brayden, wait!"

He glances at me, pauses for half a second, then keeps walking. I practically leap off the concrete steps and race toward him. I sprint around his truck and slide in between him and the door as his hand lands on the handle.

"Cynthia," he begins.

"Don't leave," I pant. "Not like this. Please."

"Don't worry," he says, "I'll drop all your equipment off at your house. Then, I'm out. It'll be like I never existed."

"That's not what I want."

"You got what you wanted, Cyn!" He tries to move me, but I've plastered myself to his truck. "You won, your old band will come crawling back to you and everything will be exactly how it was. Congratulations."

"That's not what I want," I repeat. Tears slide down my cheeks. "Didn't you listen to the song?"

He chokes. "Yeah, I did. God, Cynthia! That's the worst part. You used me! You made me fall for you, then you made me play a love song for your asshole ex-boyfriend!" He successfully dislodges me and opens the door. "Don't you see how messed up that is?"

I'm full on crying now. Hugging myself and everything. I close my eyes.

"I wrote that song for you." I say.

The car door slams. Any second now, the engine will roar to life and he will drive out of my life forever. I did this to myself. I deserve it. But still, it hurts.

Any second now.

Any second now.

Except, it doesn't. A hand finds my waist. Fingers life my chin. And lips press against mine. Lips I know. Lips I recognize. Lips I love.

It takes a second for my brain and body to catch up with each other, but when they do, it's explosive.

I cry and kiss and grab him all at once. Pure ecstasy. I can't let it end. I can't break away, because it might be a trick of the mind. Just my imagination. So just in case, just in case... I hold on for dear life. If he disappears, I want to go with him.

When he pulls out of the kiss to breathe, I clutch him tighter and he smiles.

"C'mon," he says, "let's go home."

Seventy

Brayden

Sex.

It is such a simple thing really. Mechanics that anybody could manage. And yet, for months, no years, I have been complicating it. Making more of it in my mind than really necessary.

It turns out, sex isn't complicated at all. Love is. Or it was. The journey to this moment, right here—complicated. I don't know why. It didn't have to be. If I had been honest about how I felt, it would never have gotten so messed up. And Cynthia… a world of complication in her, but she did what she could to help me understand the depth of her love. I understand it now. I do.

She doesn't speak during the entire drive home, but her eyes never leave my face, and every time I glance her way, the corners of her lips curl in an uncharacteristically shy and sweet way. The complication of love.

We unload equipment in calm, peaceful silence. There's no way she'd let me leave it in the truck overnight. I expect her to want to set everything up, or at least the drums, but when I start to unzip a case, she grabs my hand and gently pulls me away, toward the couch. With every backward step, she undoes a button or unhooks a clasp, until she's standing in front of me baring more than her body. Baring all her soul, pooled up behind the icy wall in her eyes. Eyes that I get lost in. I'm the one staring now, but I'm not ashamed or scared or nervous. I am simply… in love.

When I touch her, she shivers.

"Are you cold?"

"A little," she whispers.

I guess there's a first time for everything. I grab the blanket from the back of the couch and drape it over her, then hold her close. "I'll warm you up."

When it's over, she falls asleep, her naked body curled against mine. I can't sleep. I am awake, unafraid, buzzing with life. I am electrified by those blue eyes. She is still and silent, except for the occasional soft murmuring breath. Silence like I haven't experienced in months fills the space.

I love the silence.

About the Author

Sarah is a high school teacher and mother of two whose short fiction has been published in several anthologies. Her contemporary YA novels and short fiction fiercely tackle the gamut of tough issues that affect real teenagers. You can find her in Kansas City with her two boys and her husband, where she's often crocheting, singing along with music that is entirely too loud, or snuggling with her cat, Osiris.

You can connect with me on:
https://sarahkaminskiauthor.wixsite.com/website

Subscribe to my newsletter:
https://mailchi.mp/2144bc9871ba/2ichfp7xkm

9 798899 162280 6